Happily Undead In Dark River

Grace McGinty

Also by Grace McGinty

Hell's Redemption Series: The Redeemable/The Unrepentant/The Fallen

Damnation MC Duet: Serendipity/Providence

The Azar Nazemi Trilogy : Smoke and Smolder/Burn and Blaze/Rage and Ruin

Dark River Days Series: Newly Undead In Dark River/Happily Undead In Dark River/Pleasantly Undead in Dark River

Black Mountain Mates: Hunting Isla

Eden Academy Series: The Lost and the Hunted (Prequel)/Heart of the Hounded (Prequel)/ Rebels and Runaways (Book 1)/Sweethearts and Savages (Book 2)

Shadow Bred Series: Manix/Frenzy/Feral

Stand Alone Novels and Novellas: Bright Lights From A Hurricane/The Last Note/ Inside The Maelstrom Part 1 and 2

To My Readers.
You guys are freaking amazing.
Thanks for making my dreams come true.

Happily Undead In Dark River

1

When I woke up this morning, I didn't think I would be playing croquet with flamingos and eating jelly donuts, but that's just the way it was when I visited Nico for our compulsory counseling sessions. I was beginning to think that Nico might suffer from some kind of existential ennui, being so old and stuff, or maybe he just liked being quirky? Either way, I never knew what to expect when I walked through the electric pink waiting room. Would it be a serious session where he'd delve into my emotions—how I felt about being turned into a vampire, betrayed by the woman I called a friend, almost murdering my boyfriend? Or would we be blowing full body bubbles and trying to trap each other in them?

Today, we were in the town square. Nico aimed his giant

pink flamingo mallet and hit the ball against the peg. "Yes! I won. As the kids would say, in your face, Raine!"

He spun around and around with his mallet above his head, looking so completely ridiculous that I had to laugh. Nico was competitive, especially when it came to bizarre sports. "That's very bad sportsmanship, Nico. You should work on that."

He grinned, showing huge fangs. He held out his hand, and I shook it. He was ancient but he didn't feel that way. His hand was warm and strong. Rough in a way that said he'd lived the hard life of a barbarian when he was younger. In the soft evening light, I could see the pale rows of the tattoos on his face that spiraled down his body, a whirling geometric pattern that I kind of wanted to trace. He was boyishly hand-some, but that innocence belied a power that could consume a person.

I pulled my hand away, clearing my throat. Four. That was the number of men I had at home, cherishing me every chance I got. I did not need to make it five. I started packing up the croquet set, humming It's Raining Men under my breath. Nico watched me for a moment, then helped me collect the rest of the hoops.

"So I hear tonight is the big night for you and the Sheriff," he said conversationally. I nearly tripped over my feet. He was careful not to make it a direct question. Nico's vampire gift was terrifying really. If he asked you a direct question, you could only answer with the truth. There were some truths I wasn't ready to answer just yet.

I nodded. "Yes, he's finally taking me on that date he promised me a month ago."

And hopefully, we'd take our relationship to the next level. We'd yet to hit that home run, and I was beginning to think he just liked torturing me with his body.

Although, he had been busy. Dark River was getting a visit from the Vampire Nation, and a full complement of Enforcers, who were the vampire version of the Babadook. Everyone was busy making sure there was nothing that would draw the gaze of Lucius, who I'd discovered was one of the elected heads of the Vampire Nation and an all-around sadistic a-hole.

"He is a good man, your Sheriff. I am glad he has taken the time to woo you properly."

I made a general noise of agreement and hoped that was the end of this line of inquiry. Not that I was embarrassed by Walker, but Nico was... well, Nico. He was an enigma, and I could never be sure if he liked me as a friend or wanted something more.

I cleared my throat again. "Are you prepared for the Vampire Nation?" It had become a bit of a catchphrase around town lately, as people went about their lives with a giant ACME anvil hanging over their heads.

Nico made a rude noise in the back of his throat as he held the door to his office open for me. "I am not worried about Lucius or his arrival. He will be disdainful of what we've created here, no matter how hard we polish the town. It is just his nature."

I raised my eyebrow. "You sound like you've met him?"

Nico just gave me another enigmatic look and continued back toward his office. I sighed. "You know, I'd like your interrogation power sometimes. It would be nice not to be in the dark all the time."

He gave me a sad look over his shoulder as he packed away the equipment. "Do you really mean that?"

"No." The word was out of my mouth before I could stop it. "I think the world is run on little white lies, and the truth all the time would crush a person. You'd have to always be on guard."

With a smile that didn't reach his eyes, he shut the door on the equipment cupboard and my questioning. "Exactly." When he turned back to face me though, his normal congenial look was back in place. "You should go and get ready for your date, Raine. I hope your night is filled with happiness and romance."

With that, he walked into his office and shut the door. I had a feeling I'd made him mad, or hurt his feelings or something. Normally I would have brought him a unicorn poop cupcake from The Immortal Cupcake, but Angeline was still gone and the store remained closed.

My heart ached thinking about Angeline and the reason she left. Alice's death. I choked back the feeling and stepped back out onto the sidewalk. Brody was there to meet me, like always. The smile on his face chased away any bad feelings.

He wrapped me in his arms and nuzzled my neck. I laughed as his long dark hair tickled my face. "Brody! You're back!"

He'd gone back to his Pack to warn them that Lucius and the vampire nation were coming, taking Tex with him. I'd missed my shapeshifters. Especially Tex, because he was also my housemate. I'd gotten used to him moving around the house, playing his guitar, leaving his towels on the floor. I didn't want to tell the guys, but being alone gave me anxiety after Alice's attack a month ago. Luckily, four boyfriends meant that I was rarely alone.

Brody kissed me hungrily, and I kissed him back. "I'm back. So is Lover Boy. I left him in the car because I'm Alpha and I wanted to make out with you first. Did I abuse my position? Why yes, yes I did. Besides, he can go make kissy face with Judge."

I could hear Tex's heartbeat behind me and I grinned. "I will, but first I wanted to see my mate," he whispered close to my ear.

Brody let out a grumbling growl, but he was grinning against my lips. "That's it. That's the last time I crack the window for him," he grumbled.

I was whirled in Brody's arms until Tex had me pressed against his chest. "Hello, mate." He whispered it like a promise of dirty, dirty things. "Did you miss me?"

I kissed his chin and then sucked his full lower lip between my teeth. "I missed you more than you can imagine. No one snored on the other side of the bed, and I actually got a full ten hours sleep."

Brody laughed, and Tex smiled. "That mouth." He kissed me hard and then slid his hand down to mine. "Well, I missed you. Especially that thing you do with your tongue."

I rolled my eyes in his direction, even though he couldn't see it, but his words sent heat to my belly. That he'd sense. Life was so unfair sometimes.

We walked across the town square toward Brody's car. It was a 1967 Chevy Impala. Yep, like the one on Supernatural. Brody was a massive Supernatural fan. I watched it for the storyline. Yeah, that's it. The storyline.

"I hear you're going on a date tonight with Sheriff Tight-Pants," Tex said as he slid into the passenger seat and pulled me onto his lap. Not exactly legal, but hey, I was dating the police force of Dark River.

I shook my head and let out an exasperated huff. "Does everyone know my every move?"

Brody laughed, shifting the car into gear and pulling out onto the near-empty streets. Dark River was a town filled with vampires who could move around at the speed of light. There wasn't a lot of call for vehicles when you could run eighty miles faster than a bullet train. Except for Brody's Impala and Walker's squad car, there were never any cars on the roads.

Brody turned off the radio and shrugged. "Well, yeah. Welcome to small town life, Rainey. But the Sheriff told us in our group chat."

I turned to Tex, because let's face it, if anyone was going to convince them to start a group chat, it was the technologically proficient one in the group. "You guys started a group chat without me?" I stuck out my lip and pouted.

Tex rolled his eyes. "Please. The only thing we talk about is you. It makes it easier to ensure we all get a bit of one-on-one time and other stuff. Besides, you don't even use your phone."

I mean, he was right. I hadn't used my cellphone at all since Walker had given it to me a couple of months ago. Who did I have to call? Everyone who knew I was alive resided in this town, and when Brody went back to Pack lands, he had limited cell reception. "Even Judge?"

Tex laughed, and it was echoed by Brody. "Even Judge. It was hard to get him to buy one, and let's just say, he is still adapting to the touch screen technology. But he's on board."

I patted at Tex's pockets, looking for his phone. "I wanna see."

"You keep moving around like that, you're gonna see something else," he grumbled.

"Oh, haha," I said, but then my hand skimmed across his hardening dick and he sucked in a breath. Or maybe I sucked in a breath. I squeezed my hand around his cock through his jeans. "Well, this doesn't feel like your phone."

Tex looked pained. "I don't know. Maybe you should put your mouth near it and see if it makes a call."

Brody was giggling hysterically now, and Tex was saved by our arrival at my cottage. The red door beckoned me home, and every time I saw its black little walls and white trim, I felt so loved. The guys had bought the cottage for me and Tex. I still wasn't sure how I felt about that, but it had been the nicest thing anyone had ever done for me. I was slowly decorating the inside, painting the walls and finding pieces of furniture from the surrounding towns.

Brody came around and opened my door, and I slid out from my spot on Tex's lap, making him groan.

He hopped out, unfolding his cane in front of him. Once he was through my door, he had the floor plan memorized enough that he didn't need the cane. He propped it on the other side of the door and slid off his shoes.

"Home sweet home," he whispered. My heart stuttered. We hadn't spoken about it, but eventually, Tex was going to have to make contact with home and talk to his parents before they thought he'd been swallowed by the Canadian wilderness too. Maybe he needed to go back and visit. The thought of Tex going home made my heart restrict in my chest. What if he never came back? Mate or not, I was asking him to leave behind everything he'd ever known for a life of uncertainty.

Tex was suddenly behind me, pressing my back into his chest and wrapping his arms around my hips. "What are you worrying about, Mika—I mean, Raine?"

He was still adjusting to the fact that I was now a totally different person. In all honesty, I was still adjusting, so I could forgive a few name slips now and then.

I spun in his arms and kissed him softly. "Nothing. I better go get ready for my date. Can't keep the good Sheriff waiting."

He tilted his head toward me. He knew I was fobbing him off, but he let me. "I think the Sheriff has waited long enough. I wonder if vampires can get blue balls?"

I punched him in the arm, then kissed him hard. "I'll let you know later?"

Tex was the only one of my lovers that I didn't have to worry about jealousy becoming an issue, even though he was my mate. No, that wasn't true. They all had the capacity to get jealous—probably why they'd started a group chat—but Tex didn't mind sharing me inside the bedroom and out.

"Want me to do your makeup?" he asked, and I laughed as I headed toward the bedroom. There was an old saying where I came from. Never let a blind man do your makeup.

2

When I emerged from the shower, Tex was gone, but Brody was sitting on the kitchen counter with a beer in his hand. He handed me a glass of wine and followed me into my bedroom. He laid on my bed and watched as I went through my wardrobe, probably waiting for my towel to fall and expose my naked ass.

"How did it go with your Pack? Are they preparing for an influx of vampires not restricted by the Concord in the area?"

He nodded and swigged his beer. "Yes. Some of the old ones remember the time before the Concord. They took the town's warning seriously. We'll fortify our boundaries, have evacuation guidelines in place. But we trust Miranda's wards."

I pulled out lingerie and a little black bodycon dress. I

hadn't gone to Ella's boutique all month, not since Alice's trial. It felt weird, like I was somehow responsible for Angeline's world imploding. Angeline needed Cresta and Ella more than I did right now, and she'd known them longer. It was just better this way. I could lean on my guys. Angeline had no one to lean on. Plus, I was a chickenshit and wanted to avoid the inevitable awkwardness.

I dropped my towel and grinned at Brody's groan. "Do you really need to date Mr. Straight and Narrow? Stay home and I'll give you my version of a tongue bath?"

I laughed but knew he didn't mean it. He liked Walker; they'd been friends for a long time. I still wasn't sure why Brody wasn't more jealous of the little lovenest I'd created here, but he wasn't. He was the one who referred to Judge and Walker as my undead life partners. Not in front of Judge though. Judge had commitment-phobia so bad, he basically broke out in a ball rash at the word marriage. I slid on my underwear, which was a glorified strip of mosquito netting, and then my garter belt. This time Brody sounded pained. "Seriously? Where did they come from? Why do you never wear stockings and suspenders with me?"

I slid my bra over my arms and walked over to Brody. "Do me up?" He grumbled something about putting on women's bras going against the bro code, but his fingers were deft. When I was all strapped into my torture device, I paused.

"Brody. Do you think that because I will never change, my boobs won't sag when I get old?"

Yeah, that was the kinda shit I thought about now. Don't judge me.

"I guess so? You'd have to ask the Do—" He snapped his mouth shut. We were so used to asking Alice, aka the town's doctor, questions; it was weird that she wasn't here. "Ask Walker or Judge. Pretty sure they've seen their fair share of vampire boobs in their lives." His hands snaked around to squeeze my breasts, scraping his fingers across my lace-covered nipples. "Though I am happy to do a scientific study for the next hundred or so years, personally."

I shivered as pleasure ran down my spine but stepped away. "Nope. Not right now. You guys always end up destroying my lingerie and this is my last set," I mock scolded because I loved that shit. "But from now on, I'm never wearing a bra. Like ever. I'm free!" I unclipped my bra and threw it on the bed. "Burn them. I feel liberated!" I spun in circles so quickly, my boobs flew out like wings, making Brody fall back on the bed laughing.

I pulled out my stockings from the drawer and handed them to Brody. His eyes got heavy and he slid bonelessly off the bed, coming to kneel at my feet. He put one hand on my stomach and pushed me back until I was sitting in my bedroom armchair. Pushing himself between my knees, he pulled the stocking over my toes, rolling it up to my ankles, then lifted my leg and put it on his shoulder.

I sucked in a breath as he ran his tongue up the inside of my calf, unrolling the stocking behind the warm slide of his tongue. Up past my knee, to the inside of my thighs. He stopped mere inches from the heat of my pussy, and I groaned in frustration. "I heard saliva stops static electricity," he murmured as he blew a hot breath at my wet panties, and then moved back down to my other foot.

"Really?" I whispered.

He shrugged. "Who am I to argue with science I found on the internet?" Then he repeated the process with the other stocking. Holy Jesus. By the time he reached the top of the other side, I was willing to forgo my lingerie. But he just looked up at me through hooded eyes, his grin decidedly devilish. He gave me a quick kiss at the junction of my thighs and then slid out from between my knees. I gave a pitiful mewl, which only seemed to make him laugh more.

He held up my dress. "Here we go. Don't want you to be late." He looked at his watch. "Walker should be here in ten minutes."

I stepped into the dress and allowed Brody to pull it up over my hips. He zipped up the back and there was a hot look in his eyes that had nothing to do with the fact he was just between my thighs. "We are so fucking lucky." He leaned forward and kissed me. "I'll go wait in the living room and grill him about his intentions towards our mate."

That was the second time he'd referred to me as 'our mate' and I wondered if it was more than a turn of phrase. But now was not the time to ask. I slid on the high heels Ella had given me for my night out in Calgary and went to do my makeup. I looked in the mirror and was once again glad I didn't get turned when I went through my acne stage a couple of years ago. On the plus side, when Cresta waxed my legs, it meant they wouldn't grow back for a decade. Hashtag Vampire Win. Apart from the homicidal maker, the fact I could never see my family again or go out in the sun, and that I was now under the purview of a race of being that believed in the death sentence the way I believed in chocolate for breakfast, then the whole vampire thing was super peachy.

I brushed out my ombre red hair and put on the red lipstick that matched the darkest of the reds. I ran some mascara over my lashes, and that was it. I couldn't do Cresta's makeup sorcery, but considering Walker had seen me when I was puffy from crying and hadn't showered in a week, this was a definite step up.

I walked out into the living room to see both Walker and Brody there. I sucked in a gasp when I saw Walker. He was dressed in gray tailored pants, brown leather suspenders, and a white shirt, the sleeves rolled up to his muscular forearms. He looked good enough to eat.

"Wow," he whispered, echoing my thoughts. "You look amazing."

I blushed. "Right back at you."

Brody laughed, hustling us toward the door. "You guys are both so cute, I swear I'm about to die," he said in a Valley girl falsetto. "Go and have fun. Have her back by sunrise, otherwise, I have it on good authority she'll turn into a pumpkin."

Walker patted him on the back extra heartily. I thought I heard something crack. "Don't wait up, old man."

He held out his elbow, the most glorious smile on his face. I felt like my heart was racing. We walked down the short front path to the Harley parked on the street.

"Oh boy," I whispered. I'd wanted to hop on the back of Walker's bike ever since I heard that he owned one. I wished I'd worn a slightly longer dress though. He threw his leg over the sleek, black machine, and I swear I had an orgasm just at the sight. The Harley Davidson was so unlike Walker's personality, it made me wonder what else he kept on the down-low. But right now he looked like a wet dream.

"Are you just going to stand there drooling on the pavement, or are you going to hop on?" he teased.

He didn't need to ask me twice. I was glad for the little extra height the heels gave me as I swung my leg over the bike and molded my body to his back. Then he started it up.

"Oh shit!"

He squealed out of my little cul-de-sac, and my hair flew behind me like blood on the wind. Always wear a helmet kids, unless you are now an immortal freakin' vampire. It was amazing. Although we were driving slower than we could run, there was something about the rumble of the bike between my thighs as I had my arms around the waist of a sexy-as-sin man who I knew owned handcuffs. Life was kind of good right now.

He drove us to the diner, which was not unusual. There were very few places to eat in a town filled with vampires. Bert and Beatrice's Diner. The Immortal Cupcake, which was now closed.

But what was weird about the diner was that it was completely empty, and there was very little light coming through the front glass windows. I slid off the bike and onto the sidewalk in front of the diner. Walker was there in an instant, holding the door to the diner open for me. The tinkle of the bell didn't fill me with dread today. As I stepped through the door, Bert was there. In a tuxedo.

My mouth unhinged. Bert was older, with a girth almost as round as he was tall. But there he was, looking completely like a penguin in a bow tie and grinning like crazy.

"Your table is this way," he grumbled despite the grin. That was just his natural pitch. He had curmudgeonly as a default. He led us to the back of the empty diner to a table set with a white linen cloth and dripping in candlelight. A bottle of wine sat chilling in an ice bucket.

"Did you convince Beatrice and Bert to close the diner? This is amazing." Honestly, there was a better chance of getting Walt to close Disneyland for the day. If Walt Disney was a vampire. Actually... "Was Walt Disney a vampire?"

Both Walker and Bert stared at me. "What?"

I waved a hand. "Nothing. You look very handsome, Bert."

The old vampire blushed, pouring our wine and then hightailing it back to the kitchen, probably to lose the bow tie.

I smiled at the man across from me, the flickering candles making him look even more handsome, if that were possible. "This is very romantic, Walker Walton."

Now it was his turn to blush, and he squeezed the back of his neck. "I wish it was more. You deserve more."

Walker had been my staunchest supporter since my turning, determined to find my killer. There was still so much I didn't know about him. When was he born? Had he been married? When was he turned? But there never seemed like the right time to ask someone how they died. Given his reaction to my uh, murder, I had an inkling it wasn't a happy story.

Beatrice appeared from the kitchen with a bowl of freshly baked bread and several small dishes of dip.

"Oh, look at you two. Just the most adorable picture."

I loved Beatrice. She reminded me of someone's great-aunt. Brash, but loving. She'd stood by me since my turning, all through the thing with Alice, even when the rest of the town turned their backs on me. Sure, most of them had come around now, but it had hurt back then and while I'd forgiven them all, I hadn't forgotten that I'd been a victim yet they'd treated me like the villain.

I ate with my fingers, and Walker watched me like I was on the menu.

"So, when's your birthday?" I asked, probably impolitely around a mouthful of feta dip and crusty bread. Seriously, Bert and Beatrice were a wonder.

"July 21st. I was born in 1821, before you ask."

Woah. I mean, in comparison to Nico, he was a baby. But I never thought I'd be dating a nearly two-hundred-year-old man. Who's your daddy? Amiright?

The rest of the meal was one of the most pleasant of my life. We talked as if I were still in college like we were normal humans. We avoided most hard topics, like my family and his turning. We also didn't talk about the Vampire Nation's upcoming visit. Instead, I now knew his favorite color was blue, he liked garlic and cheese pizza which I thought was funny as hell, and that he'd always wanted to be a Sheriff, but it wasn't his vocation until after he was turned.

He'd grown up in New York, a poor Irish immigrant, though there was no trace of an Irish accent now. He'd married a famine girl. They'd never had any kids though, and he now knew it was because he'd survived the pox as a child.

I felt a brief pang of sadness that I would never have kids with Walker, or Tex, or have little Brodys. Then I mentally slapped myself. I wasn't even old enough to drink. I was too young to think about kids. But there was a niggling bit in the back of my brain that thought one day, I might have wanted them. And maybe one day, Brody and Tex would too. I mean,

Brody was Alpha. He was going to have to reproduce, right? That's what always happens in those romance novels. Then he'd have to leave me. The sadness went from a pang to an all-out ache.

Walker frowned, reaching over the table to twine his fingers in mine. "Hey, what put that look on your face?"

I was saved from answering by the bell over the door tinkling. Not unusual, but inevitably the banshee scream to important moments in my life.

X stumbled over the threshold. "Raine. Just the girl I was looking for. Wow, this place is dead, Love. Deader than usual, I mean."

Then he fell forward, hitting his head on the corner of the table closest to him and landing on his face.

3

I was on my feet and beside him as his head hit the floor. It was then that I saw his back was oozing blood. The whole back of his black shirt was soaked, and this close, the scent was so overwhelming that I was surprised I hadn't smelled his blood as soon as he opened the door. I was surprised the whole town couldn't smell it.

My fangs dropped down fast enough to puncture my lip, and I licked at the blood. I didn't know what to do. I couldn't check for a pulse. Did I lick the wound on his back? Why wasn't it healing?

A gust of wind heralded the arrival of Judge, though I had no idea how he even knew that X was here. Maybe he could scent X's blood from my house? I had so many fucking questions and no answers.

"Why isn't he healing?" I asked the most important one first.

Judge's face was shut down into a terrifying mask. "Traitor's Blade."

The words sent cold terror trickling down my spine, even though I had no idea what they meant. "How do we stop him bleeding like that?" I was starting to freak out, with flashes of the month before—of almost exsanguinating Walker—starting to blur over the reality of now.

X made this awful gurgling sound, and I knelt beside him. "Hey, it's okay. We'll get you fixed up. Stop being such a wuss, 'tis but a scratch," I teased, but there was an edge of panic to my voice that I couldn't quite hide.

"Just because... I'm English... doesn't mean I watch Monty... Python," X gasped out on labored breaths, which made me laugh but feel infinitely more worried.

Judge looked over my head at Walker. "We need to get him to the Doctor's office, now."

Walker nodded, but his gaze flashed to me. They meant Doc Alice's office. It had been sealed up since her trial, and the town hadn't gotten a replacement doctor. "Raine, I think you should stay here."

A part of me just wanted to be weak and agree. But X had been looking for me for a reason, and I wanted to know what it was. So I shook my head. "I'm coming with you."

Both Judge and Walker looked like they wanted to protest,

but X gave another death rattle, shaking them into action. They lifted him, one at each end, and Beatrice was there holding the door open. I hadn't even heard her come out of the kitchen.

I raced ahead to Doc Alice's old office, pushing every memory I had of the building before tonight right out of my mind. I kicked open the door and turned on all the lights. The guys were right behind me. They slid X onto the examination table face down. "I need a suture kit and the cautery machine," Judge barked, and Walker flew around the room like the wind. I had no idea what either of those things looked like and I felt completely useless.

Judge was talking me through it though. Maybe I looked like I was freaking out. Because I was freaking out. "The Traitor's Blade is a dagger designed purely for Lucius by one of his witch consorts. It can issue mortal wounds on a vampire that never heal, meaning it's a very powerful weapon. The Vampire Council was up in arms about the whole thing of course, and Lucius took a blood oath never to kill another vampire with it. So instead, he uses it to punish traitors by stabbing them somewhere non-life threatening, banishing the person, and allowing them to die a slow, miserable death by exsanguination if they can't find a witch to heal them. Most witches hate vampires, with a few exceptions."

"Like Miranda?"

"Uh, yeah." Judge winced a little. I'd met Miranda almost two months ago when she'd placed a ward around my apartment. She and Judge had been... a thing. It had been tense, awkward and almost the end of Judge and me.

X groaned again, and I firmed my jaw. "Should we call Miranda again?"

A hand reached out and gripped my calf muscle. I looked down to see X staring up at me, his face the gray of someone who was bleeding out. "No... Miranda..." he gasped out.

I ran a hand over the short stubble of his head reassuringly. "Okay, okay, Big Guy. No Miranda. I was in no hurry to repeat that awkward little dance anyway."

X grunted, and I raised an eyebrow at Judge. "They have, uh, history," he answered, taking the medical equipment Walker was holding out to him.

I narrowed my eyes at Judge. "Don't we all?" Judge pretended not to hear me as he set up the equipment with deft hands. Like he knew what he was doing. "Do this often?"

He didn't look up, pulling on gloves despite the fact no one here could get infections. "A few times."

The pointed tip of the cautery machine started to glow, and it finally dawned on me what the hell it was. "You're going to burn the wound closed?" Okay, that might have come out a little like a pterodactyl screech.

Judge gave me a disapproving look, and Walker edged toward me. "No. This isn't the Wild West, Rainy Day. I'm going to cauterize the veins closed then suture the wound. It will take months to heal, but eventually, it'll get better. Unfortunately, there's no anesthetic for this. Walker, hold these forceps here."

Walker did as he was asked, and I was glad for it. I didn't do well around gaping wounds, which made being turned into a vampire kind of ironic. Once, my mom had gotten new knives from one of those late-night infomercials where they cut through tin cans and stuff, and I'd been desperate to try them out. I'd misjudged slicing a carrot and cut off the tip of my finger. I'd puked, passed out and they'd found me two minutes later in a pool of vomit, with my finger bleeding and the tip still on the chopping board next to the carrots.

I saw the muscles on X's back twitch, his low grunt of pain the only sign they were literally burning his flesh back there. I dropped down so I was face height with him.

I desperately wanted to ask if he was doing okay, because that's what came naturally in these situations, right? But even I knew how stupid that sounded.

"Just so you know, the slit in your back looks a little like a vagina right now."

Judge stilled, blinking at me, and even Walker looked at me like I'd lost my mind. But X's mouth twitched in a smile and almost laughed. "Keep Judge... away from it... then," he panted out.

I laughed and put my hand on his head. "I promise to protect your virtue while you are down."

I wasn't sure what Judge did, but X suddenly hissed and latched onto my wrist, his fangs piercing my skin messily.

Walker threw down the forceps, but I held up a hand to stop him. "No, continue. It's okay."

There was pleasure in a bite, and it was awkward as hell to be turned on while a guy was getting his back sewn back together. X's dark eyes watched me carefully, his fangs so deep into my vein I was a little worried he would hit a tendon.

"Not gonna lie, X, this is not the way to woo a girl. Your flirting skills are rusty as hell." X tried to mumble something back, but I waved a finger in his face. "Uh uh, it's bad manners to talk with your mouth full."

X's eyes sparkled like the devil lived and breathed inside him. Which was better than the dull look of near death. He ran his tongue around the points where his fangs were sunken into my skin, the look in his eyes getting even hotter.

Then it hit me. "Holy shit..."

It was like molten lava coursing through my veins, if molten lava was equipped with tiny little tongues that deliciously licked all over my body. My whole body felt like jelly as pleasure and euphoria swirled over my skin.

I dimly heard an angry Walker demanding to know what he'd done, and Judge's equally disapproving voice. "His tongue has venom. It gives his victims intense pleasure. Like horny goat weed crossed with the world's greatest aphrodisiac."

I came in a rush; my skin felt too hot, my muscles too lax. I could see why Judge called it a venom and not a drug. If I was an unsuspecting victim, I'd let him suck me until I was dry. But I wasn't an unsuspecting victim, so I poked him in the eye, hard.

He reared back, his eye screwed closed but his grinning mouth still coated in my blood.

I gave him a death glare. "Thanks for the orgasm, but next time, you should ask. This isn't the tenth century, asshole." With that, I wiped my blood from his bottom lip, stuck it in my mouth and sashayed out of the room like I owned it.

As I shut the door, I could hear X's happy sigh. "I think I might love her."

Then I heard the unmistakable thud of someone's fist connecting with flesh. I guess X was feeling better.

I was back in front of Bert and Beatrice's diner before Walker caught up. His face looked grim, but he twined his fingers in mine. "Which one of you hit him?" I asked lightly.

Walker made an unhappy humph. "Both of us. I'm usually against unnecessary violence, but that guy only responds to a fist."

I smiled softly at Walker, the pacifist, and I wondered if he was right. I'd only met X a few times, but there were brief flashes of something soft in the man who was tough as a craggy mountain. But I didn't contradict Walker, as I hopped onto the back of his bike. "I'm sorry he ruined our date," I whispered as I rested my cheek against his back.

He cupped a hand over where mine joined around his waist. "No matter. I have millennia to go on a million dates with you. I intend to make each one better than the last. So I guess I should thank X for setting the bar really low," he said with a low chuckle.

I grinned against his back. "At least it was memorable."

I missed his response as he kicked the Harley into life, its low rumbling purr soothing my frayed nerves. Walker took the long way home, driving around in the darkened shadows of Dark River, which was now comforting rather than terrifying. Finally, he surprised me by pulling up in front of my cottage instead of his. He slid from the bike, picking me up and placing me on my feet. Apparently, a roaring orgasm and then a long ride on a bike made your thighs a little flaccid.

Speaking of flaccid... "Are you going to come in?" I fluttered my eyelashes, hoping I looked coy and not like I was having a seizure.

He wrapped my hand in the crook of his elbow and walked me to my door. "Not tonight, Raine. I should get back and see what X's arrival means for the rest of us. He's never the herald of good times. Besides, tonight was amazing, but it wasn't quite perfect. And I want it to be perfect."

I grinned at him. "And I can wait. Goodnight, Walker. I had an amazing night, despite the blood and gore."

"Me too. Actually, there's one more thing." He stepped closer, crowding me into the closed door. He slid his hands down my spine and under my ass. Then he lifted me against the door, his lips a fraction from my own. "Just one more thing."

He pressed me hard into the door as his lips devoured me like a starving man. His fingers curled in my hair, holding me still as his tongue plundered my mouth. I kissed him back, tangling my tongue with his and grinding my hips against his very obvious erection.

Finally, he let me slide down his body and I whimpered. "One day soon, Raine. One day very, very soon."

Then he was back on his bike, kicking it to life and roaring away like the bad boy he wasn't. Damn.

The door suddenly opened behind me and I fell backward into the arms of a grinning Brody. "Well, that was kinda hot right there. I'm beginning to see what the Drifter and the Pup are always talking about." He took a long lungful of air. "But you smell like sex and blood. I mean, not unusual in Deadsville, but the blood doesn't belong to any of the usual suspects."

I slipped off my heels and walked into my kitchen. Mine. I still couldn't believe it. "It's been quite a night."

He poured me some more wine. "Mmm, I heard. Tex called me when Judge skipped out like his tail was on fire. Something about X and bleeding to death? I'm guessing that wasn't figurative considering he's already dead?"

I downed the entire glass of wine in one gulp, and Brody obligingly refilled it. "Uh-huh. He was close to being re-dead. He's okay now. Okay enough to suck a pint of blood out of me and give me an unexpected orgasm with his tongue venom."

When Brody raised his eyebrows, I sunk back into my wine. "It's a long story."

Brody just laughed. There wasn't a jealous bone in that one's body. "Well, if you add him into your happily ever after, it'll be interesting to have two venomous partners in your harem."

"What?"

The front door opened, and we both whirled around. Tex slipped through from the darkness, his hair mussed from the wind or whatever he and Judge had been doing before X decided to drop dead on the floor of the diner. I was always amazed when I watched Tex navigate the house, or navigate life in general. He walked directly towards me, even though I hadn't spoken. Sure, being half shapeshifter had helped supplement his lack of sight, but even when he was a kid, he'd walked with the same confidence as the sighted.

He headed right for me and I waited still, desperate for the hug that I knew was coming. Of all my lovers, er, life partners, Tex was the most affectionate. And I craved his touch in the same way he craved mine. He reached me and wrapped me in his arms like he was trying to make us one person. He nuzzled my neck, and I kissed his head.

"Hey. Did you walk here?" He let out an affirmative raspberry on my neck, and I giggled like a schoolgirl. It truly was embarrassing. "You know I hate it when you walk alone. You're basically a delicious snack in a town filled with dieters who have bad impulse control. It would only take one lapse in judgment and they'd steal you from me forever."

It was a disagreement we'd had a couple of times already. I loved the town, but they were all predators and I could only trust them so much. Especially now. The thought of losing him, losing any of them, made me agitated.

And like always, Brody somehow just knew what I was feeling. Like he had a direct line to my emotions. "The Pup is fine, Rainey. But the sun is coming up, and I think we should all go get some sleep. What do you say?"

I nodded and twined my hand in Tex's. I stepped toward Brody and kissed him softly on the lips. Tonight I was brimming with an appreciation for the good-natured shapeshifter Alpha. "Let's go to bed."

I led them both to my bedroom, even though Tex had his own, and Brody helped me undress, unzipping my little black dress, and unhooking my garter belt and stockings. He groaned a little as he rolled them down, but didn't make a move. He just took care of me. God, I loved him, even though he was going to break my heart into a billion pieces one day soon.

Tex's nose twitched. "Why are you sad?"

Brody looked up at me from where he was kneeling on the floor, pausing to hear my answer. I shook my head, and then remembered Tex wouldn't be able to see it. "I just remembered I'm dead," I said softly.

That seemed to be enough, because Brody picked me up

and placed me in the center of the bed, and hopped in beside me, curling his overly hot body around my own. Tex hopped on the other side, his body pressed along mine until I was sandwiched between their warmth. By morning, I would no longer be the cold of a vampire, but like a stone warmed in the sun, I'd feel human again. At least until the night and they left me.

Tex kissed my eyelids, and then my lips. "Sleep, Mika. We'll guard your dreams."

With a long sigh, I did exactly that.

4

When I woke in the morning, the bed was empty but several voices were coming from the kitchen. I threw on one of Tex's band t-shirts and walked out into the kitchen. I needed coffee. Stat.

Walker was waiting at the kitchen bench, my favorite mug in hand, and I could have kissed him. So I did. Yay. Standing on my tippy-toes, I pecked his lips, lingering a little. His lips were soft but hesitant, and when a throat cleared behind me I understood why. Maybe I should have worn underwear.

I turned and saw X grinning from behind me. I guess he'd just gotten an eyeful of my ass. My cheeks flushed, but I gave him a cool look. "I hope you are here to apologize?"

He raised an eyebrow. "For what?"

I shook my head and took a long sip of my coffee to fortify

my patience. "For ruining my date by almost dying. For biting me without asking my permission. For giving me an unwanted orgasm."

"Is an orgasm ever really unwanted?" He grinned. I pursed my lips and he sighed. "Sorry, Love. For biting without your permission at least. That was wrong. For ruining your date though?" He looked over my shoulder at Walker. "I did get stabbed in the back with a blade that will ensure the wound never fully heals, just for you, so you'll have to give me some leeway there."

He didn't seem in the least bit apologetic. I looked at his hard, scarred face, the tattoos that ran up his neck and down his arms, tattoos and scars he must have gotten as a human. He must have lived a rough life filled with violence before his turning. Getting a man like that to bend would be almost impossible. But I'd be damned if I didn't want to try. So, inexplicably, instead of getting mad, I rolled my eyes and went to the fridge to find a yogurt. None of that light crap they make you eat when you diet. A full fat, full cream, sugar-laden concoction that was amazing. No such thing as undead diabetes, thank god.

I grabbed a spoon and pointed it at him. "You bring up an interesting point. Why did you get stabbed in the back with the Traitor's Blade, and how was it for me exactly? We are basically strangers." I jumped up onto the bench beside Judge, who'd been silent so far. He leaned over and kissed my cheek, and I smiled at my sexy drifter. His midnight eyes ate me up, and suddenly I wanted to be back in bed. That was just the effect Judge had on me. And apparently on Tex, if his twitching nose and hooded gaze was anything to go by.

"Sure thing, Love. But then you gotta explain to me how you've bewitched this many incorrigible bachelors. Maybe you have a venomous vag—" Walker cleared his throat, and X grinned. "Tongue. Maybe you have a venomous tongue too?"

My laugh echoed around the kitchen. "Some of us just have a winning personality. You should work on that, X." I leaned my head on Judge's shoulder as I ate my yogurt. "What's X short for anyway? Xavier? Axolotl?"

"Executioner."

I looked between him and Judge. Pieces started to click. "Judge. Executioner. Who was the Jury?" All mirth left both X and Judge's faces, which was an answer in itself. "It was Miranda, wasn't it? Impartial Jury."

Judge gave a short nod, but X's face remained shut down. So much history there, a mystery that I wanted to solve but I knew I wasn't going to like the answer. If ignorance was bliss, then sign me up.

"I'm going to assume that Executioner wasn't the name you were born with?"

X's lips twitched. "Harry. But Harry is dead; I don't go by that anymore." His face was scary at that moment, so I nodded. X it was.

Brody was sitting at the table, eating toast and reading the paper through the whole exchange, appearing oblivious or at least unconcerned, until he spoke up. "You were saying about how you got the knife wound?"

X sighed, and leaned back on his chair. "I would kill for a cup of tea right now. You got any English Breakfast?" At my blank look, he continued. "Lucius found out that I'd been working with Judge on the side, not declaring all the results of my investigation, namely the issue of you." He looked me in the eyes and I realized his eyes were a nearly black shade of brown. "He found out that I warned you the Vampire Nation and its Enforcers were coming. He decided it was a betrayal of the code. I've been extradited. Banished with a knife in my back. So it looks like I'm bunking with you, Sweetcheeks." He looked longingly at my bare legs where they dangled over the end of the bench, though my ankles were crossed so I was being as respectable as a person could be while not wearing pants.

Someone let out a cough that sounded a little bit like "No fucking way," and I struggled to keep a straight face.

"Judge has a spare room for you, I'm sure."

Walker was shaking his head. "We need to ask the Council if you can stay first. We are on unstable ground with them already after we kind of forced Tex on them."

"Hey!" The man in question protested. "I am not an unwanted stray puppy, despite what the Alpha Dick says."

Brody laughed, punching Tex in the shoulder fondly. Judge kissed my cheek and went over to our tattooed anomaly. He reached down, placing his forefinger under Tex's

35

chin until he could lean down and kiss him softly. Watching the casual intimacy between the two of them hit me in the gut every time. It was always a weird combination of yearning, lust and something indescribable that filled my chest.

"A completely wanted stray puppy, don't worry," Judge murmured.

My eyes drifted to X, and he was watching the scene as well, but his face was inscrutable. He didn't seem disgusted, or jealous or anything I could easily name. If he felt any particular way about the relationship between Judge and Tex, he was holding it close to his chest.

Everyone else was used to it now. Brody was still reading the paper, and Walker was standing beside me. I hadn't realized I'd stopped with the spoon halfway to my mouth until he leaned in and stole the spoonful of yogurt.

"Hey!" I whispered, but he just waggled his eyebrows and licked his lips. I watched the tip of his tongue trace his full lower lip and groaned. Seriously. If I had my way, I'd never get out of bed. Too many hot guys in your life was hell on your motivation to put on pants every day, you know? He knew all too well the direction of my thoughts, and his hot look promised that one day he was going to use my body like it was his own personal toy and that I would love it. Yeah, a look could say all that.

X was shaking his head. "This place is worse than the brothel I was born in. Don't worry, Sheriff. I'm pretty sure your Council will accept me into their fold. You see, I fill a need that they have right now."

"What's that? Because I can tell you, we don't require a hangman," Walker said, his tone almost peevish. Something about the mercenary got under the skin of my good Sheriff.

X smirked. "Killing is just one of the skills in my ball bag of goodies, Sheriff. I also happen to be a trained surgeon. Medically licensed and everything. Well, I was when I was alive. And I hear you are now in need of a town doctor."

My jaw unhinged, the spoon hanging out. When I'd met Judge, and mistaken his moniker for his profession, I'd been surprised and disbelieving. But the idea of Judge as an upholder of the law was infinitely more believable than X being a doctor, fixing boo-boos. I looked at Judge, and he nodded.

"Seriously? You want to settle in Dark River, give up all your rights to drink and fuck whoever you want whenever you want? Plus, you know, the no-killing thing." The idea of X becoming a wholesome member of the community like Bert or Walker or even Antonio over at the dry cleaners was insane. Even Judge had balked at the idea. "I can't believe you were a doctor. Unless you were removing kidneys for the black market?"

Tex laughed from where he was leaning against Judge's hip. X looked at them again, face still unreadable. "Nope. I was completely legitimate. I had a practice on Harley Street and everything. Very reputable."

I called bullshit, but I was prepared to be wrong. If it meant it was easier for him to stay in Dark River, I wasn't going to protest.

We all sat in silence, stunned by the killer's admission he was a healer, or because there was nothing to say, I wasn't sure.

"Lucius is close, isn't he?" Brody asked, sitting up from his relaxed position, going from laidback lover to shapeshifter Alpha in a heartbeat.

X nodded solemnly. "I say he'll be here within a week. I'm sorry I'm not still there to feed you information," he said, directing the last comment to Judge.

Judge clapped him on the shoulder. "You've done enough. It was time to get out."

Hmm. More secrets. I jumped from the bench, landing as gently as a cat. Vampire Boon #267. "I have to get ready for work. My boss is a real slavedriver."

I'd been given a temporary post at the Sheriff's office, doing dispatch and filing. But I mean, there was hardly anything to do. It was a tiny town. Mostly neighbor disputes, liaising with the clans and supernaturals in the area, reports to the Council, and the odd murder like mine. Nothing that really needed a secretary. I missed my job at The Immortal Cupcake, the books, and the late-night movies. I missed Angeline, my friend.

I shuffled into the bathroom, weighed down by the sadness again. I locked the door so no one tried to follow me in. Sometimes I just wanted to wallow, without an obligatory orgasm while pressed against the shower tiles.

The guys were pretty good though; they seemed to know when I needed space, and when I needed them to barge past my barriers and hold me close. It was a fine line and sometimes I didn't even know.

When I emerged thirty minutes later, I was alone in the cottage. My phone dinged beside the bed. I looked down and found they'd added me to their group chat.

WALKER: Hey, going to work. See you there, Raine. *Kissy face*

JUDGE: TAKING X TO SEE THE COUNCIL. WILL DROP BY LATER TO TAKE RAINY DAY TO THE DINER FOR LUNCH. MISS SEEING HER FACE WITHOUT YOU ASSHOLES AROUND.

TEX: You don't have to yell, Judge. *Laughing emoji*

JUDGE: I WASN'T SHOUTING. I WAS TYPING.

BRODY: Don't bother with the text etiquette, Pup. It's a wasted lesson.

BRODY: Rainey, me and Tex are going back out to see the Pack. Be back before sunrise tomorrow. Xoxo

RAINE: Okay guys. Be safe and come back to me. Xoxox

·   ·   ·

I hated it when they left without saying goodbye. I had an irrational fear since my death. That something might happen, and I'd never have gotten to say goodbye. A little PTSD to talk over with Nico next week.

I'd slipped on a bra and underwear when the front door opened and then suddenly I was squished between two bodies. I knew the smell of their blood, the thump of their hearts. My shifters.

Tex nuzzled into my neck, just like Brody always did. "Couldn't leave without saying goodbye."

Brody reached his long arms around us both, pressing me closer without pushing Tex away. "Never goodbye. Only see you soon." He kissed me gently then let us go.

Tex remained wrapped around my body. "I hate leaving you, every single time I worry you're going to disappear forever," he murmured against my skin. So maybe we both had PTSD.

I ran my hand over his hair. "I'm not going anywhere. I'm really hard to kill, apparently."

He huffed against my skin. "Not funny, Mi—" He swallowed down my old name. "Raine. I don't wanna test how hard you are to kill."

I wrapped my arms around his waist and held him tight against me, feeling the steady thud of his heart against my cheek, the warmth of his muscles pressed against mine, the smell that was just inherently Tex surrounding me like a blanket. "I promise I'll be good. I have Judge and Walker. They'll keep me safe. You don't have to worry anymore."

He stepped away, the smile on his face not quite wiping away the worry around his eyes. "You're my mate. I don't think you fully understand that yet, but it means I'll always worry when I'm not here to protect you. Even if I am the least capable of your lovers."

Brody clapped him on the back. "Don't underestimate the ferocity of a mate-bond, Pup. I hazard to guess that if Raine was ever in danger, you would be the most dangerous of us all." He smiled over his shoulder at me. "But we are burning moonlight, and we have a Pack meeting at an ungodly hour. All this vampire shit is messing with my sleeping patterns."

I walked them to the door, and they hopped into Brody's ridiculously hot car, but not before each of them kissed me like it was going to be the last time.

I watched them leave, staring into the distance until I could no longer hear the rumble of the Impala. I walked average Joe-slow to work. I finally understood what Walker had been talking about when I'd first discovered that we could run faster than the human eye could follow. When you're too focused on getting somewhere as quickly as possible, you miss out on all the small things that make life so enjoyable. Like the fact that Elsie, a vampire who owned the convenience store, had acquired a garden statue of two gnomes fucking.

I stopped and stared at the offending statue. The globes of

its little butt were polished to a high pink, its blue gnome pants around its ankles. You know what, I probably could have missed out on that little thing without too much regret. Shaking my head, I ran the rest of the way to the police station. That was enough life for one day.

I pushed open the heavy metal door to the station. Walker was still here; I could hear him rustling around in the filing cabinet. I put my phone in the top drawer, but not before checking the group chat. Silence.

"Did Brody and Tex get off okay?" Walker yelled from the storeroom where he kept all his files.

I grinned. "Oh, I got them off just fine. We tried the screaming eagle position, dicks everywhere."

Walker stuck his head around the door jamb to look back in the office, his eyebrows almost touching his hairline. "You did what now?"

I waved a hand. "Nothing. I was kidding. The guys left fine ten minutes ago. I just hate it when they aren't here. They only got back yesterday."

Walker came out, a file tucked under his arm. He wrapped the other arm around me and pulled me close to his chest. "They are probably safer on Pack lands than they are here."

That was a sad truth. I was exposing them both to the possibility of death just by keeping them close to me here in Dark River. And it wasn't just the Vampire Nation and the Enforcers that could be a problem, but any one of the residents of Dark River could just snap. I could just snap, no matter how in control I felt now.

I nodded against Walker's chest before finally pulling away and going to sit at the makeshift desk they'd created me along one wall. Nico had given me one of his cheesy nineties inspirational posters. Unfortunately, it wasn't the iconic 'Hang In There' kitten. It was an empty boat in the middle of a crystal blue ocean. It read 'Destiny: The choices we make, the chances we take, determine our destiny.' It was all very inspiring, but it made me wonder if being here, in Dark River, was my destiny? I mean, I was happy, wasn't I? I had some good friends and some great, uh, boyfriends, so maybe this was all preordained. But then I looked at that empty boat in the middle of the vast ocean, and wondered if it ever got lonely?

The phone pulled me out of my existential angst. It was an old rotary phone that I didn't even think would still work on modern lines. It was some kind of magic.

"Sheriff's office, how can I help you?"

A disgruntled male voice on the other end of the line huffed, "Well you can start by sending the Sheriff over to arrest this crazy woman." I could hear someone screeching on the other end that they weren't crazy, the caller was crazy, and sounding a little bit insane.

"Certainly. What seems to be the issue?"

"I busted Betty-Lou shitting on my lawn." I blinked,

pulling a face at Walker, who could hear both sides of the conversation with his enhanced hearing.

"Ooookay. The Sheriff will be right around." I hung up as the screaming started again, and looked at Walker. "Shit, I forgot to get their address."

Walker waved a hand. "It's fine. Eugene lives next to Betty-Lou, and I'm almost positive that was him. Not that many voices in the town that I don't have them memorized. Want to come and help with the poo-flinging crazies?" He leaned down and kissed me softly. I threaded my fingers in his soft, dark hair and pulled him closer. I explored his mouth like it was the first time we'd ever kissed. I ran my tongue over his lower lip, then slid it across his fangs, making him moan into my mouth. He shuddered and pulled away. "It takes every ounce of my control not to slide you onto this desk and fuck you like an animal."

"Yes, please?"

He grinned at the hopeful note in my voice. "One day soon, I promise. First I have to go deal with Eugene and Betty-Lou, and the case of the mysterious poo."

I shook my head furiously. "As interesting as that sounds, I better hold down the fort. I'll hear all about it later when I type up the report."

Walker sighed, pushing his cute little Mount-Me hat onto his head. God, he was really something in that chocolate brown uniform. We were going to have to defile it very soon. "Wish me luck," Walker said, giving me one last kiss.

"Good luck."

I went back to typing up seventy-year-old reports and saving them to a storage drive. I was pretty certain Walker was making work for me to do, but that was okay. At least I felt like I was doing something constructive. Finishing my report from yesterday on an argument about who got to have a prime piece of land on the corner of the Main Square, I pulled the next file down.

It was from eighty-five years ago. Walker only started as Sheriff eighty-seven years ago, so this one must have been in the first couple of years as a Sheriff. I opened the file, and looking back at me was a beautiful dark-haired woman. She had big sad eyes, but there were slight wrinkles around their edges that told me she'd known laughter and happiness in her mortal life. Rosalita Fuentes. I skimmed through the details page. Turned in 1920, maker undisclosed. I skimmed down a little more. Joined Dark River in 1925, sentenced to death in 1928.

I read the notes in Walker's strong hand. It hadn't changed in eighty-odd years.

"*Perpetrator was doing well within town limits. Exhibited good control. Felt strong enough to return home to visit family. Exsanguinated former husband and all five children. Handed self in for punishment. Highly distraught.*"

Holy shit. Holy shit. That could have been me. My heart tore in two for the unknown vampire. I turned over the page, and there was another photo clipped to the file above the transcription of the Council's ruling and her execution date. The photo was of Walker and Rosalita, smiling at each other. They'd obviously been a couple, given how their hands were threaded together, and they were grinning like school kids.

My heart broke a little more for Walker, who'd been so happy, and the way he'd handled my turning made a little more sense. But he'd never mentioned her. Not even once.

I finished typing it up and tried not to fixate too hard on why he'd kept her a secret from me.

5

I'd left the file on my desk, closed, like there was a monster between the covers of that manila folder. Maybe I'd ask Walker about it, or maybe not. I didn't want to dredge up something that was obviously painful for no reason, but on the other hand, I desperately wanted to know more.

I went back to boring data entry until the front door of the office screeched, and in swaggered the bad boy of my dreams.

"Hey there, Rainy Day. You ready for a break?"

I swear, he made my heart flutter every single time he walked into a room. It was ridiculous and a little high school, but the man made me swoon. I stood up and slid my phone into my back pocket. "I'm starving," I said, and it came out way more like a purr than I'd intended.

Judge's eyes hooded, and he bit his lower lip. Which just made me want to do the same thing. I sashayed across the room, and into waiting arms.

"Ah, Sugar, there's nothing more I'd like to do than bend you over your stuffy Sheriff's desk and fuck you while I taste your delicious blood, but I left X outside, and he's like a toddler you can't leave unattended for too long."

I heard a chuckle from outside the door. "Don't hold back on my account, brother. I might just join in?"

Judge rolled his eyes and mouthed, "See?"

I laughed and kissed him, sucking his full bottom lip between my teeth and scraping my fangs along the soft skin inside until it bled. Then I sucked harder, and he moaned. Hell, I moaned too. Even X moaned, and he couldn't see what was happening.

I gave Judge a smug grin and stepped away. "We better go before X makes a spectacle of himself."

Judge held the door open for me, and I stepped out into the warm darkness of summer. X was leaning against the wall of the Sheriff's office, a smirk on his razor-sharp face. "I know your town frowns on biting people, but how do they feel about public masturbation?"

"Not positively, I don't think?" I said, grinning because I couldn't help myself.

He nodded with mock seriousness. "I'm willing to test the theory. If you and Judge could just stand over there and do that thing you did in the good Sheriff's office, that would be great." He reached for the zip on his worn, tight jeans, and Judge punched him in the arm.

"No one wants to watch you pull your sausage, or whatever it is you Brits call it."

"Whack my willy?" X suggested.

I giggled. "Beat your meat?"

"Flog the one-eyed toad?"

I honked out a laugh. "Seriously? That seems a little violent."

X gave me a lascivious wink. "That's how I like it, Love."

Well, that thought made heat pool in very inconvenient places. Judge just walked faster, rolling his eyes so far back he could probably see his brain. I hurried to catch up, before X caught something telling on my face, like lust or drool. Gah, there was something about him, about his rough edges and that coiled air of violence, that seriously made me pant. It reminded me of Judge, but if Judge was like a torrential river that sucked you down, then X was like the sharp rocks that shredded your body.

We walked across the square, and I noticed people instinctively avoided us. Where Judge might have been taken in as the Drifter—a solitary entity that made them uncomfortable but that was it—the two of them together screamed threat. In a town full of predators, they were the biggest, baddest monsters. Or maybe they were avoiding me —it wouldn't be the first time in the last few weeks. It was like no one knew what to say to me anymore. Or maybe they blamed me for almost killing Walker, and Alice's execution.

When we opened the door to the diner, I expected the silence. I was almost becoming immune. Judge tipped his invisible hat to Beatrice, who waved us down the counter to three spare stools right at the end. It was Judge's spot, the place he always sat when he wasn't with me and the guys. They both waited until I sat down, old school chivalry that I now expected from Judge, but was a bit of a surprise from X.

"So, what's going on with you and the human?" X asked Judge, looking at the menu. "Do you think they do a full English breakfast here? Black pudding?"

"Umm, I don't know about the blood sausage, but what's goin' on with Tex and me isn't really your business," Judge said, but there was no heat in his words. I realized these guys weren't just old colleagues, but old friends.

X traced his finger down his menu and stopped at bacon and eggs. "That'll do. You know I don't care either way, mate. Don't get your undies in a bunch. I just wanna know if you guys are doing the two-man tango or if it's more serious, like you and Red over there. Because, I gotta say, you went from confirmed bachelor to shacking up with the little woman and some man candy awful quick."

Judge was looking directly at me when he said, "Some people are worth changing for." Then he went back to looking at his menu like he hadn't just confessed the Judge version of 'I love you.'

But the look on X's face said he knew, and so did I.

"Whiskey-nips?"

"What?" Was he having a stroke?

"Do you have nipples that give whiskey? Is that your new vamp power?"

I scoffed and flipped him the bird. "Amazing personality, remember?" Luckily, I was saved from his smartass comeback by the arrival of Beatrice.

"Hello, Lass," she said, smiling softly. I loved Beatrice. "Ah, good to see you're still alive, you good-fer-nothin' degenerate."

What in the Furby-loving hell?

X just laughed so loudly, everyone in the diner turned to stare. "Ah, Beatrice, you saucy fucking wench. It was touch and go, but I'm hard to kill."

Beatrice waggled a finger at him as she filled all our mugs with coffee. "So is a cockroach, lad. So is a cockroach." She grinned at me, and I thought that Beatrice might actually be fond of him. "What can I get for you? I'm going to tell Bert to spit in this one's food, so I recommend not getting the same thing as him."

X began giggling so hard, he could hardly breathe. Beatrice looked bemused.

"Just pancakes, thanks, Beatrice." I looked over at Judge and mouthed, "What the fuck is happening?"

Judge just shook his head in bemusement. "The usual please, Beatrice. If Bert needs a hand with the spitting though, you just let me know."

She walked away, without asking X for his order, but I had a suspicion he would somehow get what he wanted anyway.

I wanted to ask what happened with the Council, but not with so many supernatural ears around. Which left a conversational void for a question I really wanted to know the answer to. "So, what was the go with you guys and Miranda? Were you a thruple?"

X screwed up his nose. "A what?"

"A committed ménage," Judge answered, surprising the shit out of me. It was a day for surprises apparently. He shrugged. "Tex talks about it. He says we are a Quiple or Quinple? He thinks you should start dating X so we can be a Sexuple."

X just stared at him, then looked at me. "What the hell have you done to him, Love? It's like he's been body-snatched." He took a long sip of coffee. "I loved the cold-hearted witch. She loved the pretty Southern boy. He only loved himself. And now you, it would seem. It didn't end well, as you can imagine. But we were the Council's favorite clean up crew, so we were kind of stuck in that toxic cycle." He stirred his coffee, even though he was drinking it black. At that moment, without the perverted sense of humor, lost in a little heartache, I could see the Harley Street surgeon beneath the Jack the Ripper killer. "I need to talk to the proprietress of this fine establishment about getting tea. This shit is like sludge. Excuse me."

I watched him go, walking straight past Beatrice and out the front door. Guilt ate at my gut. I'd known it was going to be a sore subject, but I'd poked at the wound anyway. I looked over at Judge, his eyes were characteristically blank. He reached out and covered my hand with his. "It's okay, Rainy Day. He'll calm down, and will be back being the smartass prick he normally is. Miranda and him, it was messy. He loved her so damn much, and I had no fucking idea. He's not the easiest guy to read."

I bit my lip. I was still going to have to apologize. "What happened?" Judge's jaw tightened. "Hey, you don't have to tell me. The past is the past, right?"

He pulled my stool closer, so our hips were touching. "He pursued her for years. Maybe a decade. She wanted nothing to do with him. You've met her. To her, he was too thuggish. Too flirty. Too interested. I... did not take to my new position as a killer for hire so well. I was moody, standoffish. I wasn't interested in her flirtations, and that just made her more inter-ested. More persistent. But I had no idea that he wanted her for anything more than a convenient fuck. I had no idea he loved her. Sometimes we'd scratch that itch that came up when you are on the road a lot with another person, but it was never when X was around. Not on purpose, but it just worked out like that. Now I know it was because Miranda knew of his feelings." He sighed, and there was a world of regret riding on that breath.

"Anyway, we had a really bad run-in with an entire nest of rogue vampires. I was down, so was X, and we fucked. I mean Miranda and me"—he paused, looking at his mug—"not X and me. I'll never forget the look on his face, you know? He'd been slashed to pieces days before by rogues, but it wasn't until that moment that he looked truly shredded. Anyway, the rest is history. We continued to work together until it was so tense we started making mistakes. Miranda is too valuable to the Witch Cabal, so they called her back, we disbanded and I got the fuck out of the Enforcers. I got back in touch when you got murdered. It didn't add up for me, and there was only one man I truly trusted to look into this stuff with me."

I nodded. "Thank you for telling me." I leaned forward and kissed him softly. It didn't matter to me, not really, not anymore. But I was happy he trusted me with this little piece of his past, when getting information from him was normally like extracting teeth from a crocodile. I lifted my hand and waved to Beatrice. "Can we get those meals to go, please?"

Beatrice nodded but moved off to take someone else's orders. I stood up and reached over to kiss Judge's cheek. His midnight blue eyes burned into mine, as if he was trying to tell if I was really okay with the whole sordid story. I was. It was a tale as old as time, and he was as old as dirt. If he hadn't been caught in one love triangle in all that time, was he even really alive?

"Can you find X and bring him back to my house? I should apologize. But first..."

I dashed out the door. I had a stop to make, and I wanted to do it alone.

6

I still loved the stained glass windows out the front of The Immortal Cupcake, formerly the best bakery/bookshop in North America. But instead of being lit up from within, the images of horses and oceans etched in the window seems lifeless. Dead.

I still had a key to the back door, so I walked down the back alley to the rear entrance door. Up the stairs was my old apartment, still coated in Walker's flaking blood. Shaking my head to chase away the memories, I let myself in. It felt wrong to be in The Immortal Cupcake without Angeline. Without the other people of Dark River bustling around, waiting patiently for some kind of baked confection.

I strolled through the darkened kitchen, and into the main cafe area. I wanted to cry. So many good memories tainted by one hour of badness. I'd started a new life in this very room. Refound happiness right here. Now I could never be comfortable here again.

"What are you doing here?"

"Holy Jesus fucking a frog," I screeched, startling at the voice in the darkness. I spun around and saw Angeline standing in the library. Her hair was stringy and standing up on end, and she was in yoga pants and a misshapen sweater that hung to her knees. She looked like shit, though I felt like shit for even thinking it.

Her lips twitched. "That's very blasphemous, Raine." Her voice was flat, grief darkening the edges.

"Shit, sorry. I mean, you scared me, that's all."

God, it was good to see her. I'd been worried about her, even though Cresta and Ella had said she was fine. I wasn't sure I had the right to be worried about her anymore, but I couldn't help it. She just looked at me, and I shifted uncomfortably from foot to foot. The silence was getting awkward. We both spoke at the same time.

"I should go—"

"Raine, I—"

I waved at her. "You first."

She nodded and sighed. "I don't blame you. Logically, I know that none of this is your fault. But every time I look at you, I see her." She swallowed hard. "Coming back here was hard enough. To come back here and see you every day would be torture."

I was pretty sure my heart would have hurt less if she'd

just punched her fist into my chest and pulled it out. It was like someone telling you, 'it's you, not me' after a date, or your parents telling you that you were the reason they got a divorce. I wanted to rage about how that wasn't fair, that we were friends and that it was in no way my fault. Instead, I just nodded once. "Okay."

I turned and walked toward the front door. What else could I say that wouldn't exacerbate her pain?

"Wait, what did you come here for?"

I pointed to the coffee table and my teacup that was still sitting there. It was my favorite, picked up from the internet. Angeline had loved them so much she'd stocked a few in the cafe.

"Oh." She picked it up and handed it to me. Then she went behind the counter and got me another one from the stock, along with my favorite tea. I felt a little like the puppy that was abandoned on the side of the road, but with a box and a blanket to assuage their guilt. She passed me the whole lot. "Take this one too. I know you had your eye on it."

I took them from her, careful not to touch her, and I slid them into my handbag. I didn't know whether I was supposed to say goodbye or see you later. Because it wasn't goodbye. We had to live in the same tiny town together for eternity. And she didn't want to see me later. She never wanted to see me again. So instead, I just left as fast as my legs could carry me, which was fortunately at the speed of light now.

My Converses smelled like melting tires by the time I got

back to my cottage. I couldn't hear anyone inside, which was good because I flopped on the couch and tried not to think about the last fifteen minutes. Maybe the last hour.

"You really shouldn't leave the door unlocked. All sorts of cretins can walk in," X said from the darkness. I hadn't even heard the beat of his heart or smelled the scent of his blood. I covered my startled response with a yawn. It was really smooth.

I shrugged. "What are they going to do? Murder me? Been there, done that." I sat up, finding him sitting in the dark recess of my kitchen window seat.

He stood, looking massive in the darkness. "There are worse things that can happen to a person than death, Love. Just lock the doors." He prowled toward the door.

I stood up. "Wait!" I grabbed my handbag and went into the kitchen. "I stopped and got you some tea. I wanted to say I'm sorry, I guess. I shouldn't have poked at something I knew you guys didn't want to talk about. Stay. We'll start again, without murderous makers and ex-lovers. Just Raine and X."

He let out a small, mirthless laugh. "What about Mika and Harry?" But he turned and strolled back towards the kitchen. I turned on the lights.

"Harry and Mika are dead. All that's left are pieces of them, stitched together to make a new life. When I dream, I still dream as Mika. I think it will be a while before she's dust, but there's no room left for her here."

I got the teacups out of my handbag, rinsing them under the tap.

"You smell sad," X said conversationally. I wasn't sure how I smelled sad. Shapeshifters could scent my moods, but not vampires. At least to my admittedly limited knowledge. Did he want me to answer that? The silence drew out, and I turned.

"I ran into Angeline after you left."

He frowned. "The bird who was your maker's lover?"

I made a small affirmative noise. Hopefully, he'd drop it, but it would be karma if he didn't.

"Want me to kill her for you?"

I nearly dropped the teacup in my hand. "What? No!"

"Offer stands."

I smiled over my shoulder at him. Was that the X equivalent of flirting again?

I put water in the teacup, and opened the microwave and set it to cook. X was on his feet and beside me in an instant.

"What the hell are you doing, woman?!"

I reared back. "Boiling the water?"

He muttered something that sounded a little derogatory and stopped the microwave. "You don't heat water for tea in the microwave, you feckin' heathen." He pulled a saucepan from the cupboard next to the stovetop. "Guess it would be ridiculous to hope you had an actual kettle, but this is better than heating in the feckin' microwave. In china!" He grumbled some more as he moved the teacups away from me, like he was protecting his young. I couldn't help it, I started giggling and couldn't stop.

He gave me a disgusted look. "Don't laugh, woman. That was a travesty. I bet you don't even have a teapot. This continent is basically the Wild fucking West still." He continued to mutter and I could only laugh harder. He picked me up, and walked me out of the kitchen, setting me on a stool. "You can come back when you are apologetic for what you've done."

Then he looked at my teacups and laughed. "Which one do you want? The one that says 'Go Fuck Yourself'? Oh look, it says 'Bitch' on the saucer. That's quaint." He picked up the other one. "Or the one that says, 'You've been Poisoned' and the saucer says 'Bye Bitch'. No, I want that one. You can go fuck yourself, Bitch."

He got out a second pot, calling me a barbarian once or twice more, then spooned in the loose leaf tea. Finally, he poured over the boiling water. "At least it isn't bagged shit. One point to Gryffindor for that one."

"Did you just make a Harry Potter reference?" For some reason, this huge, scarred, skin-head looking killer making Harry Potter jokes just slayed me. I lied—you could die twice. I could barely stay on the breakfast stool, I was laughing so hard now. My stomach ached and tears streamed down my cheeks.

X was still scowling at me, but the corners of his lips were twitching. "We don't all live in the Dark Ages in the middle of the fucking Canadian wilderness, Love."

He let me laugh myself out until I was hiccupping as I tried to suck in enough oxygen. Not that I needed it. Laughing as a vampire was a biologically weird thing.

"Ya' done?"

I nodded, wiping my face on my arm. When I looked up, X was giving me a strange look.

"I can see it now, you know."

I self-consciously rubbed my nose. Because boogers were a real possibility right now. "See what?"

"Why he loves you."

My laughter drained from my chest as we stared at each other for a moment, the scent of tea perfuming the air. I wondered if I'd read the situation all wrong. I wondered if Judge had read it wrong all those years ago. Was it not Judge that X was jealous of, but Miranda? The looks he gave Tex suddenly took on a different light.

"Do you love him?"

He raised his eyebrows. "Judge? Sure. I love the man. Do I want him to suck my cock? Not right now, no."

I huffed out a laugh. "And you called me a barbarian."

He placed a china teacup in front of me. "No. For better or worse, it was that heinous witch that I loved. She tore my heart out and stomped on it, and now all that's left is a dark pit where it should be."

I went to lift my teacup to my lips, but he grabbed my

wrist and stilled my hand. "Good lord. How have you survived this long? You need to let it cool, because a scalded esophagus is not fun, even for vampires. If you want a throat injury, I can think of more enjoyable ways to get it." I dropped the teacup back into the saucer with an audible clink.

Judge strolled into the cottage like he owned the place, which technically I thought he might. Well, at least a partial share of its purchase price. "This is cozy." He came over and kissed my cheek. "Whatever he's told you, it's all lies."

I grabbed his hip and pulled him closer. "He said he didn't want to suck your dick."

Judge gave me that grin, that one that tempted you into sin. "Well, Sugar, that's the biggest lie of all."

X just gave him the two-finger salute and yawned. "I was teaching your girl how to make a decent cup of tea in this fucking frontier town."

Judge raised his eyebrows, and I waved him away. "Don't get him started. What I really, really want to know is what the Council said about Doctor Strange over there?"

"I bet Bendydick Cucumbercrotch would know how to make a decent cup of tea, Love. He's British after all." X took a sip of his tea. "It's safe to drink. Your Council wasn't over-joyed by my arrival, I guess you could say. But they have a need, and I have a skill. They are trying to be all kumbaya and bullshit here, and don't want to turn down applicants for their town. Though they might make a special exception for me."

Judge filled in the blanks. They voted and were dead-locked. They decided that the acceptance of two former Enforcers would just bring the eye of the Vampire Nation back to the town over and over again. The other half decided that having two Enforcers could only strengthen our stance. The Vampire Nation already had us in their sights. There was no point hiding under the covers and hoping that it wouldn't happen. That last bit sounded like Nico.

I stood and downed my tea in one gulp, mostly because I was in a hurry, but a little bit because I enjoyed X's outraged face. They say that your outraged face and the face you make when you orgasm is the same.

I kissed Judge, nipping his lip. I looked over at X, who was doing his best to look bored with the whole thing. "I better get back to work. Come over for dinner tonight? Both of you."

X nodded, and Judge wrapped me in his arms. "We'll be there. Just because X pisses off the Sheriff so bad."

Incorrigible. Seriously.

7

The rest of the day passed like normal. In all honesty, after the last twenty-four hours, I needed a little normal. Apparently, Betty-Lou hadn't shit on Eugene's lawn. It was raccoon poop. I had a feeling that Betty-Lou might start now though. Walker told me all about it, and I thought perhaps Eugene had a thing for Betty-Lou, who was a slightly dumpy, plain vampire but had a smile so brilliant it could light up a stadium. If I was Eugene, a boring accountant, I'd have a thing for her too. But someone needed to give poor old Eugene some hints about picking up women, because accusing them of defecating on your lawn was not the way to go about it. By the end of the story, Walker was laughing so hard he was crying, and I was curled in a ball holding my straining stomach muscles. I decided, in that happy moment filled with laughter, not to mention Rosalita

Fuentes. I'd finish writing up her file, put it back in the storage room, and pretend I'd never seen it. If today had taught me anything, it was that there was danger in poking at old wounds. We all had traumatic pasts. Pain let us know we were alive. We could dwell on it, or let the scars toughen us for the next time.

Eventually, we decided to call it a day, and we walked home hand in hand. We stopped by the grocery store, picking up some bread rolls and wine, and a couple of steaks to barely cook.

Walker stopped at his house to shower and get changed, and I walked the extra few yards by myself. I stopped and drew in the warm, sweet night air. I missed the sun so badly. The feeling of warmth on my skin, like a layer of light. But the night was beautiful in her own way. Everything was a wash of blues and blacks, the stars ever-changing. Soon. Soon I'd be able to see the sun again.

My phone beeped in my purse and I pulled it out.

Brody: The Pup has a surprise. You guys are going to be so impressed, especially Rainey.

Me: What is it?

Tex: It's a surprise!

Me: Is the surprise you guys are coming home early?

Brody: No, but we are on our way home. We've done what we could. We are about an hour from Dark River.

Me: Then what is it?!

Brody just sent me the emoji with the zipped lips, and I smiled. I hated surprises. It was weird using my phone again, and the constant temptation to call home was still there but not quite as strongly. Reading about Rosalita murdering her family was enough to warn me off. I wasn't special or unique. I still hungered. I liked to think I would never hurt my family, but I couldn't ever be sure.

I set the groceries on the bench and poured some more wine. It was a wine kind of day. I let myself relax into the food prep. I mean, it wasn't hard. I wasn't making a twelve-course degustation menu. There was just something soothing about such a human task. I didn't need to eat anymore, except for other people I guess. My fangs ached at the thought. It had been too long since I'd had blood. Because I had access to both Brody and Tex, whose blood was as wild and fulfilling as they were, I didn't suffer from the hunger pangs a normal fledgling vampire would have. I'd gotten so lucky, ending up here in Dark River, which Judge liked to remind me of periodically. This was as close to a utopian version of a vampire community as we were ever going to get.

The door opened and closed, and Walker appeared, freshly scrubbed and handsome as hell. He was wearing a tight gray tee and dark blue jeans. His hair was still a little damp and he just took my breath away. My knife stilled where it was chopping salad ingredients, and I drank him in.

"You look..." Delicious. Breathtaking.

He strolled over, stepping into my space and wrapping his arms around my waist. "You do too."

I scoffed. I was still in the clothes I'd worn to work, no shoes, the polish on my toes starting to chip. I wasn't in any way beautiful or glamorous at that moment, but Walker was looking at me like I might be a goddess he wanted to worship on his knees.

Actually, I wouldn't mind that.

He rested his hands on my hips, leaning forward to kiss me tenderly. "What time is everyone coming over?"

"About four I think, why?"

He looked at his watch. "Just wanted to know if we had time for this." He grabbed me and lifted me onto the bench. I wrapped my legs around his waist, pressing my heels into his ass. He ran his hands under my shirt, sliding the tips of his fingers up my spine, making me shiver. He kissed my temple, the curve of my jaw, the pulse point in my neck. When he scraped his fangs along the column of my throat, I moaned.

His hands slid up my thighs, pulling me closer to his body. He lifted my shirt up until it bunched above my breasts, and ran his tongue down the curve of my breast until teeth scraped against my nipple. I moaned again, louder this time so it echoed around the kitchen.

"If I knew it was going to be this kind of feast, I would have left my pants at home," came X's sarcastic voice.

Walker looked up at me from where his face was still pressed against my boob. "I think I might hate this guy."

I laughed and ran my hand over his soft brown hair. "Stay the night?"

He shook his head, but there was a moment of hesitation that wasn't there last night. I was wearing down my straight-laced Sheriff, one sexy moment at a time.

Judge strolled in behind X, took a look at me on the bench with Walker still between my knees giving the sarcastic Brit a death glare, and held up a bottle in his hand. "I brought really strong moonshine. This shit will kill a horse. Brewed it myself in Bert's back shed. It makes X tolerable, I swear."

"The only thing that would make him more tolerable is a ballgag," Walker whispered in my ear, but he stood up to his full height, straightening my shirt and lifting me from the bench. I laughed and gave him a quick side hug. X was a six foot five cockblock for sure.

I waved them into the living room as Walker grabbed three beers from the fridge. He handed two to me and picked up the steaks. "I'll go put these on the grill."

I tilted my face up for one last kiss, which he happily provided. "Thanks. Throw a couple of extra on for Brody and Tex? They should be here soon."

He was still muttering under his breath about X as he walked out onto the back deck. The first thing I'd purchased for the house had been a grill for out back. My dad had always said that a home without a grill was no home at all. Might have been an exaggeration, and probably just because he wanted a new grill and my mom had said no, but the idea had stuck.

As always, thoughts of my parents made the pain of their loss fresh again. But I refused to not think of my family. I wouldn't forget them.

I wandered into the living room, handing X a beer and standing on my tippy toes to kiss Judge. "You guys are early," I chastised gently.

Judge kissed the top of my head. "Mmm, sorry about that, Rainy Day. It looked like you and Walker were finally about to go all the way."

I hummed noncommittally. I wasn't so sure about that. Walker had iron control—honestly, I didn't know how he did it—and he also had a very clear idea of how he wanted our first time to happen. But they'd definitely interrupted some good third base action, the bastards.

"I'm happy to pick up where he left off," Judge whispered in my ear, sending heat straight to my belly. I looked up at his burning midnight blue eyes filled with promises of pleasure. They were promises he kept every single time. I winked and sat down on the couch.

X was cursing up a storm under his breath. "There's enough sex pheromones to start an orgy in a nunnery in here. Do you guys ever quit?"

I just grinned. "Don't be jealous, Big Guy. Green is not a pretty color on you."

I probably shouldn't have challenged him like that. Four men were enough, thank you very much. Except for that little part in the back of my mind with a direct line to my lady bits which whispered that five might be better. X was so wounded, hiding his pain under all that sarcasm and innuendo. Maybe he just needed someone to see him, to love him. And god knows I found him sexy as fuck. That accent...

BAD RAINE. NO! Stop looking at the giant killer like he is a T-bone and you are a junkyard dog on heat.

I realized Judge and X had been speaking this whole time. Oops. "... check out my new office tomorrow night. I can't believe it myself. Thought for sure they were going to kick me out on my arse."

"Wait, sorry. Hold up. The Council said yes? You can stay as the town's doctor?"

X grinned. "That's what I just said. Weren't you listening, Love?" His knowing grin told me he knew exactly where my thoughts had been, the big bastard.

I took a big gulp of wine. "What else did they want in return?" I couldn't imagine them taking a risk on X without some kind of surety.

"They wanted Judge to put a ring on it too."

"You're taking the pledge?" I couldn't keep the surprise out of my voice. He'd been hesitant to commit to the town, even if he did follow their rules while he was here. Judge was a drifter, a constantly moving storm. Deep down, I'd always been prepared for him to move on when it got too tough. But he was committing to staying?

All my thoughts must have played in my eyes because he looked at the floor. "They gave me an offer I couldn't refuse."

"Which was?"

"Pledge or leave." He looked up at me with those haunting blue eyes. "I found that I wasn't ready to leave, so I pledged. You're looking at the newest citizen of Dark River, Sugar," he said, his voice light. I wanted to pin him to the couch and make him tell me how he really felt about being forced to stay, or if he was happy about it because he was happy here. Because he was content with me and Tex.

"Second newest," X corrected. "My first order of business is to give everyone in town a very thorough physical. Care to step into my office, Love?"

I grinned, shaking my head. "I'm undead. I'm pretty sure I'm the epitome of health right about now. But maybe you should start with Judge?"

X shook his head. "Maybe I'll start with your Sheriff. See if we can't extricate the giant stick that has become lodged in his rectal cavity."

"Hey!" I said, defending Walker. X might be cute, but Walker had stood by my side through the hardest moments of my life.

X had the good grace to raise his hands. "I'm just kidding, Love. I actually like the grumpy bastard. And if I'm honest with myself for once, I think I might just be a little bit jealous." He didn't look like he was kidding at that moment.

I was saved from answering by the sound of the Impala pulling up in my driveway. I jumped to my feet, grinning.

"Brody and Tex are home!" I raced toward the door, bouncing on my toes. Sure, it had only been like twelve hours, and I was acting like a golden retriever who'd gotten into the Red Bull, but I didn't care. They were back safe, and they had a surprise. Basically, it was a double whammy of awesomeness.

The door opened and Brody's grinning face lit up my world. He raced forward and kissed me as if he'd missed me as much as I'd missed him. For god's sake, I was truly pathetic. "Where's Tex?" I asked when he pulled away, and his smile got impossibly wider.

He stepped to the side, and I screamed.

"What the fuck is that?!"

8

Brody grinned as a huge motherfucking snake slithered into my house like it owned the place. I stood at the back of the lounge like a fucking sissy, hiding behind Judge and X.

"That's your significant other," Brody said, and I did a double-take at the snake.

"Tex?" I knew he was half shapeshifter, but I honestly didn't think he'd have the ability to transform into a twenty-five foot long fucking Nope-Rope as wide as a goddamn tree trunk. "Tex turns into a freaking prehistoric Anaconda?"

I ignored the fact that X was laughing and softly singing about his Anaconda not wanting 'none unless you've got buns, hun.' Instead, I was transfixed by the sinuously moving reptile in front of me.

"He's not an Anaconda. He's just a really huge python, I

think?" Brody offered super unhelpfully. The snake, I mean Tex, stopped in front of me and reared back until it stood up as tall as a man. It curled its tail in so it was like a big round ball of snake.

Then it transformed in a flash, back to Tex. Naked as the day he was born and grinning like a fool. I couldn't help but grin back.

"Did you see? I was a huge damn snake! I can't even describe what it's like, Mika. But I can see, kind of. Different kinds of senses but better than I can as a human. I can only shift into one form though. The Elders think it is because I'm only part shapeshifter. Or that I may only be a two-natured shifter."

"Two-natured?"

It was Brody who answered. "Shifters who only have one form. Like werewolves or lion shifters. We shapeshifters slip between forms like changing a suit, but the two-natured possess the souls of both an animal form and a human form."

I wrapped my arms around Tex's waist, hugging him tightly. I could only imagine what it would have been like to see something, anything, after a lifetime of darkness. His long, lean body was heavily tattooed, and my eyes once again fell on the snake on his neck. His first ever tattoo. Had he known subconsciously that he was some kind of snake shifter?

It was too much of a coincidence not to be true. "So Tex isn't really a shapeshifter like you? He's a two-natured shifter with a whole other soul or something? Is he still protected by the Pack?"

Tex's arms tightened around my waist, and Brody came over to kiss my head. "Of course he is. I doubt the vampires make the distinction. Maybe the Vampire Nation, as they have to deal with the ruling bodies of the world's other supernaturals. But to your Town Council? He's mine now. Shifter or shape changer, makes no difference to us. He is family. He is Pack."

God, I loved this man. I leaned back and kissed him gently, hoping the small caress expressed my big emotions.

"Do you think Lover Boy could put away his one-eyed snakelet now? I like you, Red, but I don't want to stare at some other bloke's naked ass all night."

I ran my hand down Tex's spine and over the globes of his ass. I happened to like his naked ass, and I was getting hungry.

"Rainy Day, you gotta stop giving him that look, otherwise I'm going to take you both into the other room and fuck you senseless."

X blushed, throwing his hands up in the air. "I'm out. I'm going to sear cow with the Good Sheriff."

He stomped out of the room, but not before I noticed a suspicious bulge in his jeans. Did he like the idea of Judge fucking me and Tex? He said he didn't swing that way, but I wondered if he wasn't a little bit of a voyeur. Boy, did that just make me even wetter.

Brody groaned, spinning me out of Tex's arms. He kissed me hard, a branding sort of kiss that promised he was going to fuck me in the most primal, earthy way he could. I kissed him back and moaned as his hands slid up my skirt to my underwear. He slipped a finger inside the elastic and moaned against my mouth. "You smell so fucking good right now. I just want to say to hell with dinner and eat you right here on your dining table. I don't think I'm the only one either." He removed his fingers without as so much as stroking my aching pussy. I pouted. "We decided no group sex for now outside of your little thruple with Tex and Judge. Not until you know where you stand with Walker. Also, whatever is going on with you and the blushing Brit."

I pulled away and crossed my arms over my chest. "You guys decided, huh? What about what I want? What if I wanted to fuck all five of you while rolling in a pile of potato chips and chocolate cake?"

Brody laughed. "I'd say that was a weirdly specific fantasy and then start baking a really fucking big cake." He pulled me back into his arms, and I looked past him at Tex and Judge, who were both tense. Always sending Brody in with the touchy news. "It's not forever. We can live out your orgy sploshing fantasies one day soon, I promise. But until Walker makes his move, we don't want to invite any jealousy into this alternative little scenario we have going on. Because we are happy, Raine. Even Walker. No one minds sharing you, because when you're happy, you are the most beautiful creature walking the planet. In a way, you've created your own Pack here and sometimes that means withholding your own desires for the emotional wellbeing of the group."

Dammit, I was going to cry. It was hard to pout and be angry when he was just so fucking sweet and sincere. This is why they always sent Brody with the bad news. "Fine. But you two"—I pointed at Tex and Judge—"are in so much trouble tonight. Eat three steaks. You are going to need your energy."

They both visibly relaxed and Tex laughed. "Do you wanna have sex on top of those steaks too? Because I have to admit, I am down for that."

I sashayed over, leaning in close to his ear. "Maybe," I whispered huskily. Then I bit his earlobe just this side of a little too hard and walked out onto the back deck.

We ate steaks and salad outside, drinking glassful after glassful of Judge's moonshine. And boy, was it powerful. Vampires couldn't get intoxicated off normal liquor but after a shot, both Brody and Tex were drunk off their asses. After two, I was tipsy. After three, I was standing on the handrail around the back porch, dancing to Bad Guy by Billie Eilish. Apparently, I was a lightweight even as a vampire.

I jumped down and pulled Tex to his feet. "Dance with me, Tex," I purred, and he happily obliged. It wasn't really a song made for dancing; it was a song made for fucking. But we tried our best to do both, even though we were both swaying.

He pulled me close to his long, lean body, turning our drunken swaying into some kind of dance. The feel of his heat along my body made my blood sing, the predator in me getting hungrier and hornier as the song went on. I stood on my toes and licked the snake tattoo on the side of his neck, making us both groan.

He held me tighter to his body. "Do it, Raine."

He didn't have to ask me twice. I ran my hands under his shirt, tugging it off until I could see his tattooed torso. Fuck, he was beautiful. Like a long, lithe work of art. Tex's hands ran up and down my spine, keeping me close. I licked his nipple, making him hiss out a moan, then moved a fraction higher and slid my fangs into his chest. I suctioned my mouth over the spot and dragged hard. I wasn't worried about exsanguinating him from this spot, and I moaned loudly as his blood began to flow through my veins. Oh fuck. It had only been a couple of days, but it felt like decades. Heat flooded my pussy as the pleasure of his blood began to settle over my skin. It was even more potent today, the alcohol in his system doubling down on mine until I was lightheaded.

I could feel the hard press of his dick in my stomach and I rolled my body against him. He threw his head back, and the sound of his pleasure had me reaching inside his jeans. I wanted to make him purr out that noise and know it was because of me. Because of the pleasure I was giving him.

Because I was fucking powerful and I loved this man. I pushed him back against the rail of the deck, and his hands went out to steady himself. I tugged out his cock and it was hot and smooth in my hand, precum already glistening on the tip. I wanted to reach down and lick it, but I wanted to taste his blood more. I stroked his dick firmly, just the pressure he liked it. I knew what he wanted now. Knew what they all wanted. I felt like a wanton goddess, but just for them.

"Fuck, Raine," he groaned in a pained whisper. "I want to bury my dick in you so bad right now, mate."

I made a happy humming noise but didn't release my grip on his dick or his chest. I stroked faster, harder, our bodies so close that it was hard to move my hand between us. I sucked as fast as my hand moved until Tex was gasping.

"I'm going to come," he groaned, and I reached down and gripped his balls with my other hand, squeezing until he roared. I pulled away so I could see his face as he spurted cum all over his abs, the blood from my bite on his chest running down to create a mixture of bodily fluids on his upper abs. It was the most beautiful fucking thing I'd ever seen. I was beginning to see two of Tex though, swaying on my feet.

I could scent Judge as soon as he crowded behind me. "Bed. Now."

I spun around, kissing him with the taste of Tex's blood still on my lips. I was smiling so wide I thought I would crack my face. "I'll just say goodnight," I whispered.

I raced over to Brody, kissing him hard. "Fuck, you are the

sexiest woman I've ever met, Red. Go have fun, but you and I are long overdue and I'm coming to collect," he growled in his sexy Alpha voice that sent shivers along my skin.

"I can't wait."

Then I went over to Walker, a little nervous. I always felt a little guilty for these kinds of displays in front of Walker. I got what Brody was saying now, about waiting to see where Walker stood. Damn that clever Alpha. I leaned forward and kissed the corner of his lips. "Goodnight, Walker Walton. I'm sorry our chance was ruined earlier."

His eyes had that soft glow they got when he was worked up, and he gripped my wrist and pulled me close. He kissed me with enough sexual frustration to suffocate a horse. "Soon. Soon I am going to make love to you until you don't know anyone's name but mine. But go and have fun with your mate and Judge." I searched his face for jealousy, but all I could find was longing. I gave him one more quick peck on the lips, looking past him to X.

X was staring at me, his eyes hooded with lust. But he didn't have any smartass quips to go with it. I winked at him and flashed inside.

I had a date with a man sandwich.

9

When I got into my bedroom, I found Judge pressing Tex into the wall, kissing him like he was trying to show my shifter who was boss. There was no doubt in my mind though. Judge was the master in this room.

"Starting without me?" I purred, though I didn't want them to stop. They were glorious to watch, like two coiled beasts set on devouring each other. "Not complaining, but can you guys do it naked?"

I sauntered over to the bed, peeling my clothes off as I went until I was naked when I crawled onto the bed. I was a little drunk, and I felt sexy and invincible. Liquid courage chased away all my sober inhibitions.

Judge was gripping Tex's chin, and he pulled away, turning to look at me. "Fuck, she is sexy tonight, Lover Boy."

He still used his original sarcastic name for him, but now it was almost a term of endearment. I didn't doubt that Judge felt something for Tex. Whether it was the same as what he felt for me or not, I didn't know. "She is naked on the bed, her knees slightly parted so I can catch a glimpse of her delicious cunt. Can you smell her desire in the air? Do you want to taste?"

Tex groaned loudly. "Yes!"

Judge let him go, and he nearly ran to the bed. He knew instinctively where I was; he always did. I was his homing beacon. He'd found me, even when he'd thought I was dead. We were lovers, but we were also so much more. We were mates.

He stripped off his clothes and prowled onto the bed, flattening himself over my body. He kissed me softly on my lips, a tender kiss filled with feeling that slowly morphed into something hotter, harder. He kissed his way back down my body, stopping at my breasts to lap at the aching peaks. Then he continued down my ribcage at a torturously slow pace, dipping his tongue into my navel before trailing it down over the curve of my hip. Pulling himself up onto his elbows, he paused just above the apex of my thighs. His breath cooled the pulsing heat of my core. I moaned, desperate to feel his lips where my body ached.

Judge stood behind him, watching us both with his cock in his hand. His beautiful naked body was all hard contrasts in the moonlight. He looked wild, a primitive beast in a human suit. Then Tex lowered his mouth to my pussy and anything but that sensation escaped my mind. He flicked his tongue against my clit in a distinctively snake-like gesture, before pressing hard against it with the flat of his tongue. A feral moan escaped me, and I ground myself hard against his face. As Tex ate me like I was his last meal, I writhed on the bed, chanting his name like it would conjure the orgasm that was buzzing around my body like an electric shock.

Finally, I screamed, pleasure crashing over me, and my thighs gripped his head gently. Well, gently for a vampire. He looked up at me, a feral grin on his face, my juices making his cheeks shine. He wiped his cheeks on my thighs, then licked off my juices. It was the hottest thing I'd ever seen.

Judge leaned forward and ran his hand down the long line of Tex's back, over the hard muscles of his ass. "Tonight?" he asked him, and Tex nodded.

Judge's eyes met mine, and there was a tender look in them that was coupled with scorching heat. "Tex and I have been taking it slow. He hasn't let me fuck his delicious body yet, insisting that you, his mate, should be there for his first time. I agreed. We are not a couple, Tex and I. You are the glue that holds us together. We are a unit. All our firsts should be together." Judge crawled onto the bed, his hand moving from Tex's back to my thigh. "Are you with us, Rainy Day?"

I looked at Tex, saw the desire, the anticipation, the fear, the love in his eyes, and I thought my heart was going to crack open and leak all over these two men.

"Yes. Always." I leaned up and kissed Tex tenderly. "I love you, you know that right? I've loved you since I was eight years old. You are my mate. Forever." He kissed me back like he was trying to transfer every ounce of emotion in his body onto my lips.

"Make love to your mate, Tex," Judge murmured, and Tex wasted no time. His painfully hard dick slid into my body one agonizing inch at a time until he was buried deep. We both let out little whispered sighs at the rightness. He pulled out, and this time he slammed himself home, making me gasp out a moan.

"Fuck," Judge whispered as his hungry eyes watched Tex make love to me, alternating between hard punishing thrusts, and tantalizingly slow withdraws. He was driving me insane.

I followed Judge's confident movements through hooded eyes as he tore open the skin of his forefinger with his fangs. He held still as blood welled on his finger. Vampire blood would increase Tex's pleasure. He slid his finger into Tex's mouth as he curled his body over Tex's back, blocking my view. But whatever he was doing back there made Tex shudder and buck inside me, hitting a spot that made me mewl and my eyes roll back in my head.

Shifting back to his knees, Judge gripped Tex's hips, holding him still as he slid into his body so gently. Tex gasped, his eyes slamming shut as his whole body went rigid. I leaned up and bit his chest again, the other side this time, letting the vampire venom double down on the endorphins flowing through his bloodstream. Tex's skin rippled with pleasure, and Judge hummed approvingly. He slid inside Tex another tantalizing inch and I realized I was holding my breath. Tex moaned and collapsed on top of my body.

"Fuck," he whispered on a breath, and I wrapped my arms around his chest. I met Judge's eyes, and he held them as he slid out of Tex, and then back in faster, over and over again until Tex was grunting in my ear and whispering expletives over and over. He seemed to gather his wits, propping himself back on his arms and staring down at me. "I love you," he whispered, and then he slammed into me on Judge's next stroke. The increased force behind the thrust made me see the fucking face of God as he hit places that made my toes curl.

We moved like that for an eternity and seconds, Judge setting the pace, his head thrown back. He looked so powerful at that moment, his control over our pleasure making him our master.

Orgasm after orgasm crashed over me until Tex was shuddering inside me, pulsing cum inside me until he was a sweaty, shuddering mess. Judge, satisfied that he had our pleasure in his tight fist, fucked Tex faster, harder, making him whimper in pleasure against me until he too was coming on a roar.

He collapsed on top of us both and I was glad I didn't need to breathe anymore. Judge shifted onto the bed and Tex rolled to the other side of me so I was sandwiched between them. Their arms touched, Judge's fingers running over Tex's forearm tenderly.

"Wow," Tex whispered. If I could have summoned oxygen, I would have agreed. Judge got up, disappearing into the darkness of the house. He returned with two washcloths and cleaned us both up before we all fell into a blissful, drugged sleep.

Until we woke up three hours later and did it all again.

10

I groaned as Tex's phone went off at five p.m. the following day. I snuggled back under the blankets, sinking into the hard warmth of Tex's body. Tex found his phone in the drawer, looking pale and hungover, his shoulder-length hair sticking up in all directions.

"'Lo?" he yawned, his eyes still sticky with sleep.

"Tex? Did I wake you?" My body stiffened at the voice that came over the speaker. "Am I on that FaceTime? Frank, how do I get this off FaceTime?" I shook my head, stuffing my fist in my mouth to stop myself from crying out.

"Mrs. McKellen," Tex said quickly, his eyes shooting to me, and then back to Judge.

Judge pulled me back into his body, pulling my fist from my mouth and covering it with his own palm. "Shh, Rainy

Day. It's okay. Shh," he soothed, and now someone else could be in control, I let the tears burst forth.

It was my mom. On FaceTime. If I leaned just a little to the left, I could see her face. Judge held me tighter as if he could read my thoughts.

"Enough of that Mrs. McKellen thing, Tex." I could hear the smile in her voice, but I could also hear the sadness that was never there before. "Look, I was talking to your mother and she told me that you'd met someone up there. A man."

"Uh, yeah," Tex said, seeming uncomfortable for the first time. I looked at Tex. I hadn't even realized he'd spoken to his parents, let alone come out to them. Was this his plan to never go home? Just get banished?

"I know that they didn't take it well, Tex, and I don't understand. I don't understand how they could just let you go, and I keep thinking that I would give my life for just one more second with Mika." Her voice broke, and my body started to shake with the force of my sobs. Judge was whispering softly to me, but I couldn't hear what he was saying. I was focused on the one person I missed more than any other.

"It's okay," Tex murmured softly. "I knew what they would say. I expected it. I'm really happy here, I promise."

Mom gave a shaky breath. "I just wanted you to know that you have a place here with us if you ever want to come back. If your parents have anything to say about it, they can take it up with me." She sounded like the fierce woman who'd taken down my second grade teacher who kept me in class during playtime because I couldn't get my K's around the right way. My mom in a fury was a sight to behold.

"Thanks, Mrs. Mac," Tex said softly, his eyes shining too.

My mom gave a soft laugh, and I knew the sound as well as I knew my own. "You know, I always thought you'd end up with Mika? You two were so cute when you were kids. I would never have guessed you were gay. But I fully support you, we all do."

Tex shifted uncomfortably, and I realized he was still on FaceTime. "I'm not gay. I'm bisexual." He looked over the phone toward me. "I loved Mika. I'd loved her since I was ten years old, and she was following me around and dancing like a lunatic to my dad's records. I don't think there will ever be a day I don't love her."

Mom began to cry softly, and my heart shattered. It was dust in the cavity of my chest. "Me too, Tex. Me too." She cleared her throat and continued. "Well, I just wanted to let you know. Don't be a stranger. Come home whenever you need to. Bring your new beau. We'd love to meet him."

Tex's eyes shot to Judge automatically, before he looked back at the screen. "Maybe, Mrs. Mac. Do me a favor?"

"Anything, you know that."

"Check in on my parents for me. I know you don't agree, but they are a product of their generation. I'm not mad, and I wouldn't want you to ruin a long friendship being angry for me."

"Oh, Tex," my mother whispered. "You were always such

a good boy. Such a sensitive soul. I'll watch over them. I mightn't agree with their decision, but they were there for me these last few months. I owe them that at least."

They quickly said goodbye, and Tex hung up. Judge released my mouth and the keening noise that came from my throat was inhuman. Tex pulled me up and into his arms. I sobbed into his chest, into the chest of the only other person in the universe who knew what I had lost.

My sobbing had drawn the others from wherever they were in the cottage, Brody looking bleary-eyed but X looking fierce. I noticed he had a knife in his hand, looking for unknown threats. If I could have drawn breath around my wracking sobs, I would have told him that the only threat to my wellbeing was my broken heart. Judge was standing, speaking to them softly, explaining.

Brody came over, kissing the tears from my cheeks. "Oh, Sweetheart. I am so, so sorry. Want me to go and get Walker?"

I shook my head. Walker would already be at work. He didn't need to leave because I was having yet another emotional breakdown. I didn't want anyone but my mom. The one person I could never have.

X slipped the knife into the back of his pants and clapped once. "Okay, Love. If I've learned anything in life, it's that you need time to grieve. But wallowing in the darkness on sheets that stink like stale sex is not the way to do it. The pretty shifters are going to run you a bath, I am going to make you a cup of tea, and then you are going to tell me everything there is to know about your mother." He paused. "Clothing is optional."

I realized I was naked, and X could see the long line of my spine and my naked ass. Again. I was too sad to be embarrassed, but Judge, who was also naked, shooed him out of the room.

"I hate to agree with the bossy bastard, but a bath would be a good idea right now. Let us take care of you again," Brody whispered against my cheek.

I nodded and he disappeared out of the room, and I heard the rattling noise of the water in the pipes.

"You didn't tell me you'd called your parents," I said against Tex's chest, feeling the thump of his heartbeat against my cheek.

He tightened his arms around me. "I didn't want to upset you. I figured if I couldn't come out now, I would never come out, you know? This just served a dual purpose. But I could still call my parents and you're..."

"I'm dead."

He made a low, sad noise in his throat. "Yes." He squeezed me so tight, it was like he was trying to draw me into himself. I snuggled against his chest, my heaving breaths drawing his scent deep into my lungs.

Brody returned, lifting me from Tex's chest. "I can walk, you know?" I protested weakly.

He nodded. "I know, but why deprive myself of the chance to hold a naked Raine in my arms?" I rolled my eyes but wrapped my arms around his neck. He carried me like a baby to the bathroom. The tub was so filled with bubbles that when Brody put me in, I was hidden from head to toe. The warm water loosened my tight muscles, the heat chasing the chill of grief from my bones. Judge appeared at the door.

"Brody. Walker called. The Vampire Nation is less than an hour away. The Council has called an emergency meeting. He wants you and me there. X should stay behind; not all Council members were impressed with his pledging."

No one mentioned Tex. In this fight, he was cannon fodder. Brody hesitated. "Did you tell him about Raine?" Judge shook his head, and I understood why. Walker needed to be 100% focused on this right now. Me and my dead drama could wait until we were all safe.

I pushed softly at his thigh. "Go. This is important to your Pack and ours."

His jaw flexed but he nodded. He leaned down and kissed me softly. "I'll be back. Call me if you even think you might need me."

"I will. I'll be fine. Tex and X will be here."

Brody raised an eyebrow. "That's what I'm worried about. I trust the Pup with my life, but the Brit?" He screwed up his nose and it was adorable.

I looked at my Alpha. "My gut says I can trust him. I'll be fine. Go."

He nodded once, and turned, shedding the playful lover persona, and the power of the Alpha filled my little cabin.

Judge watched him go, then looked down at me. "You okay, Rainy Day?"

I nodded. "I will be."

He leaned down and kissed my head. "I'm going to do my best to make you happy, okay? I never want to hear you cry like that again."

I gave him a lopsided grin. "No promises. Now go. Walker needs you guys."

Judge left too, and I slid further down into the bubbles. It felt like someone had their hands in my chest, gripping my lungs. I couldn't take a deep breath. Tex walked in, his nose twitching. He was still naked and glorious in the soft bathroom light. He counted the steps to the bath under his breath, reaching down with his hands to find the edge. Then he hopped in, making the water slosh over the edges. His legs slid either side of mine, bubbles clinging to his cheeks making him look like a very naughty Santa Claus. It was so ridiculous, I had to smile.

"Come here, Rainey. I need you in my arms." Luckily the bath in my cottage was one of those huge old clawfoot tubs that you could basically swim in. I crawled through the water toward him, turning to sit between his thighs, spooning my body against his and resting my head on his chest. He kissed my temple. "I love you."

"Me too." I closed my eyes and pulled myself out of my own head. I stopped thinking about everything that had happened, all that I had lost, all that I could possibly still lose.

Instead, I thought about the heat of the water encasing my body, the way the bubbles tickled my skin. I thought about the strength of Tex's arms, the vibration of his chest against my back as he hummed a song under his breath. My body began to relax, one muscle at a time.

By the time X strode into the bathroom like he owned it, I was basically boneless. I double-checked the bubbles were keeping me reasonably decent.

X held a tray in his hands. It held a steamy cup of tea, a couple of slices of toast, a glass of milk and the huge block of chocolate that I kept stuffed in the back of the cupboard because Tex had a sweet tooth and would have devoured it all in a day. Apparently, there was no hiding things from X though.

He folded himself to the floor with ease that should have been impossible for a man that big. He picked up a piece of toast and held it out to me. "Eat." I lifted my hand to grab a piece of toast, but he moved it away. "Your hands are wet. I'll hold it."

So I took a bite of the proffered piece of toast and blushed. It felt too intimate to eat from his hand. But it also felt right. I felt Tex inhale behind me, and I knew what he was smelling right now. Desire.

His hand slid up my body to rest on my stomach lightly. "Describe X to me?" he whispered, and I looked at X's startled face.

"He's big," I said, holding X's eyes. "He has a lot of tattoos

95

and scars. A big scar down his jaw, like he's only just missed getting a knife to the jugular. His jaw is sharp, just as sharp as yours. He has three big black roses on the column of his throat, a skull, a knife and something sinuous peeking up from the neck of his shirt. He has startlingly dark eyes, but when he's this close, I can see they almost look like molten dark chocolate. His nose is crooked, like it's been broken and reset too many times." I stopped, clearing my throat. "His shoulders are huge, about twice the size of even Judge's. He must be like seven feet tall."

X chuckled low. "Six foot six, actually. I'm not a giant."

I disagreed but okay. "There's not an ounce of extra flesh on him though. He's all corded muscle, like he spent his time lifting cars before he was turned. Or working out a lot. He is 0% body fat. He looks like death walking." I smiled. "But when he drinks tea, he lifts his pinky finger out straight."

Tex laughed softly, more a sensation than sound. X scowled at me. "It's correct table etiquette, Love. It's not my fault you Americans drink like you are slurping from a bucket."

He held more toast out to me, and I obligingly took a bite. I couldn't read his thoughts in his dark eyes, but his face was stoic. He could have been feeding a llama at the zoo, rather than a naked girl in a bath.

"Want to tell me about your family? Sometimes, telling people about them keeps them fresh in your mind. Some vampires will tell you it's best to forget, but you'll always feel the emptiness where they used to be, so I always thought it was better to keep them alive in your heart. Tell me the good and the bad."

So I did. I told him what my mother looked like, the soft, floral dresses she liked to wear in summer, and her favorite fluffy angora sweater for the winter. I told him about the time she caught me kissing Tex behind the big oak tree in the backyard, making the boy in question laugh and tighten his arms around my torso. I told X about how much she had loved my father, that I'd sometimes catch them dancing around the living room or making out like teenagers on the couch when I was supposed to be in bed. I told him about how she cooked every day for six weeks for the construction worker who lived by himself across the road and broke both arms in a worksite accident. I laughed about the time she accidentally hit another car in the carpark at Walmart and drove away instead of giving them her insurance, until her guilt had driven her so crazy she'd gone back and waited at the car she'd dinged in the car park for four hours until the person came out so she could explain.

I unloaded onto the broad shoulders of X, every feeling, memory, wish until Tex was snoring softly behind me and the water was completely chilled. Eventually, I realized the bubbles were all gone, but X had never let his eyes drift past the edge of the bath.

"She sounds like a good woman." There was something haunted in his eyes. "You should get out of the bath before you turn into a mermaid and your shifter turns into an eel." He rolled to his knees, not even a little stiff from sitting on cold slate tiles. For the first time, he let his eyes drift to the bathwater.

He swallowed hard. "What magic do you possess, Raine Baxter?" He leaned forward and kissed me softly on my lips, barely even brushing them. Then he was gone.

Fuck.

I had developed a crush on the Executioner.

11

You could almost tell when the Vampire Nation stepped across the town borders. It was like the whole town rippled with fear. Goosebumps chased across my skin and I shivered like someone walked across my grave. Well, my proverbial grave.

I was dressed in a long-sleeve bohemian blouse trimmed in lace and tight black leather-look pants. I was really feeling the vampire aesthetic today. I coupled it with bright red lipstick that matched the lightest part of my ombre red hair, the armor of strong women everywhere.

I slipped on my pretty studded combat boots, and I looked like I was ready to kick someone's ass. But I wasn't really. In a fight, I would be worse than useless. Being a vampire hadn't suddenly given me the ability to kick ass or twirl swords like Joan of Arc. I could run fast, but not faster than any other vampire, and apparently, it hadn't made me anymore graceful. I still ran like a duck. Just a really fast duck.

I stepped into the kitchen to find Tex fully attired in his usual black jeans and band t-shirt. I'd been steadily refilling his band t-shirt collection with online shopping. Today he had a shirt from a band I'd found on YouTube, and the lead singer was the dead ringer for Tex. It had a skull and coffin on the front and I loved it. Actually, buying stuff online was one of my new favorite pastimes. It wasn't fantastic for my bank account though. You could only become one of those rich, eccentric immortals if you were born before the age of online shopping with same-day delivery. Not that anyone ever delivered out here. The Council had a post office box in the next largest town to ours. Not even the Postal Service stopped in Dark River.

X was with him, dressed exactly how he normally dressed. Killer couture. He sat on one of my timber chairs, tipping it back until I was worried that the chair legs would buckle under his weight.

"They're here, aren't they?" I asked X, who nodded, his brow creasing right between his eyes, pulling his long, dark eyebrows closer together.

"What do we do now?" The idea of the Vampire Nation being here, complete with Enforcers, made my anxiety ratchet up a thousand notches. I felt raw already after the thing with Mom. Now I was jumping out of my skin.

X shrugged. "We wait." His tone was blasé but I could see the tightness across his shoulders, along his spine. It was echoed in the stiffness in my spine. Tex sat down and I wandered over to sit in his lap. He wrapped his arms around me and the tension in my body eased. This was what the mate bond did. It soothed and healed.

I watched YouTube conspiracy videos on Tex's phone, watching the group chat for any news. But so far, there was nothing. X sharpened his knives on a whetstone, the slow scrape of the metal disconcerting but also a little hot. Damn. Who knew killers were my type? We sat in companionable silence until there was a heavy thumping knock on the door. X was on his feet, his huge hunting knife gripped in his hand.

"Stay here," he growled low, and now I really knew why Judge made him stay here. Not because he'd offended the Council, but because he trusted X with my safety, and Tex's, above anyone else. It made me trust the former Enforcer even more.

Tex slid me off his lap as he stood and poised himself in front of me. "I don't recognize the scent," he whispered in a low voice.

I heard X open the door, and whoever was on the threshold gasped. "X. What a surprise. Though, not really considering you are such a traitor. Pieter, get the Master," the voice said in a quieter voice. "I'm sure he'd want to know for what, or should I say for whom, his golden child fell from grace." His voice was louder now. "Are you not going to invite us in, old friend? It has been a day for surprises. This little shithole certainly has some interesting inhabitants. Judge too. Who would have thought it, hmm? Will I find the witch in the next cottage over?"

I needed to see the owner of the voice, and I shifted toward the foyer, peeking around the wall. I could only see the broad expanse of X's shoulders as he blocked the door.

"You aren't welcome here, Raul," X said, his voice so cold that it sent shivers down my spine.

Raul, whoever he was, laughed. "We are the Vampire Nation; we are welcome everywhere. Now move aside before I have you executed for inhibiting an investigation by the Vampire Nation."

X shifted another hand behind his back, unsheathing a second knife from what I realized was a back holster. It made sense; it wasn't like he was pulling them from between his ass cheeks.

"Fuck off, Raul, you smarmy old bastard."

"That's what I hoped you'd say. Please place X under arrest," Raul said to someone, and I couldn't stand there and do nothing.

I leaped into the hallway, Tex's hand reaching for me but missing. "Wait. X, let them in. We have nothing to hide here," I said loudly. I grabbed Tex's hand and pulled him close. "Don't leave my side, okay?" I whispered. He squeezed my fingers so hard I thought they might break.

"Never."

X looked over his shoulder at me, worry marring his normally nonchalant face. He shifted back to me faster than my eyes could follow.

Raul strode in like he was a god, but he looked exactly how X had described him. Like a smarmy old fuck. He had an aristocratic nose and eyebrows that kind of blurred into one. "And who are you?"

I squared my shoulders. "Raine Baxter. This is my home." I was proud that my voice didn't wobble as much as my knees did.

"And your pet? Human? I thought this town frowned on eating humans? We certainly frown on you not killing them afterward. Though there is something to be said for Renfields."

I scowled, ready to make the hugest mistake of my life and tell Raul to go fuck himself when X interrupted. "He's half-shifter. Protected by the Alpha of the Western Canada shapeshifters. Our treaty forbids us from injuring any of their people. Especially vampires like you." X's voice was basically dripping with malice. "You may be an Enforcer for the Vampire Nation, but not even the Nation is above the treaties of the Convocation. Or do you only answer to Lucius now? Shall I tell Titus your allegiances?"

Raul sneered, his lip curling above huge canines. "Do not pretend you have the ear of Titus, you filthy traitor."

X just grinned, looking supremely confident. "Don't I? Are you sure?"

I had no fucking idea what was going on. Who the hell was Titus? What was the Convocation? I was basically drowning in a tidal wave of my own stupidity.

Raul grunted something that sounded completely unflattering. "We will see what Lucius says when he gets here, hmm? Maybe he'll take your toys off you just because he can? Just because he likes to watch you squirm like the maggot you are."

Oh, that was it. I might be insignificant, and couldn't fight to save my life, but I couldn't stand here and let him speak that way. Fortunately, a smooth, familiar voice spoke from the doorway. "I do hope you aren't speaking for me again, are you Raul?"

There was casual cruelty in the familiar voice that didn't belong. I looked around Raul's shoulders to Nico.

Only, it wasn't Nico in the finely tailored suit. Oh, they looked the same, right down to the light tattoos on his face. But this Nico had a cruel twist to his mouth, and his eyes were cold, dark flint.

Raul blanched. "No, sir. I would not."

Not-Nico walked in, smiling pleasantly at me like he was a contestant in the Miss America pageant. It was all wrong. Wrong, wrong, wrong.

"Nico?"

I heard Tex's sucked in breath. "Holy shit."

X swallowed hard, his muscles flexed so hard I could see his muscles quiver in his back. "Lucius."

He smiled almost fondly at X. "Ah, X. It's good to see you looking so well." He sounded so sincere despite the fact that he'd stabbed X in the back with the Traitor's Blade. What a fucking sociopath. Lucius's gaze landed on me. He gave X another long look. "Well? No? Damn witch," he muttered under his breath and pushed past Raul.

He looked me over appraisingly. "Nicolai is my twin, as you probably have surmised by now. And you are?"

"Raine Baxter."

He raised his brows in surprise. "Oh? You are the one that all the fuss was over? No offense, but I thought you must have been a great beauty."

Well, ouch. Did I care that a sociopath thought I was ugly? Fuck. No.

He drifted closer, and both Tex and X went rigid beside me. "Perhaps there is something else about you that has them all so protective. As loath as I am to say it, perhaps Raul is right. Perhaps I would like to take you from our friend here. But I would let you keep your half-blood pet. Wouldn't that be lovely?" he cooed.

"No. Thank you."

He laughed again, and it was a cruel, awful sound. "You speak like you have a choice, fledgling."

There was some kind of kerfuffle outside, and the real Nico appeared in my doorway. He still looked vicious, but there was passion in his eyes, not that cold barbarism. "Raine has a choice. Everyone in this town does. You do not have carte blanche to take what you want, Lucius, even if you believe you do. You still answer to the remaining members of the Vampire Council. Raine has done nothing wrong. She is not under the purview of the Enforcers."

Lucius gave me a sneer. "Not yet. Everyone slips up eventually, even in this little false utopia you've created." He stared down his twin, cocking his head. "You care for her too?"

Nico scoffed. "She is a vampire under my care. They all are. The only thing I care about is making sure you go back to where you came from, leaving my vampires unmolested by you and your thugs."

Now that hurt. He didn't mean it. I knew he didn't, but still, hearing him saying the words bruised something inside my chest.

Lucius laughed, looking over Nico's shoulder to where Judge and Walker stood. Walker looked stoic, but Judge's eyes begged for bloodshed. "I think that some of my thugs have already been molesting this one." He smirked, looking between Judge and X.

Nico didn't smile. "They are no longer yours, brother. They are mine."

Lucius walked out the front door, clapping Nico on the shoulder. "We'll see, brother. We will see."

Nico sent me a longing look and followed after his twin, no doubt to stop him from terrorizing the rest of the town.

Walker went with him, but not before mouthing, "Are you okay?"

I nodded and gave him a weak smile. It had been a big fucking day, and my emotions were bordering on total meltdown.

Judge came in, slamming the door in Raul's face. I gave him a lopsided grin that quickly turned watery as adrenaline spiked through my veins. Judge quickly had me in his arms. "Fuck. They are terrorizing the place out there. They shook down Bert and Beatrice's Diner, smashed everything. They've completely decimated the Doc's office looking for 'evidence.' What a fuckin' joke. They've frisked down everyone they could find and have been going door to door hoping someone will crack and spill something they can use to take the entire town down."

I shook my head. I now knew why everyone had gone rigid with fear at the very mention of the Vampire Nation and the Enforcers.

"It is hard to be on the other side of the door," X said quietly. He turned to me. "How could you be so bloody stupid? Now Lucius knows your name, knows your face. Saw the way his brother looked at you. You'll forever be on his mind now, a way to needle his twin for the rest of his immortal life." He let out a frustrated huff.

To be fair, adrenaline probably increased my rage at that moment. But I just saw red. I shook out of Judge's arms and stood toe to toe with the arrogant dickhole. "Look, you arrogant asshole. I wasn't going to let them take you away to be executed because you didn't want Lucius to see my face. How do you think I would live with myself for eternity if I let that happen?" I poked him in his chest, which hurt my finger but still made my point. "I don't know what you are used to, but I protect my friends. So you can stop being so bloody stupid," I finished in his poncy British accent.

He glared down at me, his nostrils flaring rhythmically. Then he leaned down and kissed me, the hard line of his lips punishing. I gripped the front of his shirt and kissed him back, no softness between us. Just fear and desire, and a shit-load of lust.

I vaguely heard Judge whisper to Tex, "When did this happen?"

"In the bath, I think."

It shocked me out of my rage, and I jumped away. My eyes felt too big in my face, as I looked between X, Judge and Tex. "I... Uh..."

Then I hightailed it back to the bedroom like my ass was on fire.

12

It took three hours to suck up the courage to head back out into the main part of my house. I was surprised to see everyone was there, even Nico.

I looked at him, noting the differences between him and Lucius. "Was no one going to tell me that Nico had an evil twin?" Nico should have told me; he knew how worried I'd been about this mysterious Lucius.

"I didn't want him to taint the way you look at me like he has done with everyone else for so long. You were so new, you didn't know the whole sordid back history, the cruel things he had done in my name. For the first time in so long, I just wanted to be Nico." He looked so forlorn, it was almost heart-breaking. "Do you forgive me?"

It wasn't a throwaway question. I narrowed my eyes at him as I was forced to say the truth. "Yes. As much as I hate being the stupid one in the room, I can understand why you didn't want to tell me." I looked to the rest of the guys in the room. Both Judge and X looked uneasy. Was it because of the kiss? "Is there anything else I need to know?"

Judge cleared his throat. Well, this couldn't be good. "Lucius is my grandsire." He looked at X and winced. "Our grandsire. Our makers were nestmates. Normally, he would be able to compel us to do things, but Miranda put a permanent anti-compulsion geas over us when we worked together. We could never be compelled by anyone of our maker's line while ever our maker was alive. Fortunately, mine is dead," Judge said bitterly. "Which means Lucius's control over me disappeared as soon as she was a husk in her grave, and so did Miranda's compulsion geas. X isn't quite so lucky."

My head was spinning. "What does that even mean?"

"It means, Love, that Miranda left a little bit of her witchy jizz in me and it means that Lucius can't compel me despite being the equivalent of my vampire grand-daddy. I don't have to worry about Lucius telling me to cut your pretty throat even though my degenerate maker still exists. It's why I can walk into your apartment while others can't, and luckily I wasn't here when she made the new ward because otherwise it would zap me in the nuts too." He chuckled. "What a fucking bitch."

I had to agree.

I looked around the room again, so many concerned faces. Walker's was the worst. When he looked at me, it was like he was already witnessing my second death. I didn't blame him. I seemed to have brought trouble with me when I died outside the town not that long ago. It was attracted to me like ants to honey, a constant threat just hanging there, waiting for me to fuck up somehow. I'd never really shaken the specter of death.

I went over and wrapped my hand in his. "It'll be okay, I promise. They'll get bored with bullying the town, and then they'll leave. There's not enough here to keep them entertained."

Walker's jaw tensed. "I want you to leave. Go to Brody's Pack lands until they do go. Take Tex and run."

I was shaking my head before he'd even finished. "No, I'm not letting them chase me out of my home. It makes me look guilty and I have done literally nothing wrong. None of us have. If they're here in the official capacity that they say they are, they're constrained by the rules as much as the rest of us." I also might have been talking out of my ass. I really needed to read more of that book about the history of vampires. But I'd left my copy at Angeline's apartment, and whenever I was in the room with Walker or Judge, we ended up making out instead of talking about the laws of the Vampire Nation. This was what I got for being a horny bitch. "Who's Titus? What's the Convocation?"

For some strange reason, everyone looked at Nico. I raised my eyebrows at him. "Titus is my older brother. He sits on the governing body for all supernaturals, the Convocation. All paranormals have a seat, and it is where treaties are formed, disputes are heard and resolved, lives are played with like it is a game of chess."

I shook my head. "Do you have any other powerful siblings that I should know about?"

Nico smiled and shook his head. "That's it. We are very old; that is why we have reached such heights of power."

I frowned. "Yet you created a little village in the middle of nowhere instead?"

Walker rubbed my back. "Nico once sat on the Vampire Nation."

I couldn't connect Nico with the cruelty of the Vampire Nation and Lucius. There were flashes of his brutality though, like when he was saving me from Doc Alice. He'd wanted to tear out her heart.

"Yes, used to. A long time ago now. It wore away at me until I left." He looked so beaten then, so exhausted by life. I sent him a sympathetic look, even though I really wanted to hug him right now.

"Is Titus like Lucius?" I shuddered to think that our very highest ruler had such casual cruelty.

Nico smiled, it reaching his eyes. "No. Titus is a thinking man, very evenly tempered." His smile slipped. "But you don't rise to those heights because you won a popularity contest. He is as brutal and unforgiving as any in power. But he can be reasoned with, and he doesn't torture the populace for the fun of it like Lucius."

Well, that was a win I guess.

I went over to the couch. I needed to sit down. Or sleep for a hundred years. Before my butt hit the cushions, Brody had vaulted the back of the couch and was sitting behind me, making sure I landed in his lap.

"Sorry, Red. But I need to hold you in my arms. Just pretend I'm the couch cushion."

I laughed. There was nothing about Brody's corded body that was even remotely couch-like. Still, I rested my head back on his shoulder, and I looked into his searing gaze. "If we are doing confession time right now, I feel like I should tell you guys that I kissed X. I think I might have a crush on him. I love you guys, so I don't know how I'm meant to handle this kind of thing in our, er, unique situation."

Brody's brows hit his hairline. I closed my eyes and counted to five, then looked around the room. I met everyone's gaze. Judge and Tex already knew. But I met Walker's eyes. I still hadn't had my moment with Walker, and here I was kissing other men. Guilt rode me hard, and I looked at the floor. I would lose it if one of them kissed another woman; I would not be half as understanding as these four men. Men who loved and protected me, who worshipped my body at night and cared for me during the day. They didn't ask for anything from me other than my loyalty, and I couldn't even give them that.

Brody's hand ran up and down my thigh. "Relax, Raine. This is not exactly a surprise. You and X have chemistry so thick it's a wonder anyone else can breathe. You know I don't mind. I want you to be happy. If the big dumb Brit does that for you, then I am happy for you too. As long as he doesn't cut into my Raine time." He kissed my neck, his stubble tickling my jaw. "We do this kind of thing in the shifter world."

"Have more than one mate?" I looked at Tex. Did he have another mate out there, someone who was more suited to him? That he could take home to his parents, have babies with?

"Ah, Red. No. For us, there's only ever one mate. But for the females, they can have two or three mates, even more sometimes. Nature's way of ensuring genetic diversity, I guess? But for the males, there can only be one mate. One love."

His tone was off. I looked over my shoulder at him, but his face was its normal congenial expression. I wasn't Brody's mate. Eventually, he'd find the woman who was, he would settle down and breed other little shapeshifters. Did I have the ability to feel happy for him the way he was happy for me?

I could, but my heart would break into a million pieces first. I pressed myself back against him, and his arms tightened around me.

Walker was still looking from me to X. His green eyes traced the lines of my face, and I wondered if this was one step too far. It was the first time we'd added someone outside of the original four of us. My first vampiric lovers. I wasn't worried about Judge. He loved X. He was happy to share, maybe because it felt less like commitment? Brody was the same. But with Walker, this could break the fragile thing we had.

He looked at X. "And you? Why did you kiss her?"

X shifted uncomfortably from foot to foot. "She pulls at this thing in my chest, like I couldn't help it if I tried. And fuck knows I tried. I didn't want to fuck a girl who I'd have to schedule time with, you know? I thought you lads were crazy. But the more time I spent with her, the more she pulled at me until I couldn't help but kiss her sassy fucking mouth."

Well, wasn't that romantic? I rolled my eyes and scoffed.

He flashed his fangs at me. "But she seems to be this weird mixture of loving and crazy, and I can't resist that. So, if it is okay with you dickheads, I would like to see where it could go between us. It might go nowhere. Maybe one kiss will have gotten her out of my system. It's not like she's made of crack."

Judge laughed and slapped him on the shoulder. "Sure thing, X. Let me know how that goes." He looked at me and smiled. "If it matters, you have my blessing to date the idiot."

Tex walked toward me and kissed my cheek. "Sharing's caring, isn't that what you used to say?" He grinned, and I had the feeling he wasn't talking about sharing me. What a fucking horny snake. I didn't think X swung that way either, but then there was a time I would have said that about Judge too. Guess sexuality was more fluid in the vampire world.

Eternity was a long time to be stuck in a societally confined idea of sexuality. Tex winked and stood. "I'm going to bed. Today has been wild and I didn't get much sleep last night." I blushed bright red. Yeah, today had been wild.

Judge kissed my cheek. "I'll go to bed too. Rainy Day, you're always welcome."

Nico cleared his throat. "Wait, before you go, I would like to, uh, I would like to, at some point in the future, not right now—" He took a deep breath. "I would like to court Raine, if she would allow it."

Judge patted Nico's shoulder as he walked past. "We know, old man. We all know."

My jaw was hanging open, and even Walker was smiling at Nico. "We've been expecting it. But take my advice, don't rush it."

I mean, I knew, but I didn't realize the guys knew too? Was it that obvious? All of Brody's offhand remarks made more sense now.

All the blood in my body must have been in my cheeks at that moment. Everyone was watching me, waiting for an answer. "One day soon? After this is all over and everything settles down and we both have time to breathe."

Nico gave me that soft, sad smile. "Soon, Raine." Then he flashed out of the room, the soft clicking of the door shutting the only sign he'd ever been here at all.

We all stood in silence for a moment, an awkwardness descending that hadn't been there for a while now.

"I think we should all stay here tonight," Walker said, clearing his throat loudly into the silence. "I would feel better if Raine was properly protected at all times."

Brody shrugged. "I agree, but I call shotgun on the left side of Raine's bed."

I was acutely aware that Walker still hadn't said anything about X. Walker came over and pulled me from Brody's lap. "I want whatever makes you happy." He kissed me softly. "I think you could do better though," he teased, echoing words that Brody had said so long ago about Judge.

"Better like you?" I whispered back.

He leaned forward and kissed me. "Let's go to bed. I just want to snuggle my girl tonight. I'll even put up with the fleabag hogging the other side of the bed."

We were at my bedroom door when X finally spoke. "What about me?"

Brody laughed. "You can have the couch, new guy. Though there's probably room in with Tex and Judge?" He waggled his eyebrows. "You can go and ask if they'd care to spoon?"

X raised an eyebrow. "Maybe I will." Wait, did that mean...?

Before I could ask, Brody scooped me up over his shoulder and slapped me on the ass. "Let's go, Lover Girl. There's enough sausage in that sandwich already."

I lifted my head from where it was dangling over Brody's

back and pointed at X. "We are going to talk about that, I promise."

He laughed and laid down on the couch. "You can count on it, Love."

Brody carried me all the way to the bedroom. Someone had changed my sheets, which was great after last night's debauchery. When Brody set me on my feet, I was too tired to undress. I just crawled onto the bed and flopped down onto my stomach. Brody crawled over the top of me, kissing my nape. "It's been a big day, hasn't it, Baby?" He peeled off my blouse, and then my pants, his hands softly manipulating my body where he needed it to go. "First this morning, and then all that shit with Lucius, and then X?"

Walker paused where he was unbuttoning his Sheriff's uniform. "Wait, what happened this morning?"

I swallowed the lump that formed in my throat. I was kind of glad today had been so intense. It forced my unresolved emotions back into the box where I'd stuffed them. "My mom called Tex while we were in bed."

Walker's eyes went impossibly wide. "Did she hear you?"

I shook my head, the sadness beginning to seep out of the edges of that box. "No. But Walker..." My voice broke a little, and he was in front of me, gathering me against his strong chest. He knew how hard it had been for me to lose them, more than anyone else in Dark River.

He kissed my face, dropping tiny little kisses across my

cheekbones, my eyelids. Those tiny, tender kisses expressed how he felt better than any words ever could. Finally, he kissed my lips equally softly. I didn't want soft though. If I had to feel, then it was going to be lust, love, fiery passion between two people who loved each other even if they couldn't say the words yet. Fingers ran up my spine. Maybe between three people.

Walker didn't ease his kiss when Brody sat up behind us, his hands tracing my spine, the curve of my hips, over the slope of my ass. He leaned forward and bit my ass cheek, marking it and making me suck in a hissed breath. I pulled away from Walker, and we both looked down at the teeth marks on my ass and the completely unrepentant face of Brody.

Walker shook his head, grabbing my chin and turning my face back to his. He kissed me harder this time, tasting my moans with his tongue. Brody slipped his hands between my thighs, running up to brush the side of his hand against my wet core.

I moaned and Walker's arms tightened around me as he pressed me harder to his chest. He didn't seem to mind sharing me with his friend, though while Brody was naked, Walker was still in the pressed brown pants of his uniform that I just wanted to tear from his body.

Walker laid me back down on the bed, and then they both just stared down at me until I began to squirm. "Beautiful," Brody murmured, and Walker hummed his agreement.

He reached for the edges of my panties and tore them off like they were made of crepe paper.

"Fuck," he breathed, and then he was over me, kissing me again, his dick painfully confined behind the zip of his pants. I kissed him back, desperate for the contact.

He eventually dragged his mouth away, kissing down my neck, between my breasts, ignoring the aching peaks of my nipples, much to my frustration. He hovered above me, his shoulders pushing at my inner thighs as he just looked at the most intimate part of me. Then he gently sucked my clit. I bucked off the bed against his face.

He ran his stiffened tongue down my slit, turning toward the very top of my thigh. Then he struck with his fangs. The pure rawness of his bite made my core pulse with heat. I clenched my thighs against his head, riding the sensation of his bite. Brody took one of my nipples in his mouth and I arched so hard I almost turned into an origami fucking swan.

He placed one hand on my stomach, holding me still as he lapped at my breasts. I came hard, my juices dampening Walker's face. He pulled away, licking at the bite wound so it would heal. They stared down at me and then had some kind of macho wordless conversation that ended in Walker nodding once.

"Come here, Rainey. I'm going to make love to you like I've been dying to do for days, and Walker is going to watch like a puritanical voyeur."

Walker flipped him the bird, but his eyes told me how

excited he was by the idea of watching Brody fuck me sense-less. This was so hot, I was going to come again. I went to Brody, who was lying on his back now, watching me with that hooded gaze. He always made me feel so damn sexy, like I was some kind of bombshell to get a man like him. His long, dark hair flared out behind him, the soft bedside light making the harsh angles of his face even more prominent. He took my breath away.

He let out a groan. "Don't look at me like that, Red, or I'm going to come right now and embarrass myself in front of the Sheriff."

I grinned as I slid up his body until I was resting against his naked abs. I leaned forward and kissed him softly, feeling his body rumble under mine. "Nuh-uh, Sweetheart. Turn around and watch the Sheriff." He turned me until I was facing Walker. I held his brilliant green gaze, which was cloudy with lust. Brody gripped my hips, and I reached between us, holding his dick until I could slide onto it, moaning as it hit every good spot and then some spots I didn't even know I had. My eyes fluttered closed until Walker gripped my chin again.

"I want to see the look in your eyes," he whispered, and Brody's hands were moving me into a rhythm that seemed so perfect, it was magical. I was so secure in his hands, trusting him to get me where I needed to go, that I reached out toward Walker, grabbing the sides of his pants and pulling until the button flew off toward the corner of the room.

"You are going to owe me some pants, Sweetheart," he murmured, but I gave him a completely unapologetic look and pulled him closer, dragging his pants over his muscular butt. Such a fantastic ass.

With his pants around his ankles, his cock was straining against the tight cotton of his boxer shorts. He freed his cock, and it bounced against his tight stomach. Shit. I reached out and wrapped my hand around it, pulling him closer and he followed more than willingly. You grab a man by his hard cock, he will follow you into the very bowels of Hell.

When he was close enough, I leaned forward a little more, making both Brody and I groan, and put my lips around Walker's cock. He grabbed my head gently, guiding his cock slowly into my mouth, then back again. Unfortunately, or fortunately for me, Brody was getting there, beginning to fuck mc hard, pushing me until I was being impaled on both their cocks. Walker didn't have time for soft and slow, and soon he was matching Brody stroke for stroke as I moaned around his dick. An orgasm crashed over me, and my scream was muffled by the wild slide of Walker's cock.

"Ah shit," Brody groaned, his body bucking wildly until he released himself inside me. He held my body as Walker rode my face harder, faster, grunting loudly as he pulled out and came all over my chest.

Brody lifted me off his dick and settled me back against his chest, completely uncaring that I was currently coated in Walker's bodily fluids. "Damn, Red. I thought it couldn't be like that every single time, but I was so damn wrong. Every single time."

Walker disappeared and returned just as quickly with a wet cloth. He cleaned me up a bit, threw the washer into my clothes hamper then climbed into bed on the other side of me. He kissed my cheek, and I turned to face him, nestling my ass back against Brody, letting him encase my body like a huge hot water bottle.

I searched his face for any sign of regret. "Are you okay? With what just happened, I mean."

He kissed my face once more, more reverent than passionate. "I have zero regrets about anything, Raine. Not a single one." He yawned. "But I am so exhausted. Kiss me goodnight and dream sweet dreams of me fucking you like crazy and the Alpha over there watching from the sidelines." He grinned at Brody, who just laughed. I was pretty sure Brody had no dramas watching either.

My eyelids got heavy and I yawned too. Before I knew it, I was drifting off to sleep in a house filled with people who wanted to be my boyfriend. What the fuck was my life right now?

13

The Vampire Nation caused mayhem. They'd been here for days, and I'd been basically confined to my cabin with one or more of the guys in constant attendance. Just in case. Judge and X had been missing most of the time, off doing reconnaissance or something. Most of the time it was Brody and Tex, sometimes Walker during the day. Every night, they would all converge on my tiny cottage, and I'd rotate between sleeping between Judge and Tex, and sleeping between Brody and Walker. Walker hadn't repeated the sexual shenanigans of the other night, but sometimes I would catch him staring at me with a look so hot it threatened to brand my skin. X continued to sleep on the couch, and he hadn't tried to kiss me again. Maybe I'd scared him off? I know if someone suggested I share a boyfriend with four other women, I would tell them where to stick it.

Maybe X was right. Maybe I did have a magical vagina. Maybe that was my vampiric superpower. Apparently, after a certain age, we all got them. Nico's was obviously compelling someone to speak the truth, but he was old as hell and I had no doubt he had many, many others. Walker apparently drew energy from the high emotions of others, which is why his eyes always glowed whenever he was horny. He was legitimately soaking in my lustiness. X had orgasmic venom. I wasn't sure what Judge's ability was, and he wouldn't tell me, so I could only assume it was bad. He always shut down completely when I asked, and no one else would tell me either. X had to know. They'd been partners for decades.

Today, they'd decided to let me leave my cottage, and only because both X and Judge were with me, as well as Brody and Tex. Walker was busy trying to reassure the citizens of Dark River that everything was under control.

In all honesty, it wasn't. There had to be close to fifty Enforcers in town, and they were wreaking havoc. As I walked toward the diner, I saw vampires with human pets pressed against walls, drinking from them in full view of the public, flaunting the very foundation that the town was built on. Another pair were throwing things up in the air and shooting them down with bullet spray. Judging by the cracking noise, it seemed like someone's fine china. I grabbed Tex's hand and pulled him closer to me. I'd kill these murderous bastards without a thought, and that made me a hypocrite.

The inside of Bert and Beatrice's Diner was basically empty. We sat at one of the booths, an extra table propped at the end. A harried and super pissed off looking Beatrice came over to take our order.

I reached out and squeezed her forearm. "How are you going?" I whispered.

"Oh, just fine Lass. What can I get you?" Beatrice smiled back, but her eyes said she wanted to stab every single Enforcer in the town in the eye with a spoon. "Just to let you know, we are using paper plates for the foreseeable future." Her tone was nothing but pleasant, but I could sense the underlying curse in her words. I guess we knew whose china they were shooting in the square now.

I ground my back teeth, forcing myself to sound as pleasant as she did. The only other faces in town were strangers to me, so probably Enforcers. "Just the usual, thanks, Beatrice. Give my love to Bert."

She patted my shoulder. "Will do, Lass. The same all around?" We all nodded, even though X hadn't been here long enough to have a usual dish. Beatrice would figure it out.

I didn't miss that I was closest to the wall, and the guys spread out in a V around me. X sat at the end, the last line of defense.

X also didn't give a 'feckin' pigs arse'—direct quote—that the Enforcers were here. "Did you know they tore apart the quilting circle's quilts? What did they think they were hiding in there? Fairies? Brainless twats," he said loudly, and the Enforcers all stiffened. But none of them stood against him.

Apparently, X was the reason that Enforcers had such a terrifying reputation. He would appear in your room in the darkness, stake you in your sleep, and slink back out again. None of this bully bullshit. Usually, Judge had been there as well, earning themselves their reputation. Miranda would have been there too, but I was doing my best not to think about that.

Judge just quirked a brow, staring down an Enforcer who got to his feet. He walked past our table, his eyes staring hatred in our direction. "Traitors," he cursed, and spat at X, the globule missing his head, but landing on the table. X was on his feet faster than even my vampiric gaze could follow, grabbing the Enforcer by the throat and pinning him to the wall. The vamp tried to swing at him, but X was strong and had a huge reach.

X's fangs were exposed as he snarled at the Enforcer. "Excuse me? I must have misheard."

"I said you are a fucking traitor, Executioner," the Enforcer mocked. "You and him both. A joke. A fucking urban legend with no substance."

Judge stood too this time, and I gave a relieved breath that he was going to break it up. I was going to be disappointed though; he just walked over to the front door and locked it ominously.

I gave an annoyed huff. Lord save me from testosterone

overload. I scooted out of the booth, only a fraction quicker than Brody's restraining hand. I was beside X in a second, my hand wrapping around his bulging forearm. Woo boy. I needed a moment to push my flaring libido way, way down. Now was not the time to get all drippy over sexy man arms.

"Put the nice Enforcer down and send him on his way, X. They are trying to bait you, and they really need to try harder than a little bit of saliva."

The Enforcer snarled at me like a rabid animal. "How about I bend you over and fuck you in front of all your gay boyfriends, whore."

Well, I was not known for my good decision-making skills, but my mother would have been proud. Instead of punching him in the dick like I desperately wanted to do, I just smiled.

Then I grabbed the sides of his pants, yanking hard and pantsing him in front of everyone. "Sorry, Twinkle Dick. You're not packing much of a threat in those chinos."

Okay, so I still wasn't going to be known for my good decision-making skills or my witty comebacks. But damn, it was satisfying watching him blush.

Just to make my point, I tore his pants into a million little pieces. They ripped like paper and honestly, it was kind of therapeutic. I threw what was left in the air like confetti. "Bet you wish you weren't wearing a muscle shirt now, huh? Walk of shame is gonna be awkward as fuck."

X dragged him to the front door and threw him bodily

along the ground. Gravel rash on your dick was no laughing matter, kids.

I slid back into the booth, and X looked at me grumpily. You wouldn't even know that I probably just saved him from an Enforcer-style Kangaroo court and execution. Again. "It's like you are trying to paint a big target sign on your ass."

I huffed with exasperation. "Did you just call my ass big?"

Brody chuckled but didn't chime in. He loved my butt.

"You have a delightful bottom and I'd much rather it not be at the mercy of the Enforcers or Lucius just because you have some kind of savior complex."

My eyebrows got so comically wide, I could feel them basically at my hairline. "Excuse me? I have the savior complex?" I pointed my finger at his chest. "I'll have you know, I don't need saving either, so how about we both cut out the White Knight shit and we'll all be happy." He raised a single brow. Fine. "Fine, I don't need saving *often*. Just keep the machismo in your pants."

Beatrice returned to the table and set down a huge cake in the center. Then three bowls of cheesy fries and four steaks with a garden salad.

"On the house," she said. "Consider it payment for the satisfaction of watching you put that weasel in his place."

I grinned. I'd be leaving money because the Vampire Nation being in town was going to be hell on everyone's profits, but I'd sneak it to her later. She was proud and wouldn't take it if I offered it to her now.

I obviously ate the cake first, because it was freaking triple-layer chocolate cake with chocolate buttercream and coated in chocolate ganache. I would fight any person who dared to say that was too much chocolate.

I cut a piece that was as big as my head and promptly began to devour it. Judge leaned over and licked some icing that had smeared up my cheek. Forget the sausage fest I had going on—this was the real reason to become a vampire. Would my jeans be tight if I inhaled this entire cake? Nope. It would still be the slightly wobbly awesomeness that it was on the night that I was turned.

"Where the hell is she putting all that cake?" X muttered, looking slightly horrified.

Embarrassment slowly dripped into my sugar high. Whoops. I took a spoonful and held it out to X. He grabbed my wrist, taking the spoon and placing it on his plate. Then he sucked my icing-covered finger into his mouth, the sucking motion pulling at my clit like he was sucking that too. Oh yeah. His saliva was orgasm juice. He scraped his fangs along my finger and I quickly pulled it out. Nope. I was not going to orgasm here in the middle of the diner. I needed to come back here to eat. I couldn't have a 'When Harry Met Sally' moment and show my face here ever again.

X grinned wolfishly but picked up the spoon I'd offered him and curled his tongue around it.

I may have moaned a little, and Tex kicked me under the table. He leaned forward until he was inches from my face. "You sure he isn't at least bisexual?"

I shook my head. "Nope, I asked."

Judge laughed. "What bullshit was he spouting? I've found more guys tied up in our hotel rooms than I care to remember."

My eyes shot to X. "You sure he wasn't torturing them for kicks?"

X grinned. "Oh, they were definitely being punished."

Well, la sploosh. Spank my ass and call me Gumby.

Tex's eyes got significantly more 'other' and everyone inhaled deeply. Screw it. I went back to eating cake and dared anyone to make a comment about my obvious arousal. I'd moved onto the cheesy fries when the door to the diner burst open. I was surprised to see Cresta, looking completely disheveled. Her hair stuck up at odd angles, and I couldn't have been more surprised if she'd stumbled in bleeding. Cresta was always perfect, especially her hair.

Beatrice came out from behind the counter. "Cresta lass, what's wrong?"

She panted, which was a testament to how fast she'd run. "They took Angeline."

14

I was on my feet, vaulting over Judge.

"They what?"

Brody was right behind me. "Easy, Raine. Start from the beginning, Cresta."

Cresta sucked in two huge breaths, even though we didn't need to breathe. Sometimes old habits died hard, literally.

"They tossed the cafe. The books, the kitchen, the apartment. They found the garbage bin with tainted blood and found out she was Alice's partner and decided she was an accessory. They are taking her back to New York for a trial. I couldn't find any of the Council, or Walker, or anyone." It all came out in one long rush of words, but I was out the door before she'd even drawn breath. No, no, no. This was my fault again.

A hand grabbed my arm and I whirled on X. "I have to get them to release her," I said, pulling uselessly at his grip.

"Wasn't she the broad that made you cry the other day? That wanted nothing to do with you ever again?"

I nodded. "Doesn't make a difference. She's my friend."

Judge and Brody were right behind him. "Think, Raine. We need to do this right. We can't go in there guns blazing because we'll just end up at the end of the proverbial rope with her," Judge said in a hard voice.

Tex was pacing behind me, his anxiety making his heart race. "We need to get Raine off the street. They'll soon work out it was her apartment they found that crap in."

All the blood drained from my face. Shit. I was rooted to the spot, at least I was until X picked me up bodily. "Find the Sheriff and Nicolai. I'll guard Raine and the Snakelet."

Tex crossed his arms over his chest. He looked like he was going to protest the need for protection, but he held it back. It was a well-known fact that against an Enforcer, a half-blood shifter wouldn't stand a Hershey's chance in a sorority house during shark week.

Brody hesitated again. He hated leaving me when there was danger. It was written all over his face every single time. "Go find Walker. Nico. You need to do something, Brody," I whispered.

He looked like he wanted to scream. Instead, he shifted into the fox that I'd seen the very first time I met him, nipped and licked at my fingers and then took off in the direction of the Town Council building.

Judge kissed me, and then Tex. A look passed between Judge and X, and it was half plea, half threat.

Finally, X nodded. "Let's go, Snakelet. Gotta get our girl home."

Tex frowned, again looking like he wanted to protest. So X leaned down and picked him up as well, running through the back streets of Dark River like a blur. We made it to Walker's cottage, and X let himself in.

"Didn't think the Sheriff would mind a little change of location." He placed both me and Tex down on the couch, moving around the house, locking doors and windows, like that would keep the Enforcers out if they decided to come for me.

Tex was back to pacing. "Don't haul me around like I'm some fucking burden. I can protect her too. She's my mate."

I put a hand on his arm, I didn't know what to say to reassure him. He stilled but was vibrating under my palm. X scoffed. "You may be her mate, but in this situation, you are a liability. You are the most fragile creature in this whole fucking town, and she loves you so much it basically shines out of her arse. Relax, Snakelet. No one doubts that you are fierce. You are a rattlesnake in a world full of honey badgers."

I wanted to laugh that he just equated vampires to honey badgers, but good sense told me that laughing at this moment would be bad.

Yep, Tex was basically humming with anger now. A long sigh escaped X. "Fine, Snakelet. If you can get the upper hand in a fight with me, not even beat me mind you, then I will no longer carry you around like a big girl's blouse. In your human form. A snake is not going to be any good at carrying Raine away from danger, no matter how much she likes something long and hard between her thighs."

"Hey!" I protested, but X ignored me.

Tex's hands flexed, and he nodded once. Shit. He was gonna get his butt kicked. But his eyes did this weird thing, they flashed and the pupils slit. Had he just snaked out a little without shifting? Was that even possible?

He waited, his hands flexing, watching X with an eerie calmness. Then he struck; there was no other term for it. One second he was coiled and waiting, the next he was across the room, launching himself at X. But X was a skilled fighter and expected the move. He danced out of the way with minimal movements, like a bullfighter. Tex twisted his upper body in a way that was not even close to being human, and punched a surprised X in the face. He split his lip, but X spun away again before Tex could follow up with a second hit. X grinned as blood ran down his chin. The smell of his blood made my own burn. I wanted to taste it.

X was on the other side of Tex quicker than I could follow, and had him by the throat and pressed against the wall. I launched myself toward them, but I noticed that he wasn't holding him hard. Tex had a grip on X's shirt, but it was pretty useless. X grabbed both his wrists and pinned them above his head, releasing his throat. He pressed him there with his body, keeping him basically immobile. Oh boy.

"Enough." His voice was cool and authoritative and did wild things to my lady bits. "Partial shifting is quite the talent, Snakelet. If I open that pretty mouth of yours, am I going to find fangs?"

He lifted his hand to cup Tex's cheek, his thumb rubbing along his lower lip until it dragged the plump flesh down. His teeth had indeed lengthened into fangs. Not just two either. A whole row of sharp, needle-like teeth.

"Holy shit," I whispered, but they both ignored me.

X was staring down at Tex with a cool expression. "This is what I mean, Tex. She loves you enough to try and protect you from even me. She loves you, so you'll always be a liability and a savior. It's a role you have to abandon your pride for, because she needs you more than she needs any of us." He grinned. "But you did good, popped me nicely in the mouth." He laughed, and the blood was still flowing down his chin. Tex must have punched him hard for that not to be completely healed by now. I wanted to run my tongue over it, to taste X. Something about watching X pin Tex to the wall, with the scent of blood in the air, was intensely erotic. I spotted the moment Tex was calm enough to realize it, as his nose flared and his eyes looked at me over X's shoulder. They were still slitted pupils, but as I watched, they rounded back out to his beautiful unseeing orbs. His whole body was tense, but was subtly arching toward the giant former Enforcer. X looked over his shoulder at me, and his grin got impossibly more wicked.

"I think your girl likes it when I have you helpless, Snakelet." He leaned forward and paused, with no doubt in my mind that he was about to kiss Tex. He waited for Tex to protest, or move his face, but judging by the hard bulge in Tex's jeans, he'd be waiting for a cold day in Hell before Tex moved away. He pressed his lips hard against Tex's, a punishing kind of kiss that had no softness but was all heat.

I might have moaned. X grinned, and it was a wicked expression. "Come here, Raine." My feet were moving towards him before I even consciously meant to. He turned his face to me, lifting his chin. "You wouldn't mind cleaning this up for me, would you Love? I got my hands full."

I pulled his face down closer to me because the man was a giant. The blood curled just under his chin, and I licked at the trail, tracing it back to its source. His blood was like an inferno through my veins, and I moaned again. When I got to the cut on his lip, I sucked it into my mouth, making it bleed more until it was coating my tongue. He gave a low grunt of his own, and I grinned. Then I ran the tip of my tongue over the wound, healing it right up.

X gave me a hooded gaze. "She smells good, doesn't she?" He looked back at Tex. "On your knees, Snakelet." Tex hesitated, his eyes fiery and his jaw set. X gripped his face, running the pad of his thumb along Tex's sharp cheekbone. "Kneel," he said softly, but the command was still there.

I watched Tex's face for any sign that this wasn't what he wanted. He looked hesitant, but his eyes were burning and he was so hard I was worried he'd make mincemeat out of his dick in the zip of his skinny jeans. Finally, he shuddered and knelt in front of X. He was the perfect height to take X's dick in his mouth, but when Tex reached eagerly for the front of X's tactical cargos, X stilled his hands. "Not me, Snakelet. Her. Pleasure your mate."

My knees went to jelly at those growled words. Tex turned his face, sucking in deep breaths of my scent. He pivoted on his knees, but I was a lot shorter than X, so Tex's face came up just past my navel. He lifted my shirt and ran soft kisses down the curve of my stomach.

I moaned when his hands went to the waistband of my pants, and gripped his hands. "Oh my god. I don't want to say this, but we have to stop. I can't do this right now, it wouldn't be right. Angeline is out there being interrogated, Brody and Judge are trying to get her back, and I'm here about to climax from watching you guys doing"—I waved my hands in an encompassing fashion—"whatever this is. We can't."

X nodded once, while Tex nuzzled my stomach soothingly. "Okay, Love. We'll wait for a better time and place." He ran a hand over Tex's mussed head. "But one day soon, this will happen," he said softly. "And I can't wait."

He helped Tex to his feet, and we all shuffled from foot to

foot, except X who seemed completely satisfied with himself despite the huge hard-on. I dragged my eyes from his crotch with great difficulty. The taste of his blood still lingered on my lips.

"We should have tea," I said overly brightly to try and counteract the weirdness. Instead, I just sounded loud and awkward.

X laughed, and the sound rippled over me like a caress. "Let's do that."

Tex heaved a sigh. "Make mine a Long Island."

Every time the house creaked, which happened quite frequently, we all tensed, but no one returned for three hours. It was the longest three hours where I read the same paragraph of my book over and over again. When Walker came in, his shoulders curled in defeat, I knew it was bad.

"Did they execute her?"

He shook his head. "No. But they've taken her back to the Vampire Nation headquarters in New York. There's nothing we could do. They were legally within their rights to take her; they followed the letter of the law. Nico and the Council couldn't do anything." He slumped into the chair. "I couldn't do anything."

I sat on his lap, wrapping my arms around his shoulders and pressing his head to my chest. "I know you did everything you could. What are we going to do?" Because there was no way I was going to let Angeline die at the hands of the Vampire Nation. No. Fucking. Way.

Before he could answer, Brody and Judge strode in, looking grim. Brody kept walking until he was in front of me and Walker. He reached down and encompassed us both in his long arms. "I tried to appeal to our member of the Convocation, but he said it was vampire business, and not worth creating an incident over."

He looked peeved, but I understood. Kind of. The world stood in a precarious balance that I had no idea about as a mortal. Morals seem to go out of the window when it comes to maintaining power.

There was a knock at the door, and everyone tensed. "It's not Enforcers. They left with Angeline an hour ago," Judge said softly, and I let out a relieved sigh when I saw it was Nico. Or was it Nico?

"What's your favorite cupcake?" I asked. The twins were exactly alike. Their tattoos were the same, their hair color. Even their haircut, which was cropped close to their head. I had to wonder if Lucius had done it on purpose to unnerve us all.

Nico gave me a sad smile. "Angeline's unicorn poop cupcakes."

I nodded and my eyes welled with tears. I waved him in, and he looked as defeated as Walker. "I could not prevent him from taking her. The more I protested, the more he wanted her."

I reached out and held his hand, squeezing it tightly. "What are we going to do?"

There was silence around the room. Finally, Nico sighed. "I'm going to find Titus. Appeal to him on her behalf." He looked between Judge and X. "One of you should come with me. He was always fond of you two. He'll be more inclined to bend for you." Nico frowned, and it made me wonder about this mythical Titus.

"Why would he listen to X and Judge? Isn't he the big, big guy?"

Judge ran his hand down my hair. "Whatcha gotta remember, Sugar, is that the vampire world is like the seven degrees of Kevin Bacon, but really, there are only two degrees of Titus. Titus is Nico and Lucius's older brother, but he's also their maker."

I blinked, gawping at Nico. "Your brother is your maker? That seems... wrong."

Nico sighed. "It was a different time. Literally. I would have been considered an old man at thirty-five. He believed he was saving us, which he was. Immortality warps a person though," he murmured softly, obviously thinking of Lucius. Would I become that unnecessarily cruel just to feel something?

I shook my head in denial. Never. "I don't want them to go. I don't want you to go. If everything people say about the Vampire Nation is true, you guys won't come back." I swallowed back the emotions threatening to bubble over. I felt callous, wanting to keep Angeline's last hope with me, but the thought of losing Judge, or Nico, or even X made anxiety gnaw at my gut.

"We have to go," Walker whispered in my ear. I whipped around.

"Not you too," I said, shaking my head. Nope.

He squeezed me to his chest. "Angeline has been my friend for eighty years. I cannot leave her there. I'd never forgive myself if I didn't try everything to free her. You'd never forgive yourself if you kept me here. She is innocent."

I crumpled into his chest. I knew this. But the idea of him never returning was more than I could bear. I nodded, but I couldn't make myself say the words.

Nico cleared his throat. "You need to leave. Tonight. With both Walker and I gone, I don't trust Lucius not to come back and take you too, just to torment me." His brows lowered over his eyes. "It smells like a ruse. He wants to draw me out, but I don't know why. I don't want to take the risk that it's so he can take you."

I stood, my fingers lingering on Walker's chest. "Nico…"

He waved me away, his face more vulnerable than I'd ever seen it. "Brody, will your Pack take her in?"

Brody nodded. "Of course. Raine is always welcome in my Pack."

Tex grunted something, but he was looking at the ground, his hair blocking his face. The weight of things unsaid hung heavy in the room. "I don't want to run." They all started to protest, but I lifted my hand. "But I'm not stupid enough to put everyone in town at risk because I'm stubborn." I bit my lip, gnawing at it until it began to bleed. "I don't want to put Brody's Pack in danger either. Is there nowhere else I can go? Maybe I can just go and live in a cave somewhere until you guys come back and get me?"

Brody finally smiled. "You can stay with us. We are confident in our wards. Though, if you want to go full cavewoman, I know a good one up in the mountains. Might have some bearish housemates at this time of the year, but I hear they are really fluffy to spoon."

I gave him a half-hearted smile. Walker pulled his badge off his shirt. He stood in front of Judge, who was beginning to look so panicked I was sure he was going to run. "Judge, I'm deputizing you for the time being. Keep the peace. Protect the town."

You'd think Walker had just proposed. Judge's mouth hung open and his eyes were comically wide.

X laughed. "Looks like I'm taking a trip to New York, New York. I hear it's a hell of a town. Or the town from Hell. Congrats, Judge. Or should I call you Deputy Judge now?" He started to giggle at his own joke, and my lips curled until I was laughing along with him.

15

Tex was the cleverest person I'd ever met. Or the most resilient. Brody had wanted to leave immediately for his Pack lands, not wanting to wait for Lucius to double back. He had shifters out along the road, watching the Vampire Nation's cavalcade driving through Alberta. But it meant we had to leave in the middle of the day, and my brand new vampire eyes would have been burned out of my skull. So they dressed me up in a giant hat and bandaged my eyes tight against the sunlight. It was so dark, not even a sliver of light penetrated. I was completely helpless, reliant on the people around me.

It was a vulnerable feeling, and yet Tex had flown to a different country to chase me with exactly this much sight and only a vague feeling that I was alive. And he had found me. It was a miracle, or fate, or the mate bond or whatever. But I now had a real appreciation for his day to day struggles. Even with my vampiric senses.

But when I stepped outside into the sunshine, felt the bite of heat on my skin, I was glad I was so heavily blindfolded because no one would see the tears leaking from my eyes. It had been so long since I'd felt the kiss of the sun. I had missed it so much, craved it as much as I craved sustenance from blood. However, even as I basked in the sun's warmth, I could feel it burning me, my skin now more sensitive to its rays. Brody's arm was suddenly around my waist. "Come on, Red. It won't be the last time the sun hits your face, I promise. The sunburn isn't worth it."

He directed me toward the car, and I could feel the eyes of Judge, Walker and X on my back. I'd said goodbye, but I had to resist the urge to go back and say it again. It felt wrong, leaving them behind even for a moment.

I could hear Tex's heartbeat where he stood by the door of the Impala, and when I reached him, he leaned forward and kissed me. "We'll be back before you know it. Come on, in you go. A big step up, then you'll be able to feel the seats and squeeze through into the back. Brody will cover you up just in case." His voice was soft, cautious. He'd seemed off ever since Nico had suggested I stay on Pack lands. I wanted to know what was wrong but now didn't seem right. Plus it couldn't be worse than Lucius the Sociopath.

As Brody covered me with a reflective blanket, I resisted the urge to hyperventilate. I was being ridiculous. I'd left Dark River before, but never without Walker. When I asked what would happen if I lost control of my thirst and ate Brody's whole Pack, no one seemed overly perturbed. Apparently, I had cast-iron control and also two blood banks to keep me topped up so I wasn't hungry. And if it was a problem, Judge could be there in twenty minutes. But twenty minutes was enough to decimate a small village. I just had to trust that something in my mate bond with Tex, or my relationship with Brody, meant that I no longer found shifters as appetizing as normal humans. Or maybe I was just more satisfied. At least, I hoped so. I didn't think that Brody would forgive me for eating his entire family. That was not a first impression you could come back from.

The dichotomy of my nature hit me hard once more. I was a girl meeting her boyfriend's family for the first time and I was nervous as hell. I was also a vampire who was being sent to the chocolate-coated crack factory.

Fortunately, I was tired as hell. The low rumble of Brody's Impala lulled me to sleep better than a lullaby and I didn't wake until the car slowed to a roll. The sun didn't seem as hot on my skin as I sat up.

"Hey, sleepyhead. We are at the edge of Pack lands. We are just waiting for someone."

I frowned, though they couldn't see it behind the blindfold. "You know, when I used to think about being blind-folded, I thought it would be sexier. It's just annoying," I sighed, unfolding myself from the back seat of the Impala. "Who are we meeting?"

A weird sensation washed over my body, like coming too close to a live wire. Then I heard a familiar tinkling laugh. "Me. It is nice to see you again, Raine."

Miranda. Ah shit.

I kept my hands at my sides because I didn't want her to accidentally read me. She'd find out all about X. I didn't know how the Witch Miranda would react if she knew that both her previous consorts were interested in me.

I cleared my throat. "Nice to see you too, Miranda. Well, kind of see you," I said in a falsely upbeat voice. I felt vulnerable in front of her without my sight. But I trusted Brody and Tex. The scent of Brody's Alpha power was stronger here, this close to Pack lands.

As if he knew I needed him, he came over and placed a hand on my back. "Miranda will have to let you through the ward. It's spelled to keep out all vampires, except Nico, as the Dark River Town Council's representative, and Walker, because he's a charming bastard."

Miranda laughed again. "And now you. Three vampires in a handful of centuries. I wonder what makes you so special, hmm?"

She grabbed my hand and I felt something sharp pierce

my finger. I knew it would be the ceremonial knife from when she had warded my apartment. "Oh!" she whispered, and I knew she was mining my mind for hints of Judge. Instead, she was getting a whole wad of X. I tried to block my mind, but she was old and powerful, and I was just a baby vamp. Plus, I had terrible impulse control, obviously because I now had four and three-quarter boyfriends. So, when I told myself not to think about Tex and X and their weird little power play last night, it was the first thing I thought about. Maybe she'd just throw me into her interdimensional vagina slit and put us all out of my misery.

Miranda started to giggle. "Interdimensional vagina slit? Seriously? I really, really want to hate you, Raine, but you make it so difficult when you say shit like that."

She let go of my hand and chanted in whatever language her magic spoke. All the hair on my arms stood on end. "It's done." She patted me on the back, probably a little harder than necessary. "I can tell you're worried about my feelings," she emphasized the word like it was a four-letter curse. "But I really am happy that they have both found someone. Those two, they are a lot more connected than they believe and you might just be the right person to bring them together."

With that, the buzz of her interdimensional vagina slit ran across my skin again, and with an inaudible pop, she was gone. Brody's fingers curled around my hip. "Now that you mention it, it does kind of look like a giant vagina."

Tex laughed. "What does a giant vagina look like? You should describe it for us poor blind people."

Brody walked me back to the car. "Like an alien and a Shar-Pei had a baby."

The laugh that burst from me was so sudden, I choked on my own saliva. "What the hell?"

Tex was laughing too. "I'm never asking you to describe anything ever again. Fuck, that sounds horrifying." He reached out and grabbed my waist. Brody's hands protected my head as Tex pulled me into the front seat of the Impala, settling me on his lap. "Only a little further. I want to get as much of my scent on you as possible so none of these horny shapeshifters get any ideas," he whispered into my ear.

I rested my head back against his shoulder as Brody climbed into the driver's seat. "I think two horny shapeshifters is my quota." I let my body melt back into his, the small light inside me that was all Tex's glowing like a beacon.

I wanted to say we bounced down a rocky, potholed road into the wilderness, but Brody's Impala swept down the well-kept main road with ease. "We'll head to my place first, wait until you get your eyes back before I make you face the lion's den."

"The proverbial lion's den, right?" You could never be sure with shapeshifters. I knew Brody liked to turn into a housecat, but he had a tiger he was dying to show me. Maybe they met new people in lion form. It would certainly make an impression. "Do you think they'll like me?"

Tex's body went subtly stiffer beneath my body. Uh oh. Brody, however, sounded nothing but confident. "My grand-mother is going to love you, and she's the matriarch. I might be Alpha, but she would happily kick my ass from here to Houston."

The lie in his statement was in the omissions. A lot of people can lie while telling the complete truth. I'd been lawyered. I wanted to press, but we were rolling to a stop.

"Tex..." I started, but he cut me off.

"Home away from Sweet Home," he said overly cheer-fully, even though it made no sense. He all but tossed me out of the car, grabbing my hand and hustling me into the house. I think he forgot that we were both blind right now. Once inside though, I tore off my blindfolds. My eyes took a little time to adjust, but it was good to be able to see again.

I looked around Brody's house, and it was exactly how I'd imagined it would be. Rustic, utilitarian, but with odd little touches. A moose head wearing a Santa hat. A framed poster of Who Framed Roger Rabbit? A TV the size of a small house.

"Holy shit, that's huge," I gasped.

Brody strolled in behind me. "That's what she said," he rumbled into my ear, and I shivered. Only he could make a lame joke sexy.

I laid down on the floor beneath the television. "Red, what are you doing?" Brody asked with exasperation.

"Measuring. This television is legit longer than I am. Why would you need a television this big?"

Tex chuckled and winked. "To watch porn. On a television that big, it would definitely look like an alien Shar-Pei."

Brody threw a cushion at Tex's head and it nailed him right in the cheek. He stood above me, bemused. "You look like Tex in his snake form trying to work out if he can eat something."

I screwed up my nose. "You eat things in your other form?" Poor Bambi and Thumper.

Tex pointed in my direction. "Hey, don't judge. You eat people now. People in glass castles and all that."

The man made a good point. "Touché, asshole." I waltzed over and kissed him softly to take the sting out of my words. He knew I adored him though. What was the point of having a boyfriend if you couldn't call them inappropriate cuss words from time to time?

He smelled delicious. If I inhaled deeply enough, the whole place smelled amazing, as if someone was baking cookies in the house next door. But it wasn't cookies, it was blood. My fangs elongated, and I huffed. I was here three minutes and already I couldn't control myself. Brody handed me a bag of blood and put the rest of my coolerful in his fridge. Walker, ever the cautious one, had packed me an abundance. I wouldn't use that much in a month, let alone the two weeks he promised would be the maximum time he'd be gone. Especially if I was topping up with Brody and Tex.

I sucked down the bagged blood like it was a kale smoothie. Nutritious, but not particularly satisfying. I wandered around Brody's house, looking at the pictures on the walls of smiling people. Some who looked like Brody, but not many. The shapeshifters of this Pack came in every size, shape, and color. Brody once told me that his Pack saw no race, no gender. You were judged by your commitment to the Pack, to your family and to your heritage. I thought that perhaps Brody had rose-tinted glasses when it came to his Pack. Prejudice was ingrained into the very fabric of nature. It was how we survived. It was how we evolved.

"You sure your Pack won't be angry I'm here?" I asked again, and Brody came over, wrapping his arms around my waist, pulling my body against his. He buried his face in the crook of my neck, sucking in my scent.

I guess I smelled like cookies too.

"Rainey, I'm Alpha. I passed it by my grandmother, but in the end, the decision is mine. This is not a democracy, as much as I like to give everyone a choice in decisions that affect the Pack. But in the end, I have the final choice. Always. And I want you here. You are always welcome in my Pack." He kissed me then, not his normal, sweet kisses. This one left me breathless and more than a little wet.

Tex groaned from somewhere in the house and Brody grinned. "You know, we have a couple of hours and I'm thinking the Pup had the right idea. I'm going to cover you with my scent so everyone knows you belong to me."

He picked me up and carried me to his bedroom. He made love to me with such thoroughness that there wasn't a section of my body that he didn't touch or taste. By the time he'd wrung three orgasms from my body, I felt thoroughly owned.

16

When night fell and I stepped out into Nîso, the village that housed the shapeshifters of this region, I scoffed at Brody's description of 'village.' This was no tiny, rustic village. The lights that spread out below Brody's house on the hill were expansive, a sea of lights that lit the wilderness around them. It was a huge town, triple the size of Dark River.

Brody proudly told me it had everything his people needed, from a cinema to a small but well-equipped hospital. Daycares, elementary and high schools, supermarkets and even a tiny shopping mall. When Brody spoke about it, I could hear the pride in his voice. He should be proud, as should his forebears. They'd created something wonderful for their people. Something safe.

I dressed conservatively in a billowing blouse and tight

154

blue jeans. Tex stood close to me, the heat of his body reassuring. "The Meeting House is just down the road, so we can walk," he said softly. "Raine, Brody loves this town, loves every person in it. But you have to know, there will be more than a few people who aren't going to like how much their Alpha loves you."

I nodded as I heard Brody's footsteps come down the hall. I'd figured as much. Brody basically skipped across his porch and wrapped an arm around both mine and Tex's shoulders.

"Come on, Red. I can't wait to show you my town." He pulled me along by my hand. "But first, we have to meet with the Elders."

Tex strolled along behind us, his senses more useful to him than his cane now. Since his first shift into his snake form, I'd noticed that he used it less and less, like his snake form was always lingering in the background now, enhancing his other senses. I was so happy for him, I felt like my chest might explode with the sensation.

The town was filled with the same sort of houses, little cottages with wrap-around porches and good size back yards. The whole place was verdant like they'd built the houses around the trees, rather than bulldozing nature to fit their purposes. It meant that their streets weren't perfect grids, their roads were winding and disorganized, but every single one of those houses seemed inviting.

It was quiet on the streets, which was weird, but I quickly realized it was because they were normal living beings who lived their lives during the daylight hours. Everyone was having dinner, tucking their kids in bed, and watching late-night television. They weren't just starting their day.

There was something terribly lonely about being a night creature in a town of everyday people. Well, kind of everyday people. One building glowed like a beacon in the surrounding darkness. It was built a little like a church, with a steep, gabled roof and high windows. It also had huge reinforced wooden doors.

It had to be the Meeting House. There were a few cars parked outside, and people were milling around on the front steps. About a block away, Brody came to a stop and took a deep breath in. I almost saw his skin ripple as his Alpha power settled on him like a mantle. He turned to me, his eyes flashing but his beautiful smile still the same. "Let's go," he said, his voice husky.

Tex reached forward, grabbing my hand and pulling me back beside him. "It's kind of hot when he does that. It's almost a shame he's so damn straight."

Brody scoffed. "I think you have enough paramours, Pup. Almost as many as Rainey." He grinned, the cheeky bastard. He strode off, walking toward the crowd of people. I went to catch up, but Tex's hand held mine firmly.

"He needs to go in by himself. Don't make yourself a target straight up. If you walk in beside the Alpha, they'll see it as a challenge."

Politics. I sucked at it. I didn't understand the nuances of political maneuvering. But Brody did. I remembered how he'd secured Tex's stay in Dark River with just a few words and that earthy power.

I mightn't have been at his side, but I wasn't more than a step behind him when he reached the doors of the Meeting House. The group around the front doors nodded at Brody, smiling pleasantly. When Brody had gone past, they all eyed me with curiosity. Some with suspicion, and one woman with all-out hostility. I was almost seared by her death glare. Tex pulled me along behind him through the doors, and away from the weight of so many shifter gazes.

I squeezed Tex's hand, and he squeezed it back. "That's Brody's mom. She's intense. And scary as fuck," he whispered so low it was barely a breath.

"Did I piss in her coffee and not realize?"

Tex shook his head. "She's a purist. She doesn't approve of, well, basically anything. Not of me. Certainly not of you and her Alpha son."

I was still walking a few steps behind the Alpha son down the long aisle that ran down the middle of the Meeting House. It looked even more like a church inside, with long benches that ran like ribs down either side of the walkway, curving gently like an amphitheater. At the front, was an aging woman, with wispy gray hair and a familiar grin. Familiar because it was almost an exact replica of Brody's cheeky smile.

"Alpha," she said reverently, tilting her head to the side in a gesture between a nod and baring her throat.

"Matriarch," Brody replied, just as respectfully. "Elders," he said to the other older people sitting along the long table.

They all murmured "Alpha," and did the same head tilting gesture.

With the formalities seemingly out of the way, Brody's grandmother shooed Brody. "Get out of the way, boy, so I can see the woman that has captured your interest."

Brody laughed and moved to the side. The same dark-eyed stare took me in, and I bowed to Brody's grandmother. "Ma'am, thank you for taking me in."

The old woman waved a hand. "Pssh, don't ma'am me. It makes me feel old. Call me Nell." She made a humming noise. "You are a beauty. No wonder he has been skulking around the Death Dealers' village like a hound dog." She said it with great affection, and Brody rolled his eyes.

"Nico sends his regards, ma—Nell."

Nell gave a wistful sigh. "Ah, Nico. So handsome. If I didn't think my father would have chained me in a basement for a century, I would have been no better than young Brody here." She grinned. "You tell him I said hello." She wiggled her eyebrows, and I couldn't help but laugh. I liked Brody's grandmother. She was a lot like Brody. I didn't doubt that she was powerful though; the air around her buzzed with it, much the same way it did with my Alpha.

"Tex tells me you are his mate," she said, looking at the

man in question. She gave him a huge grin and waved him forward. "Come here and give me a hug. How has your shifting been? Have you been practicing?"

Tex smiled happily, walking around the table to hug the tiny woman. She wrapped her arms around him and squeezed him tight. There was such an expression of happiness on Tex's face that I found myself smiling. He seemed content here.

"It's been a hectic couple of days. I haven't let the python out as much as I would like. But I'll have plenty of opportunities over the next few days to practice."

Nell tapped his cheek. "Of course. Remember it's not *the* python, it's *your* python. He is you, and you are him. The sooner you think of yourself as one, the easier it will be to shift between forms." She looked at Brody. "I heard Lucius took one of the vampires."

Brody nodded solemnly. "Yes. Angeline, who owned The Immortal Cupcake. She was the life partner of the Doc. They are accusing her of being an accomplice."

I swallowed hard as guilt chased its way into my heart. Both sets of dark eyes flicked to me. "Ah, child. There is no need for you to feel so much. You were wronged; any results of that are not your doing. You can not blame the rabbit if the wolf gets a belly ache."

Someone behind me muttered, "You can if the rabbit was rotten to start with."

Nell's eyes narrowed. "Daughter. Is there something you

wish to say, or are you happy back there being sly like a weasel?"

Ouch. I mean, I wasn't sure if that was meant to be an insult or not, but it sounded like the Matriarch was throwing some serious shade.

I looked over my shoulder at the woman that Tex said was Brody's mother. She was a tall woman, with a long straight nose and thin lips. But her hair still hung to her waist in a long, dark sheet, and she was a striking woman. When she wasn't staring venom at me, that is.

"You know my feelings, Matriarch. I think by sheltering the Death Dealer, we are inviting trouble to our doors. She is not our kind. She has no business here. No place amongst our people." *No place with her son.* It was unsaid, but it couldn't have been clearer if she shouted it from the rooftops.

Nell nodded. "Indeed, I do know your feelings, your prejudices on this issue. Luckily for us all, our Alpha has decided. If you wish you to challenge him on the issue, you have the opportunity right now. If you would rather be a snake in the grass, then continue undermining us all. That is far more dangerous to our people than a single baby vampire in our midst." She looked at Tex. "No offense about the snake thing."

Tex snorted out a laugh. "No offense taken, Matriarch," he said, bowing his head to hide his grin.

She gave him a half-smirk. "She is the mate of one of our own. She stays."

Brody's mother scowled. "He is not our kind either. A two-form. He is not a shapeshifter."

Nell's face got scary. Like, Nico-on-a-bad-day scary. She stood to her full height, and her power swelled around the room like a physical force. The crowd shrunk back, and even Brody's mother lowered her head and tilted it to the side. "You will know your place, daughter."

That was it. It was not a threat or an admonishment. It was a fact. Brody's mother looked up, a snarl on her face. There was a low rumble that echoed off the exposed roof beams. I looked over at Brody and sucked in a gasp. Nell's power had made everyone shrink back, but Brody's Alpha power made everyone drop to their knees, even Tex. Nell didn't kneel, but she bowed her head again.

"Enough of this," Brody said quietly. "Raine is mine." There was a finality to that statement that echoed around the room. "Tex is also mine. If anyone has any issue with either of these two things, you are welcome to challenge me for the position of Alpha. If not, this is my choice. My decision. And you will obey!" His voice swelled until the final word echoed around the room.

Finally, the pressure of his power subsided around the room, pulling back into Brody like an attack dog he could command.

"Miranda has renewed the wards, at a significant cost. She assures me that they would hold against an army of vampires."

I could feel the weight of every set of eyes in that room. I could almost read their thoughts—who would protect them from the vampire inside their wards?

There were several issues discussed at the Meeting House that night, everything from an apple shortage due to severe weather in another part of Canada, to evacuation plans in case Miranda's wards failed. I'd eventually taken a seat beside Tex and settled in, resting my head on his shoulder. I was getting hungry being this close to his jugular, but I kept it in check. I didn't want to prove Brody's mother right.

Eventually, around midnight, everyone drifted away to their homes, and I stood stiffly in the back corner, trying to be inconspicuous. I'd expected resistance, but the glares I got as people shuffled out seemed to be a bit extreme considering these people had never met me. I guess Brody's mom was a little more compelling than Nell or Brody imagined.

Brody and Nell were the last to leave, talking quietly, their heads tilted close. Brody's eyes shifted to me, a small, private smile on his lips that dragged one from me too. Finally, they both walked over. Nell smiled broadly at me. "Right. It was nice to meet you, Raine. Come to dinner tomorrow night with the family."

"Uh, will your daughter be there?" I asked, wincing.

Nell shook her head sadly. "No. She has guard duty tomorrow. She is shackled by her views, that one."

With that, she left surrounded by other old women.

"No Mr. Nell?" I asked Brody on the way back to his house.

He shook his head sadly. "No. He died in the Shifter Wars when I was a teenager. He was Alpha before me."

Poor Nell. Poor Brody, to be Alpha so young.

We walked back toward Brody's house and I appreciated the silence of the town. There was no power out here, the whole place was run off the grid. Solar, wind power, hydro— this town was a testament to sustainable living. They had working farms growing and selling seasonal produce. Hunting groups cultivated and caught herds of goats, deer and wild sheep. The whole place was pretty amazing. The stillness of the night was calming out here, something else I hadn't been able to appreciate given that Dark River was at its busiest this time of night and I was basically trapped inside during the day. Just the peacefulness of empty streets.

Brody gripped my hand and pulled me off the path and onto a dirt track into the woods. "Come on, Pup, switch forms. I have a surprise for Rainey, and I can't walk there human-slow."

Tex stood on the path, looking awkward as hell. He peeled off his shirt and pants and boxers until he was standing naked in the middle of the street. Shifters, right?

Then his body stretched and contorted, and where Tex had stood was a huge python. Its body was the circumference of my torso, and it had to be over twenty feet long. It slithered over, its long body undulating sinuously. It wound its way through my legs, its scales soft and warm. It curled its tail and sat up so it was eye height. It had Tex's amazing blue eyes.

"You're beautiful," I whispered, running my hand around the slick muscle of its body. "Bet you miss having thumbs though, right?"

Brody laughed. "Come on, you overgrown slinky. I got something special to show you both." He started to run through the darkness, and I ran after him. Between one breath and the next, he shifted into his fox, his clothes left behind in the woods. I ran faster to keep up with the agile fox. I could hear the steady crunching as Tex slithered faster than I imagined possible behind us. Definitely faster than the average python.

The fox gave me a toothy grin and yipped, hurdling a log. I jumped too, laughing as my hair flowed behind me, my blouse billowing in the slight breeze. I felt free in the darkness.

17

We ran for fifteen minutes before Brody the Fox skittered to a stop and shifted back to a very naked Brody the Human. His long hair blew around his beautiful bronze skin, and he looked as wild and free as these woods. My heart constricted in my chest. I loved him. So very much.

Tex transformed behind me. "Dude. I'm a python. We aren't marathon runners, you know?" he puffed out.

Brody made a rude noise. "We're here. Close your eyes," he whispered. "Follow me."

An odd scent tickled my nose, and I felt like it was a scent I should recognize. We walked a little further, and the ground was rough and uneven. I heard Tex curse behind me, his fingers touching the waistband of my pants as he slid down the steep incline.

Finally, the path evened out. "Okay, open your eyes, Red."

The smell was sulphuric. He'd brought me to the most beautiful little grotto with a natural hot spring. The steam was visible in the moonlight, and the water was an inky mirror.

"Wow," I breathed. I was peeling my clothes off even as I said the word. I looked over my shoulder. "It's a hot spring. Lucky you're already naked," I said to Tex, whose nose was twitching.

Brody waded into the water, and he looked like a forest god. I reached out for Tex's hand, putting it on my shoulder as I stepped into the pool. The steaming water burned my toes for a moment, but my body acclimatized slowly as I walked toward Brody. He was sitting down on what must be a natural rock bench on the other side of the pool. Submerged up to his waist, Tex dropped his hand from my shoulder and I let my body sink into the water, moaning. It was so good. Every muscle relaxed into the water, I just wanted to sink further and further down. So I did. I didn't need to breathe, so I let my weight carry me to the very bottom. I looked up at the full moon, my hair swaying in the water like seaweed. Eventually, I swam back up because I knew it would freak the guys out if I stayed down too long. I was totally going scuba diving one day when I could stand the sun.

I waded over to Brody and sat in his lap. "This is perfect,"

I whispered into the cacophony of the night. He wrapped an arm around my waist and pulled me close.

"You are perfect. This is just a natural phenomenon."

He set me between his knees and rubbed my shoulders in the hot water. Oh. My. God. It was bliss. I was dead. It was better than sex. Okay, that was an exaggeration. Better than any sex I'd had before being turned into a vampire. There, that was more accurate.

Tex sat further along the bench and hooked one of my feet with his hands. He rubbed my feet while Brody worked the knots from my shoulders, and I wanted to cry. How had I gotten so lucky? How had the worst night of my life resulted in some of the best moments imaginable? There was nothing sexual about the gesture from either of them, everyone was just completely relaxed as we floated there and talked. We talked about what Tex would do now that he was a permanent citizen of Dark River and Nîso. We talked about what it was like to be Alpha, and Brody gave us both a short history of the Shifter Wars that had killed his father and their former Alpha, Brody's grandfather. Apparently, it used to be every Pack for itself, but when they decided to join the Convocation, there was an argument about how they would be represented. Should it be the wolf shifters, who were the most prolific? The shapeshifters, who were longest lived? A creature so old that it had been relegated to myth, who usually had little to do with the modern world but had strict, sometimes outdated, moral codes? Each race thought it should be one of theirs. That argument turned into bloodshed, with a war that went for nearly a decade and killed a large portion of the adult populations of a lot of different races. In the end, they found a shifter type that had no allegiance to any clan. A practical immortal. A King among shifters. A motherfucking Dragon shifter. Then apparently they created the Shifter Council, their version of the Vampire Nation, to nut out any problems before it came to war. They did it all democratic-like, by vote.

Still sounded treacherous to me.

Sometimes, we just floated in companionable silence for minutes or hours. I floated on my back and stared at the stars through the trees, Tex floating next to me.

"I think I'd like to see my parents," Tex whispered.

I wrapped my fingers in his. "They won't be hard to find. They're probably praying in church for your mortal soul," I said, failing to keep the scathing note from my tone.

Even Brody made a rude noise. Tex held my fingers. "No, I mean my real parents. Whoever gave me this ability, gave me my python."

I sat up until I was treading water. "Really?"

He nodded, though he didn't sit up. Where the hell would we even start? Could I even go with him? I ground my molars. That was a stupid and selfish thought. It didn't have anything to do with me. If he wanted to find his parents, we would find them. He would go, whether I could or not. We would figure things out, together.

"Okay," I said softly, and it had an air of finality about it. We would do it.

"Okay, Pup," Brody whispered. "Rainey, come here. You look hungry." That was a lie. If anyone looked hungry, it was Brody. Which was ridiculous because we had literally spent all afternoon having sex in his huge California king bed. I didn't want to think about why he'd needed a bed that huge before me.

My fangs punched out as I caught his scent. Okay, maybe I was a liar. I was always hungry for these guys. I swam lazily toward him, feeling like a languid sea monster. He grabbed my arms and pulled me closer. I wrapped my legs around his waist, clutching him close to my body. I leaned my face into the crook of his neck, licking the sulphuric-tainted water from the column of his neck. He moaned softly as I sucked his vein between my lips. Then I slid my fangs into his throat, slowly drawing his blood into my mouth.

I'd come a long way in a few months. When I was first turned, I'd gulped him down like he was a juice pouch. But now I savored the taste of his blood against my tongue, the buzz of the magic that swirled through me. He tasted different from Tex, his Alpha magic stronger. I moaned and pulled away, slicking my tongue over the wound in his throat. No matter how much the inner predator wanted to drink him until I was gorged on his delicious blood, the woman who loved him wanted nothing more than to take care of him forever. I turned in his lap, giving my butt a little wiggle against his hard-on. I reached for Tex, dragging him closer to me. He kissed me until I was breathless, then tilted his head to the side for me. I licked the snake tattoo, swirling my tongue over its head.

"Do you feel like you have two souls?" I asked him, not moving my lips from his skin.

"Mmmhmm. He's getting louder now, and some of the things I'd do before now make more sense. Coming to find you in Canada. My love of eggs and red meat. How I loved to lie in the sun even though my pale ass skin burns if I'm out there for more than ten minutes. They were all things that he, my python I mean, wanted but could never voice. He was trapped inside."

I bit down gently on his tattoo and he hissed, but it was a pleasurable sound. I wished I had X's pleasure venom right now. At least I could give them something back for letting me literally survive from their blood.

Tex dragged me from Brody's lap, and I wrapped my legs around his body, trusting him to keep us afloat as I drank him. I felt him nudge himself against my panties, and make an infuriated noise. "Why are you not naked?" he whined and I laughed against his throat.

Something brushed past my ear, biting me.

"TEX! Down!" Brody yelled, and Tex was dragging me under the water. I unlatched from his neck and held my breath as we sank into the inky water, deeper and deeper until we finally hit the bottom. I looked up and saw the moon wavering above us. I looked at Tex whose cheeks were puffing out as he ran out of air.

I sealed my lips over his and blew my breath into his mouth. Theoretically, it would still be oxygen, right? Not like my body knew how to metabolize it now. It seemed to be enough, and I wrapped his hand in mine and half-walked, half-swam to the edge of the pool. My eyes adjusted quickly to the darkness; after all, vampires were creatures of the darkness. When I reached the ragged edge of the natural pool, I slowly ascended, dragging Tex up with me, trying to make as little disturbance in the water as possible. When we broke the surface, Tex was gone, but his snake was there, its body coiled around mine protectively. I told my heart not to panic. He wasn't constricting. He was holding me as gentle as a lover's arms. This was my mate, just as much as Tex was. I stroked my hand down its wet scales, which made them feel almost slimy in the sulphuric water. His tongue flickered in the air, tasting for danger. My ears didn't hear anything. I couldn't see any Vampire Nation Enforcers anywhere. When something huge walked through the surrounding woods, I tensed and Python Tex reared back. A huge tiger walked into the moonlight and I instinctively knew it was Brody.

Tiger Brody snarled, and Tex loosened his grip on my body until I could climb up and out of the hot springs. "What is it?"

The tiger shook its head, snarling at Tex. Tex transformed back to a man.

"He said someone tried to shoot you." He reached out his fingers and brushed my ear. He pulled back and his fingers were smeared with blood. My blood. I was still bleeding? That was odd, vampires healed unnaturally fast. Tex gripped my hand. "We have to go. Now."

Tiger Brody leaned down and picked up something in his massive jaws. Honestly, he was huge. It was an arrow? What the hell? He rumbled something at Tex again, and Tex looked at him incredulously.

"I'm not riding you, dude."

Brody snarled, showing his fangs, and Tex dropped his head immediately, tipping his neck in that weird shapeshifter show of submission. "Okay, okay."

He climbed onto the tiger's back, his injured pride soon giving way to a stupid kid grin. "I'm riding a freakin' tiger," he crowed, and I laughed and shook my head. Until Brody grumbled and started running faster than a car. I hightailed it to catch up, and the trip back to Brody's house took all of three minutes as we cut through the forest. I could see why Brody wanted him to ride on his back—neither Python Tex nor Human Tex could run that fast.

Brody herded us both up his porch and through the front door. Then he roared so loudly I was worried it would shatter the windows. He strode into his house and slammed the door with his big tiger butt. He was beautiful in the foyer light.

I reached down and stroked his fur. "Who's a pretty kitty? Oh, you are. Yes, you are," I cooed, and Brody transformed under my hands until I was petting something distinctly lower than his head.

I was waiting for Brody's inevitable cheeky joke, but when I looked up at his face, it was fierce and scary.

"What's wrong?" I asked as Tex reappeared wearing pants, throwing some to Brody too.

He dropped the arrow on his hall table to slip on his pants.

"Ash arrow. Someone tried to kill you tonight."

18

I lay in bed with Tex, Brody in the living room keeping watch. There was a bandaid on the shell of my ear, though the bleeding had now slowed to a mere dribble.

"Do I have 'kill me' tattooed somewhere on my body?" I asked Tex. The sun was just coming up over the horizon, and I could see it peek through the curtains.

Tex wrapped me in his arms. "I don't know, Raine. I'm blind, remember? I can tell you it isn't there in Braille if that helps?"

I slapped his arm, huffing out a laugh. Smartass. Tex had wanted to call Judge, but I'd stopped him. Judge was needed in Dark River right now. I could deal with a bow and arrow-wielding hitman.

Brody strode into the room, his body still tense. "Can you

guys come out here for a second? I'd like you to meet someone."

I slid out of bed, pulling on one of Brody's shirts and a pair of shorts. Tex didn't put on a shirt, and his sweats were hanging low on his hips. I ate him up with my eyes—the sharp V of his obliques, the art that was inked all over his torso, his beautiful pale skin. "Damn, you are just so beautiful," I whispered to him, and he gave me that half-grin that melted my heart every time. He wrapped his arm around my shoulders and pulled me to his chest.

He kissed the top of my head. "You're the beautiful one. I love you."

I kind of wanted to cry. Did vampires get PMS? Maybe it was the nearly dying thing. Again.

I led Tex from Brody's room and out into the living room. Standing near the window were two women, both tall and regal, their coloring the same as Brody. One was grinning, and the other had a slight frown on her face.

Brody came over and kissed me softly. "I like you in my shirts. I'm hiding all your clothes until we go home."

Normally, I would have said something wildly inappropriate, but not in front of strangers. So instead, I grinned and waved him away.

"Raine, this is my sister Kelly." He pointed to the tall, frowning one. Then he pointed to the shorter, yet still way taller than me, grinning one. "And that's my cousin Annie."

I gave them a little wave. "Uh, hi. Sorry, I'm not... I

normally would have, you know." I generally indicated my outfit.

Annie just smiled more. "It's all good. It's your bedtime, right? I'm just glad you're dressed at all. Though I probably wouldn't have complained if Tex had come out naked. Your mate is hot. Like capital H-O-T."

Kelly reached out and gripped her cousin's shoulder. "Could you at least pretend you were born with good sense? Don't tell the nice vampire that you think her mate is hot. She might make you her midnight snack, and quite frankly I wouldn't stop her because you can't fix stupid."

Annie pouted. "Just because she's a vampire, doesn't mean she's going to eat me because I think her mate is hot. She's not a killing machine, Kelly."

My head moved back and forth between them. "Uh, thank you? And it's okay. I know he's hot. I'm not that territorial." I looked to Brody for help, but the bastard was just grinning. It was nice to see the smile back on his face.

He wrapped an arm around my shoulders, pulling me closer to his body. "They are here as your guards until I can get the whole arrow thing sorted out. You won't even know they are here." He paused. "Well, you won't know Kelly is here. Annie talks too much for stealth."

The shapeshifter in question flipped him the bird.

I hesitated. "I can take care of myself, Brody. And Tex is here as well. I don't need babysitters," I said softly, looking at the two women. "No offense."

Kelly shrugged. "I told him you'd say that. No one wants to be treated like a damsel in distress, especially not a Death Dealer. Let's face it, if you got it into your head to do so, you could take out me, Annie and the majority of this block in like five minutes."

I stared at her. Did she have the same opinions as her mother? Had Brody inadvertently put someone who wanted to assassinate me on the doorstep?

As if she could read my mind, Kelly shook her head. "I'm not like our mother. I know you're dangerous, but I don't think you are a mindless killing machine, Raine. Besides, Mom's protests are only a little bit to do with the danger you pose to the Pack and everything to do with you and Brody being—"

"Kelly," Brody bit out, and her mouth snapped shut. "They'll only be here for a little bit. I've called a town meeting, again. I try not to pull the Alpha card, but apparently, there are members of my Pack that have forgotten who is in charge."

"Brody..." I didn't want him doing any damage to his relationship with his Pack because of me. I'd be gone in a couple of weeks, but he was Alpha of this town for the rest of his life.

He kissed my temple. "It's fine, Rainey. Go back to bed, wrap yourself in the safety of the Pup's arms, and I'll be back before you know it." He pressed his forehead to mine. "I love you," he whispered. "One inch to the left last night, and you would have been dead. I would have lost you forever.

Someone in my Pack tried to take you from me, and I won't have it."

I sighed. "Okay. Just don't do anything you'll regret later," I whispered back against his lips.

He nodded and looked over his shoulder at Kelly and Annie. "Protect her." The 'or else' was subliminal. Kelly nodded once, and Annie gave him a snappy salute and a grin.

The front door closed softly, then a tiger was strolling down the street. Annie was watching him leave too. "Oh, he's going as the tiger. They're going to be in trouble tonight," she crowed, but she didn't seem overly worried. Kelly nudged her with her shoulder. Annie rolled her eyes. "Fine, I'll take the front."

Kelly nodded, giving me a small smile and striding out of the room toward the back door. Annie smiled happily at me. "I'll be outside if you need me."

"Annie, just one question. Why is it that Brody's mom hates me, if it isn't because I'm a vampire?"

She was pulling gum out of her pocket. "Because you're his mate, obviously. How can we have an Alpha pair if one of them is already dead?" She laughed. I sucked in a shocked breath and her head snapped up, a comical look of horror on her face. "Shit, you didn't know? Oh man, Brody is going to murder me. I never think before I speak. Of course, that's why he shot down Kelly. Dammit Annie, you and your big mouth." She looked at Tex, whose face was uncharacteristically solemn.

178

I stared up at him. "You knew?" He nodded. "You didn't think I should know?"

He frowned. "I didn't think it was my place to say anything. You guys would figure it out eventually, or you wouldn't. Telling you about someone else's feelings is never the same as that person telling you, you know?"

Annie was looking at me like I was an alien. "How could you not know? Can't you feel it?"

I wanted to say that until a few months ago, I'd been a human. The only time I'd ever used the term mate was when I was doing my bad Steve Irwin impression. But the more I thought about it, the more the signs became glaringly obvious. Brody knew when I was sad, or happy, or angry. The fact that when he was around, I felt more content, and I missed him so much when he was gone. Ugh, I was so damn blind.

Annie ducked out, excusing herself to go guard the front of the building. Tex grabbed my hand and walked me back to Brody's bed. Tex had a bedroom here, but I'd wanted to sleep in Brody's bed because his scent was all through the room even when he wasn't here. Yeah. In hindsight, the whole thing seemed pretty damn obvious.

I crawled beneath the covers and Tex hopped in beside me, leaving his sweats on. I stared at the ceiling, turning it all over in my brain while counting the beats of Tex's heart. "Brody is my mate too. I have an Alpha shapeshifter as a mate." Tex didn't answer, just making a small, affirmative hum. "Do you think my life would have been normal? If I hadn't come to Canada, I mean," I whispered to him in the darkness.

He wrapped his arms around my waist, pulling me into his warmth. "I don't know. Maybe? Maybe you would have gone on to major in something you hated in college, lived a life in the city that you hated, and missed all of this." He squeezed me tighter. "Well, not me. I would have tracked you down eventually. It was too late for you by then. I was yours and you were mine. Then one day we might have had kids, who turned into snakes. Boy, you would have been surprised then." He laughed, and I couldn't help but laugh along with him. I can only imagine changing a baby's diaper and boom, there's a tiny python on the changing table. That would have been a one way trip to the psych ward.

But Tex was right. This life had found me before I'd even thought of coming to Canada. Before I could even walk, because Tex had been toddling beside me when I was just a baby. I wondered how much of the supernatural had surrounded me as I'd lived my so-called normal life?

He nuzzled into my hair. "I don't regret it, you know? I wouldn't have it any other way now. Thinking you were dead was the worst pain I'd ever endured, but it led me to you and to my destiny. I really believe that."

I wondered how Walker, X, and Nico were going freeing Angeline. She was one person who probably wished I'd never come to Canada. But I knew that I was a victim of circumstance. Eventually, Alice's blood harvesting operation would have either drawn the attention of the Vampire Nation or she would have killed someone just like she did me. Judge would have still been 'The Drifter,' distrusted and outcast by the people of Dark River. Walker would never have taken the leap to love again after the death of Rosalita. Brody would have never met his mate. Nico...

I shook my head. Maybe it was fate. Who needs a normal life? I was where I was supposed to be. I just wished it hadn't come with so many people who seemed to want to kill me.

We dozed on and off, watching daytime television where the soap operas had people coming back from the dead, illegitimate babies with people's husbands, and evil twins named Cliff. I tried not to think about how much my life resembled a telenovela.

Eventually, as the sun began to wane in the sky, the front door opened. "Brody's back," Tex whispered, and my heart leaped with the same excitement that I always got when Brody came home. I was on my feet and to the end of the bed before I hesitated. I needed to talk to him, needed to understand why he didn't tell me how he felt, that I was his mate. Still, I couldn't deny myself that moment of running into his arms, so I burst through the bedroom door and barrelled into his arms. He held me close, bent me backwards until he could nuzzle the crook of my neck.

I wiggled away. "Do I smell nice? Maybe like your mate?" I said, proud of my complete nonchalance. He froze up, then gripped me closer.

"Dammit, Kelly," he muttered.

I pulled away so I could see his face. "Annie actually, but it doesn't matter who it was, except for the fact that it wasn't you."

"Raine..."

I stepped out of his arms. "Do you not want it to be me?" I asked softly. Brody had said that male shapeshifters only get one mate. He'd gone and wasted it on someone dead. He would never have shifter babies. Though not only was I dead, but I was also a whole world of trouble.

Pity party of one. All I needed was cake and black balloons.

Brody was shaking his head. "You can't ask me that. I literally cannot imagine it being anyone else. You are perfect for me. The Ancestors believe you are perfect for me. So get whatever nonsense you are thinking out of your head because it's two against one and you're outvoted," he teased softly, though there was a worry in his eyes that wasn't normally there.

"But will you and the Ancestors still feel that way in fifty years? In a hundred?"

He pulled me back into his arms. "Yes." He smoothed my hair down, even though it started to poke up like a bird's nest. "I know you won't believe that. Lucky I have a full century to convince you. The real question is, will you still love me when my balls hang to my knees?"

I laughed because if I thought about the idea of Tex and Brody growing old and dying without me, I got chest pains.

I held him close because time was short and I couldn't be mad at him, my sexy, stubborn Alpha. "We better get ready. I don't want to be late for dinner with your grandmother. She doesn't look like the type of person who appreciates tardiness."

Brody audibly gulped then kissed me softly. "This is why I love you; you're as smart as you are beautiful."

19

Shapeshifter dinners were loud. Like, break your eardrums, rock in a corner loud. There must have been thirty people at Nell's house, ranging from the ages of newborn to whatever age Nell was. I think one of her sisters was there, and she looked even older. There were so, so many children. Shapeshifters bred well at least. Well, they would, except for Brody who was stuck with a mate who was the living dead.

I stood outside, under a tree covered in fairy lights as people bustled around. Children screamed and squealed, women fussed, men cooked and Nell sat in a chair on the back porch as everyone came and greeted her one by one, a regal Queen on her throne. I'd done the same thing, and as she welcomed me into her home as if I was just another one of her family, my heart felt a little too full, like it was going to explode.

A woman who looked nothing like Brody wandered past, a crying baby in her arms and two kids hanging off her ankles screaming about something. She huffed out a frustrated sigh, and I totally commiserated. I must have made something that resembled a sympathetic noise, because she looked me up and down, then handed me the baby. I took it automatically, and the whole party screeched to a stop. Everyone stared at me like they were waiting for me to devour the child whole.

"Arla... " someone said hesitantly, unwilling to be the one who finished the sentence.

The harassed mother picked up one screaming toddler from her ankle and put it on her cocked hip. "What? It's not like she is going to eat my baby. Get a grip, people." She turned to me, her eyebrows drawn together in a deep frown. "You aren't going to eat her, are you?" she asked so softly that no one else could hear.

My eyes were impossibly wide and I clutched the baby like it was made of glass or something. I was worried I might break it, but I definitely did not want to eat it. "No!"

The woman smiled. "Good. Her name is Ellie. Don't eat her." Then she was gone with the screaming toddler, and another boy not much older clinging to the back of her shirt. I looked down at the baby, who had huge brown eyes and hair that looked like a bad politician's combover. I looked up, and everyone was still watching me. I looked back down and waved a finger. "Uh, hey Ellie. I'm Raine."

The baby blinked. But it didn't cry. I took that as a win. Everyone pretended to get on with the dinner festivities, but I could feel their collective gaze watching my every twitch. I could have told them I had about as much inclination to drink from an innocent baby as I had to gnaw off my own leg. Actually, I was probably more likely to gnaw off my own leg first.

Finally, Brody came over, gave everyone the stink eye, but smiled at me. As if on cue, the party went back into full swing. Apparently, with the Alpha close at hand to stop me if I decide to go full infanticidal, they could relax back into what they were doing. I felt like I'd passed a test, but when the baby started to squirm, I began to panic that I'd drop her. I mean, she'd never hit the ground because I had reflexes that mothers and ninjas could only dream of, but still, babies got things like whiplash and all sorts of weird things because they were basically a bag of bones that were hardly fused together. Like what the hell was with the soft spot on their head? Whose design idea was it that babies should come out with their most important organ completely unprotected?

"She wants to be up on your shoulder. She's active, even for her age. Wants to see what's going on," Brody said softly as he shifted the baby so she was up on my shoulder, and I supported her with one arm under her butt and on her back, clutching her to my chest like a stiff wind might blow her on the ground.

I took a deep breath. "She smells nice," I said softly. Another record scratch in the party as everyone picked up my words with their shifter hearing. "I don't mean like that! I mean she smells like baby powder and new car smell or something."

Geez. These people were nuts.

Brody laughed and took a big inhale. "Yeah, that baby scent. They grow out of it eventually and smell like poop and fermented applesauce all the time."

I screwed my nose up at him, and he laughed even harder.

The harassed mother finally reappeared, the toddler no longer crying but with a bottle in his mouth, and the kid had a drink in a sippy cup. She passed the toddler to Brody and put her hands out for the baby.

"Thanks for that. Don't mind them, they just have preconceived notions. I get a good vibe about you though." She winked, and wandered away, leaving the drinking toddler in Brody's arms. Brody told me people's names, what they did, where they came from, all the family gossip as we stood around under that tree. I'd never remember all the names or even half the faces, but it was still nice to be immersed in a family again, even if it wasn't my own. Brody held the wiggling toddler like a pro, bouncing him until his eyes began to droop and he started to doze on Brody's shoulder. Eventually, a man, still dressed in construction gear from whatever his job was, appeared and took the sleepy toddler from Brody's arms. "Raine, this is my younger cousin, Tye. He's Annie's brother. Tye, this is Raine, my mate."

Okay. I thought there was silence when people thought I was going to eat the baby was bad, but that was nothing in comparison to the crickets that were creating the audio track to that little statement. Tye, bless him, shifted the toddler into one arm and reached out to shake my hand. "Nice to meet you, Raine. Hope we get to see you more at these shindigs now that Brody isn't trying to hide you away up in his love nest."

Tex appeared from somewhere, two beers in his hand. He passed one to Tye, and the other to me. "Hey, I live in that love nest too."

Tye just laughed and took a big swig of his drink. "I rest my case. Hey, have you seen my delicious mate anywhere?"

I pointed to some outdoor benches where she was feeding sausages and burgers to the kids. Another three had appeared from the woodwork. Brody laughed and pointed at the brood of kids. "You better look into getting that vasectomy, or you are going to wake up one day at the vets completely neutered."

Tye looked a little green as he chuckled good-naturedly, going over to help his wife with their seven billion kids.

"This is why I'm not worried about having kids. If there isn't a future Alpha somewhere in this mob, then they are doing their job wrong." The tribe of kids running around had formed their own little Pack dynamic, and now that Brody had mentioned it, I could see their different levels of dominance. There were the kids that were the ring leaders, the ones who followed, the bullies and the ones that picked up the little kids when they fell down. Their own little microcosm of Pack politics.

Dinner was a potluck, help yourself kind of affair. Eventually, everyone stood around balancing disposable plates in one hand and a beer in the other, chatting and talking. It felt like home, like the parties of my teenage years with my parents. Especially with Tex by my side. I slowly relaxed and chatted with Annie about where she was going to school, what she wanted to do when she got older. She lamented that she couldn't eat cake and cheese fries and remain hot forever. I envied her tan and the fact she could run in the sun. I guess the grass was greener either side of the sunset.

Eventually, families wandered off with tired, full-bellied and insanely grubby kids, and then the singles wandered out in search of more thrilling entertainment or to binge Netflix. I ran around at super-speed, cleaning up the trash, and putting things back in order.

"Well, she halves clean-up time, and for that, she has my vote," Annie announced, pouring another glass of wine and offering me one. All that was left of the party was Brody, Tex and me, as well as Annie, Kelly, and Nell obviously. There was also an assortment of elderly faces that I recognized from the dais the other night. The town Elders. Well, a few of them anyway.

Nell waved me over to where she was sitting.

"How are you feeling after the incident?"

It took a little bit for me to figure out she meant being almost shot. "Oh, I'm fine. It's not the first time someone has tried to kill me this year. Actually, if you think about it like that, someone has already killed me this year, so a little nick on my ear hardly counts."

Nell laughed like I'd just made the funniest joke ever. "I like you, girl. I can see why Brody is so fond of you." Nell pet my arm gently. "Be that as it may, we sincerely regret that this has happened while you are a guest within our lands. Being a guest in a shapeshifter's Pack used to mean something, and our word on your safety meant something too. But so often these days the younger generation are losing touch with the old traditions that allowed us to thrive in even the direst of conditions." She shook her head sadly. "Change is inevitable, and good for the Pack. But the loss of our morals, our ethics, shouldn't be one of those changes. It smells like a disaster, and I think you may just be the herald."

I bit my lip, worrying at it with my teeth. "I didn't mean to? If you want, I can find somewhere else to stay? Brody said there was a bear cave around here somewhere," I joked to lighten the mood.

Nell laughed. "Bear shifters are funny creatures. Huge and playful, but get on their wrong side and you will rue the day you were born." Holy shit! Bear shifters. Brody might not have been joking at all when he said they were great spooners. I was going to have to ask... "No, child. You are the Alpha's mate, and they will have to come to terms with that. The Ancestors have chosen you as part of our Alpha Pair, and that means we will need you soon enough. But until everyone comes to terms with the fact, we will beef your security when the Alpha isn't around. Annie and Kelly, of course, but they have their own jobs. We will give you one of our Protectors too. Our version of Enforcers, I would reckon."

She let out a high pitched whistle and this huge man appeared from nowhere. Like he was just part of the porch, then just stepped from the woodwork. I leaped away and towards Brody, who chuckled.

"Holy shit, where did you even come from? Are you part chameleon?" I hadn't sensed him there at all. Not his heart-beat. Not his scent. Nothing. My own heart was pounding. Well, the vampire version of pounding. The Protector was huge and pale, not quite albino but almost. Brody wrapped his arm around my waist, and I thought he might have been staking his claim ever so subtly. I was going to have to watch more David Attenborough.

Brody kissed my temple, confirming my thoughts that he was marking me as his, and smiled at the other man. "This is Pierre, but we all call him Ghost. He is the Pack's best Protector, mainly because he moves like his namesake. It made playing hide and seek with him as a kid frustrating as hell." He chuckled, and there was definite fondness there. "Ghost, this is my mate, Raine." Ghost grunted, but reached out and shook my hand. "Ghost doesn't speak," Brody said softly.

"That's fine with me, I talk enough for two people. It's nice to meet you, Ghost. I won't bug you for too long, I promise. All of you. I'm only here for a couple of weeks, then I'll take my problems back to Dark River with me."

Brody stiffened slightly under my hand, and I looked at him and frowned.

Nell distracted me. "It's fine, child. You are now part of the Alpha Pair. This Pack is as much yours as it is Brody's. Stay as long as you wish."

I blinked. I didn't know what to say. When Brody said I was his mate, I assumed it was much the same way that I was Tex's mate. I had to love him, care for him, which was no hardship because I loved that man so much already my heart was basically bursting with it. I just hadn't realized it would come with other responsibilities.

I looked at Brody, and he must have seen the panic on my face, because he gave me a squeeze, and nodded to his grandmother. "We best be getting home. There's still some more of the town I'd like to show her before the night is over."

Nell nodded. "Yes, go show her our Pack lands. It isn't all assassination attempts, I promise."

I must have said something pleasant because I was being hustled out between Brody, Tex, and Ghost.

I looked over at the Protector. He was easy over six feet and wide like a Mack truck. I wouldn't want to meet him in a dark alley. Tex slipped his fingers between mine, and I gripped him tight. I'd meant what I said to Tex—I was at my quota for shifters. I couldn't imagine loving any other shifters the way I loved Tex and Brody. I didn't even love my vampires the same way I loved those two. It was like they'd cleaved off a part of my heart and made it their own. There was plenty of love left for everyone else, but the mate bond was a different beast altogether.

Niso was beautiful at night, the petrichor scent of the surrounding forest getting stronger, music and laughter echoing from houses on different blocks. We were walking around in the open, and I was starting to get a little antsy. I mean, I got that Brody had put his foot down, but they did almost shoot me right in front of him, so I wasn't sure if they were too perturbed by his wrath.

I looked over my shoulder at Ghost, but he was gone. Then he stepped out from between two houses. "Seriously, are you three-quarters chameleon, one-quarter camouflage pants?"

One side of his mouth curled into a smirk, and he shrugged.

"Ghost is a two-natured shifter as well, like Tex," Brody answered for him. "He was dropped here as a child, much the same as Tex. Actually, they have a lot in common."

I stopped in surprise. "Are you a python too?"

Ghost shook his head but didn't elaborate. Not that he spoke. I didn't know how he would elaborate? Charades?

Maybe I needed to learn sign language. Brody signed something to him, and Ghost nodded.

"It's considered a bit of a faux pas to ask a two-natured shifter what animal they have, but Ghost doesn't mind. He isn't a python. He's a snow leopard."

I looked at his nearly white hair, his pale, almost translucent blue-gray eyes. While I would never have guessed Tex was a snake, I could see Ghost as a snow leopard.

I gave Ghost an embarrassed shrug. "Sorry, Ghost. If I had an animal, it would probably be a Big-Mouthed Bass."

He made a hissing laugh, his face crinkling into a grin that made me smile back. Then he gave me a thumbs-up, and his face went back to intent as he searched the town around us for threats.

Brody pointed out landmarks of his town, giving me the tour guide special, but also throwing in little hints at his past, anecdotes from his childhood and teenage years that had me gripping my stomach with laughter. Twelve-year-old Brody getting stuck putting rotten fish in the air conditioning vents of a teacher's house. He stayed there until Ghost came with a bottle of Crisco and slicked him up enough to get him out. Teenage Brody, not yet Alpha, getting busted kissing one of Kelly's best friends behind the cinemas by Nell. Brody and Ghost stealing a bronze statue of the first Alpha from the town square and sinking it to the bottom of the hot springs. The more they talked, the more I realized that Ghost wasn't just the Pack's best Protector, but Brody's best friend. I'd been selfishly ignorant of the fact that he had a whole life here. A life I was keeping him away from by dragging him back and forth to Dark River.

I faked a yawn and stilled my feet. "I'm exhausted. Can we pick up the tour again tomorrow?"

Brody's brows lowered, and his eyes searched my face. I gave him what I hoped looked like a tired smile.

He wrapped an arm around my waist and pulled me close to kiss my temple. "Sure we can, Red." We wandered back to Brody's house in comfortable silence. Tex had been really quiet as well, which made me wonder what was on his mind. We were a group still filled with secrets. We were still new. I was learning four new boyfriends all at once. I had to hope that with time, I would learn them better.

I looked at Tex. Except for him. Tex I knew as well as myself already. As well as you could know your childhood friends. I knew his dreams and his fears. I knew his triumphs and failures. Sure, I hadn't known he was adopted, or that he was some kind of snake shifter. But I knew that he'd cried the first time he listened to Hurt by Johnny Cash. And my fierce friend never cried. It was a sign of weakness, and his blindness made him feel weak enough. Thinking back to that moment as an adult though, it probably wouldn't have just been because the lyrics are terribly sad. He would have been about ten I guess, and we'd finally discovered his dad's Johnny Cash American IV album. Ten-year-old Tex, who was raised a good Catholic boy, would have just been discovering he liked boys as well as girls, and the soul of the shifter inside him would have ensured he'd always feel incomplete. He must have felt so out of place. No wonder he'd cried. He'd been struggling, and I had been as oblivious as any other eight-year-old girl.

I super-speeded to his side and wrapped him in a bone-crushing hug. He squeezed me back gently. "Hey, what's wrong?"

I blinked rapidly. "I was just remembering when we listened to Hurt by Johnny Cash that first time. I just realized how hard it must have been for you growing up. I'm sorry I didn't understand until now."

He let out a deep chuckle, one that was edged in dark pain. "You couldn't have understood, Raine. I didn't understand." He kissed me softly. "You know what I remember? I remember being consumed by sadness at the words like he was speaking directly to me. Then I cried, and I never cried, and I got so mad at myself for crying in front of you. But then you came over, wrapped your arms around me even though I kinda still thought girls had cooties, and I felt like it was all going to be alright. I was scared and confused, but you were like this fucking tiny ray of sunshine and you were hugging me, and I felt like I was just soaking all that goodness into myself. I wonder if my snake knew even then that you were destined to be mine."

Now I was crying. Tears gathered at the corners of my eyes, but I didn't let them fall. I just hugged him until he kissed me one last time and let me go, grabbing my hand until we were walking along again. I realized Brody and Ghost were in front of us a couple of paces, giving us some space. Damn, I loved that Alpha, almost as much as I liked the boy that was holding my hand.

The sun was freshly in the sky when Brody stood in front of me, his arms crossed over his chest which made both his biceps and his chest look fantastic. "Okay. Out with it, Rainey."

I raised my eyebrows, sipping my wine that was liberally mixed with blood. "Hmm?"

He gave me a stern look. "What's wrong? You've been weird since we got back from my grandmother's house. Is it the mate thing?"

"No. Nothing is wrong," I said automatically. He tilted his head, reading my heart rate, scenting the lie or some other Alpha bullshit. Seriously, sometimes it was like dating a coked-out sniffer dog who moonlighted as a therapist. "Not really. Some part of me knew you were my mate too. Am I unhappy that I had to find out from your cousin? You bet your ass. But no, it's not that..." He just waited and I sighed. "It finally dawned on me that I'm a bit of a selfish asshole."

He looked like I'd slapped him with a fish, and I couldn't help but laugh. "What? What do you mean?" He came over and pulled me onto his lap.

"I mean, you have a life here, a life filled with responsibilities and people who need you. I've been dragging you back to Dark River, when you should be here, being Alpha. And then there's the whole Alpha Mate thing, it's like I've robbed your chance to have a proper mate, one where you could have kids and a family that didn't want to eat you and you didn't have to share her with a hundred other people."

"A hundred?" He laughed, but I smacked his chest.

"You know what I mean. A lot. And they aren't all shifters. We can never leave Dark River, as if Walker would ever do that, or Nico. I mean, if me and Nico end up, you know." I trailed off and Brody just waggled his eyebrows, the cute bastard. I gave him a stern look. "What I'm trying to say is that I'm making you choose every single day, and that isn't fair."

Brody kissed me, a soft tender thing filled with love and promises. Then he pushed me off his lap until I landed on my ass on the ground. "Hey!"

He shook his head at me. "You listen here, Red. You aren't making me do anything. I'm not choosing between the Pack and my mate. You aren't making me choose you as the person I will love with every fiber of my being for the rest of my life over some hypothetical perfect shapeshifter mate. You definitely aren't stopping me from having kids, if I even wanted any, which I don't. Just because I'm an Alpha, doesn't mean I am Primo Stallion."

I resisted the urge to make a dirty comment about what

was in his pants, which was good because what came next made me tear up like a big baby.

"You've undoubtedly changed the course of my life, Raine. Because now, instead of walking through life alone, I will have you by my side always, and that fills me with an immeasurable amount of pride. I will have four or five men who will help me protect you from anything life throws at you. Your love isn't a finite well, Raine. I'm not worried that it will dry out and I'll be left behind. Your Pack is my Pack too, and I love you."

I climbed back into his lap and buried my face in his neck. "Smooth-talking asshole, I love you too. So much. I just don't want you to have any regrets."

"Oh, I have regrets." He grinned. "I regret not convincing you to let me put it in your—" Something made me lean over him, touching my nose to his, kissing him to stop his words. Maybe there was some truth to the Ancestors looking out for him.

Because the moment our lips touched, the house exploded.

20

I coughed, a gust of ash pouring out from between my
lips. Light seared my eyes and I slammed them shut.

"Brody?" Someone was grabbing me, pulling me
out of the rubble. "Brody?!" I shouted again, my hands
reaching out in front of me. "Tex!" I struggled against the
hands holding me.

"Stop!" A ragged voice, more of a rough grunt than a
voice, yelled in my ear. "Ghost."

I looked over my shoulder, opening my left eye enough
that the sun seared it but I got a vague impression of Ghost's
face. "Ghost, put me down. Get Brody!"

"Will." The word was strained, like it physically hurt him
to speak. He placed me in the trees, and I realized I was
bleeding. Ghost was bleeding too; I could smell it. My fangs
elongated, but I clamped my mouth shut.

He put me down in the shade of the treeline, the sun no longer mixing with the burns of the explosion. He placed me down on top of someone else, and I could tell instantly it was Tex from the scent. Thank fucking god.

My fingers found his face. "Tex, are you okay?" I ran the tips of my fingers over every inch of his skin I could feel. He didn't answer me, and I felt a huge gash on his head, but his heartbeat was strong and I could hear him breathing. Just unconscious.

I leaned forward, licking the wound on his head, sealing the wound. I heard footsteps, and I poised my body over Tex's, my fangs bared in a snarl. No one would hurt my mate.

"Woah, woah, Raine. It's just me, Kelly," someone said, but I couldn't see. Her scent was familiar, but I didn't know her well enough to be able to pick it over the smoke that had burned my nose.

"Brody," I growled, the predator overcoming the human again. "Stay back. Too much blood."

I heard her heartbeat move away, and I sighed around my fangs. "Ghost has him. It's okay," she called, and I heard sirens and shouts. "I'm going to stay here with you, right over here. No one will come near you until you have yourself under control. But they have to put out Brody's house because it's on fire."

I nodded, and settled back over Tex, my ears attuned for even the slightest sound, but it was all muddled by the ringing in my ears, the shouts of the fire crews and the crowd gathering around. My arm wasn't working properly, hanging limply beside my body. Broken or dislocated, I couldn't tell.

When someone crunched towards us, my body stiffened again. "It's just Ghost with Brody," Kelly yelled, and I stood. I kept one foot beside Tex, needing to be anchored to him, but I needed to feel Brody myself.

I could hear Kelly warning Ghost not to go any closer to me, but he seemed to be ignoring her. I could hear his pulse as he got close to me, and the overwhelming scent of Brody's blood hit me. My hands grabbed for him as Ghost laid him beside me, and I breathed a sigh of relief as I touched his neck and felt his pulse. He was alive. "Help him," I said, my voice rough around my fangs.

"Will you attack?" Kelly asked, although Ghost was right beside me. I didn't take it personally; it was smart.

"No. Help him!"

Kelly rushed over, and I could hear her whispering to herself, or maybe to Ghost. "He seems to have a bang on his head, like Tex, and a broken shoulder. But I think you protected him from the majority of the blast. Raine, your back is all cut up, your arm is broken. You're bleeding a lot. I can see the bone sticking out the side. How do we help you?"

I reached over and ran my hand up my forearm, feeling the bone jutting from the skin. Actually, now someone had pointed it out, that did kind of hurt. "Judge," I whispered. Then I passed out.

. . .

When I awoke, it was dark. I couldn't see anything, and I sat up, reaching for my eyes. I felt the bandages, and I sighed with momentary relief. I inhaled deeply and a familiar scent wrapped around me.

"Judge," I said, my voice broken.

Judge was there, his arms wrapping around me. "Ah, Rainy Day, what have you gotten yourself into now?"

I cried. Then I cried a bit more until I'd soaked the bandages around my eyes. "Brody? Tex?"

He squeezed me tighter to his chest. "They're fine, Sugar. The Pup was out talking to Ghost, though the big white guy isn't much of a conversationalist if you're blind, so I imagine it was a one-sided conversation," he joked, and my lips tried to curl into a smile. "Anyway, he got the awning of Brody's porch in the back of his head. You'd cleaned that up before you passed out. He's here, one bed over, under observation. He refused to leave the room." I could hear the exasperation in his voice, but also the fear. Love.

"Brody?"

Judge sighed. "He was a little more banged up. Broken shoulder where a beam fell on it, and a broken ankle. But other than that, he got a rough bang to the head as well, they think where your head hit his during the impact. He's awake, and he is a bear right now. And I don't mean he's angry. I mean, he is literally a bear. He's lying on the floor and roars at any of his Pack members who enter your room unless it's Kelly or Ghost." He let out a shuddering breath

"You had it the worst, Rainy Day. Your back was completely shredded from the debris of the roof. You were out, and the back of your head was basically split open like an egg. Your arm was smashed, and I've had to put it in an old-fashioned cast like you are human, because that's how long it will take to heal properly, even with vampire healing."

He gripped me so tight I was glad I didn't have to breathe. Obviously, my back had healed completely, because his arms banded around my ribs didn't hurt at all. "Where are we?" I asked, looking around the room that looked more like a house than a hospital.

"The Matriarch's house. She insisted you all be brought here when concerns were raised about how you would react when you woke in a hospital filled with 'vulnerable Pack members.'" He said the last part a tad scathingly.

There was a grumble, which wasn't even remotely human. In fact, it was very bear-like. "Lucky I like my men big and hairy, right?"

As I spoke, the tickle of magic ran across my chest and from what I could feel, a very naked Brody was draped across my body

"Rainey," he whispered, kissing my face with a million little kisses, whispering things I couldn't understand. "God. I'm so sorry."

I double-checked my body. In the movies, that's what people said when you'd been horribly disfigured for life. But both legs were there, and my fingers still wiggled inside the cast.

"Is my face scarred or something?" I touched my face, rubbing them over my forehead to my scalp. I pulled my fingers away like they were scorched. I felt the rough stubble of my head. "You shaved my head?" I gasped.

Judge let out a sad sound. "I was a little worried your brains were going to leak out the open fracture on the back of your head. The beam that broke Brody's shoulder had bounced off your skull first. You're lucky you didn't die instantly, vampire or not. I wired your skull closed, stitched up the contusion on your scalp. We don't have to worry about infection, thankfully."

I ran my fingers over the back of my head, feeling the rough, puckered flesh of an old scar. We healed quickly, so the fact there was a scar was a testament to the fact I'd almost had my head squashed like a grape. "The scar will fade in a couple of weeks," Judge consoled. I wasn't worried. My hair wouldn't grow back for a decade. That was more of a problem, but still not as bad as being dead. As Brody or Tex being dead.

"It's okay. I'm okay, and you are okay, and Tex..."

There was a shuffling sound from the other side of the room, then everyone was shifting around as Tex climbed into the bed beside me.

"What did we say about the almost dying thing?" he whispered.

I kissed his face, not sure where though, and kept kissing until I was convinced he was okay. "I seem to just piss people off. I don't mean to keep almost dying."

Brody's low growl echoed off the walls, and it was so menacing it sent a cold chill down my spine. "Someone from within my Pack did this. My. Pack. They almost killed us both. They will pay."

I didn't know what to say to appease his torment, because I wanted them to pay too. I wanted whoever did this to hurt in the worst possible way. They'd almost killed my mates, and for that, they wouldn't be breathing much longer. I couldn't work out what part of my weird, fractured psyche wanted this bloody revenge, but it didn't matter, because every part of me was in agreement.

I wrapped my entire body around Tex, my nose pressed against his sternum, just breathing in his scent, feeling his heartbeat against my nose. Then I remembered something. Gah, I was so annoyed at the blindfold covering my eyes. I pulled at it, and when no one moved to stop me, I figured it had to be okay. And there was nothing more beautiful than seeing the faces of my mates, no matter how haggard they looked in their concern. Brody especially looked like shit, deep bags under his eyes, his hair mussed. He looked like a dead man.

Shit. "Ghost! Ghost pulled me from the building. Is he okay? He was bleeding."

As if I'd summoned the man himself, he appeared from

the darkness. Honestly, the guy was like a beacon of whiteness, so how he managed to hide in plain sight was nothing short of magic. He stood under the light, and I swear he looked a little like a Fallen Angel at that moment. But he seemed completely fine. Whole.

"Thank you."

He nodded solemnly.

"You spoke. When you pulled me out of the house." Again, another nod.

Brody's jaw dropped. "He did?" He looked at his best friend like he was staring at an alien. He signed something to him in ASL, and Ghost frowned as he signed back. "Ghost says that he did. But it hurts to speak so he tries not to. He said his old Pack got him... " Brody swallowed hard. "Debarked."

My eyes swung to Ghost, but his face was completely shut down. I had no idea what he was thinking. "Brody, while we are looking for Tex's family, can we look into Ghost's family too? I'd like to pay them a visit."

With that, Ghost curled one lip in a smirk. He may as well have laughed out loud. I winked and snuggled back into Tex.

There was a knock on the door before it swung open. Judge was tense, but Brody and Ghost were completely relaxed. There was only one person who would make them feel at ease. Nell.

"Stand down, Death Dealer. I'm not here to hurt your

mate." She came over, her eyes tracing my face for injury, pain or the meaning of life. You could never be sure with Nell. "You gave us a bit of a scare. The Alpha is ready to go door to door and sniff out the culprit in the ways of the Gestapo. I must admit, I am not overly inclined to stop him."

"As if you could stop me if that is the course of action I chose," Brody muttered. Ghost clicked and signed something to Brody, grinning, and it only made Brody scowl harder. Nell cackled heartily.

"What did he say?"

"He said he had fifty bucks on Nell kicking my ass."

Having met the woman, I wasn't going to disagree. She would have been one kick-ass warrior in her prime. But I wouldn't tell Brody that. Instead, I squeezed his forearm. "Not everyone is guilty until proven innocent. There has to be a better way than shaking down every person in your Pack until one of them cracks. Maybe we should start with your mother?"

Nell looked pensive, the creases between her brows and around her eyes seeming deeper today. "I pulled her in front of the Council of Elders while you were recuperating, but she had a very good alibi. She was at work. A dozen cameras were watching her. Do not worry, I had them verified. I love my daughter, and it is because I do that I do not underestimate her." She sighed, seeming to look another century older. "However, for all her faults, she loves her son. While she'd happily see you drawn and quartered in the midday sun, she would never harm Brody."

She had to turn out to be the mother-in-law from hell. Just my luck.

"No other suspects? Take my word for it when I say sometimes it's the most unlikely of people." Pain at Alice's betrayal, at almost being killed, crept up on me once more. Dammit. Let it the fuck go, Raine!

Brody reached out, stroking my hair—no, my stubble—as my emotions surged up. I felt sad about the loss of my hair, which was a completely stupid thing to feel sad about. I could have lost my life, or the lives of Brody or Tex. That would have been a tragedy. Some hair was nothing. But still, the red locks had meant something when I'd done it months ago. It was the birth of Raine. What did it mean that it was now gone?

"Which is rougher, do you think? Raine's head or Brody's tongue as a tiger?" Tex asked, breaking my pity spiral.

"Depends on what area you were conducting your experiment. On your hand, Brody's tongue as a tiger. On your balls—"

"Judge!" Brody and I said at the same time.

"Dude, my grandmother is in the room," Brody chastised gently.

Judge sent Nell a saucy wink. "I'm pretty sure she could give us all a run for our money."

Nell sniffed haughtily but ruined it by grinning. "I'm sure

I have no idea what you are talking about, Death Dealer." Then she sashayed out of the room like a motherfucking Queen. I didn't know how a person got her kind of brass balls, but I wanted to learn.

Judge laughed. "No wonder Nico speaks so highly of her." He leaned down and kissed my forehead, then nipped Tex's earlobe. "I need to get back to Dark River. Come with me. You aren't any safer here."

I looked between him and Brody, completely torn. He was right. I'd been here for two days, and someone had tried to kill me twice. I was significantly unsafer here. But I loved the Alpha of the Nîso Pack, and I was their Alpha Mate. Did I want to start what would hopefully be a long, long connection to this Pack by showing them I was a coward? By running away?

I reached forward, grabbing the front of Judge's shirt and dragging him down towards me. I kissed him, my tongue exploring his mouth, giving him every ounce of passion and love I possessed for the enigmatic Drifter.

When he pulled away, I sighed. "I can't. I have to stay. I have to show them I'm not weak, otherwise they'll never believe in me. But maybe you should take Tex home with you."

The man in question wrapped both arms and legs around me. "Like fucking hell," he grumbled.

Judge stared down at me, and I could almost see the war inside him. He wanted to just pick me up and carry me home,

I could see it in the way his fingers kept curling and the tension in his shoulders. But he knew I was right. "He finally told you he was your mate, hey?"

I glared at him, my eyebrows drew together in a frown. "You knew too?"

Judge nodded. "He's the Alpha of the largest shapeshifter Pack in North-West Canada, Rainy Day. And instead of being here in Nîso, Alpha-ing shit, he was in Dark River being a snack pack. I was pretty sure it was love." He laughed and danced away as Brody aimed a punch at his thigh. "I'm happy for you guys. You'll be the best damn Alpha Mate this Pack has seen since Nell, if they stop trying to kill you for a minute. You have a fuckin' huge heart, Rainy Day. Let them see it."

He leaned forward and kissed me one more time, then kissed Tex. He looked at Brody and waggled his eyebrows, and Brody gave him the finger.

One more kiss and he was gone in a swirl of displaced air. I missed him already.

21

Brody was pissed. He might not be in bear form anymore, but he scowled at every single shapeshifter we came across on our walk to the Meeting House. I was trying to do my best impression of regalness, but it was kind of ruined by the bright pink cast on my arm. Ghost was ever vigilant as he strode behind me, his eyes watching everything and everyone.

Alpha had pulled rank, dragging everyone to a compulsory meeting on the steps of the Meeting House. Apparently, it had only happened twice in his time as Alpha, and people seemed nervous. The cacophony of heartbeats in the square made me wonder if bringing me along was such a good idea. I reached over and anchored myself with Tex. He didn't deserve to be my security blanket, but he was. He didn't seem to mind though, he just squeezed my hand reassuringly. I was in one of Tex's t-shirts again because I couldn't fit my cast through any of my own shirts, and the wind was cool against my bare arms.

Brody walked up the steps to stand above everyone else. Unlike the meeting the other night, none of the Elders were up there with him. There was just the Alpha, looming over the rest of the Pack. The symbolism of the whole thing wasn't lost on me. He was in charge. No one else. I stayed at the bottom of the steps, Tex by my side and Ghost at my back, towering over my head.

Brody refused to wear his sling, but I noticed he had his arm tucked close to his body. "My Pack. My family. I must have gravely wronged you all at some point. Been tyrannical until you had to live in fear in your own homes. Neglected your needs. Abused my power over you by making you KNEEL!"

He yelled the last word, power rushing over the group, forcing them all to follow his command. Even Tex and Ghost knelt beside me, and I went down on my knee, even though he couldn't compel me to do so.

"I must have been a terrible Alpha to warrant one of you, someone I have cared for, loved like family, trying to kill me yesterday morning. To make you want to put a homemade bomb in my roof cavity like a coward, giving it enough force to destroy my home, injure me and grievously injure my mate."

His nostrils flared, and I saw him take a deep, calming breath.

"Please stand, my friends." He waited until everyone was on their feet. He looked down at me and beckoned me up onto steps with him. "I understand that my choice of mate may seem like an error to some of you. Some of you are old enough to remember when vampires were held on a far looser leash. Some of you are old enough to remember the Supernatural Wars. Let me tell you, I understand your hesitance. But trust in the wisdom of our Ancestors. We have little choice over the mate bond." I frowned a little. Was he trying to say he was coerced into our bond by the ghosts of shapeshifters past? Because that was a cop-out if I'd ever heard one. "However, even without the mate bond, I would still choose Raine to be my partner. She is smart, compassionate. She is funny, caring and loyal to those she loves. She is a worthy Alpha Mate. If you would give her a chance and stop trying to kill her at every fucking opportunity, you would see it too." I reached out and put a hand on his back, sending him calming thoughts. He gave me a quick smile and looked back at his people, his Pack.

"She is not some monster to be feared. She stands here, surrounded by temptation, but makes no move against you. I implore you to give her a chance because I do not want to be a despot. But do not forget that there are many types of Alpha in this world, and I do not want to become one that rules with fear and coercion, rather than love and mutual respect. Please do not make me become that person." His face hardened. "I will not let this Pack become a cesspool of bigotry, violence, and racism. That is not what our ancestors wanted for us, it is not what the Elders want for us, and it isn't what I want for our Pack. If you know anything about the attack on me, on my mate, please come forward. I will protect you and deal with the traitors to our Pack in the way of our traditions." Somehow I didn't think their traditions involved being tickled into submission or given a stern talking to. "Now, let us celebrate my new mate, and the fact we survived such a cowardly attack, with a cookout. Nothing brings together a Pack like a steak, even if it is just to fight over who gets the first one." There was a smattering of laughter.

He wrapped an arm around my waist and led me off the stairs. I noticed that Ghost was halfway up the stairs, not close enough to be up there with us, but close enough to be able to get to us in an instant if something went wrong. I gave him a grateful smile as we walked toward three huge grills and a couple of smokers the size of a small car.

"Is there a Mrs. Ghost?" I asked my current shadow. Ghost looked panicked for a second, shaking his head and signing quickly to Brody, who laughed so hard I was worried he was going to reinjure his shoulder.

"Calm down, big guy. I don't think she was hitting on you." He raised an eyebrow at me. "Were you?"

All the blood in my body rushed my face. "No! Not that you aren't attractive, Ghost, I mean, I was just asking, that's all. I didn't have an ulterior motive." Now Tex was laughing too, and I rammed my shoulder into the traitor. I frowned at Ghost. "You saved me, and have been basically my babysitter for the last three days, is all. I wondered if you had a wife or girlfriend, or boyfriend or goldfish or something, running around at this party that you'd rather be hanging out with?" I glared at the still-laughing Brody. "Would you quit it?"

Ghost shook his head again, his own cheeks blushing. It looked hilarious on the scary, pale goliath. He signed something at Brody, who signed back.

I really had to learn sign language.

"He said that he hasn't been blessed with a mate yet, and he is where he was supposed to be, watching his Alpha Pair's back."

"Naw. You sure you don't want to keep him?" Tex teased, and I elbowed him again.

I glared at Brody. "I can appreciate the tall, silent type right now, that much I can tell you." But I felt nothing but friendship for the fierce, tragic figure that was Ghost. Maybe I could find him a girlfriend or something. "Any prospects?" I asked Ghost as we came to a stop when someone pulled Brody aside to say something. Ghost's eyes darted over my shoulder, then quickly back to me. But I saw the move. I looked over my shoulder and saw a laughing Annie talking to Tye and his mate, absently playing with a toddler as she spoke.

I turned back to the still blushing Ghost. "Oh. Interesting." I grinned at Ghost, who was blushing again, and he frowned at me and shook his head. I patted his arm. "It's okay, your secret is safe with me." I mimed zipping my lips.

Tex tugged at my hand. "Who was it? Dammit, being blind sucks."

I kissed his cheek. "Sorry, babe. I'm sworn to secrecy."

Tex huffed. "I'm going to get a beer." He stomped off to one of the coolers dotted around the park. His cane was out, being in unfamiliar territory, but I noticed a little boy run over and grab his hand, pulling him down to talk to him. Then he very solemnly led Tex to the coolers, looked in the first one for a soda and pulled it out, handing it to my mate. Tex ruffled the kid's hair, then turned back to me, whispering something to the boy who looked at me with wide eyes. He then grabbed Tex's hand and led him back to me.

"What a good kid," I murmured to Ghost, who just nodded.

When Tex was back in front of me, I smiled at his little guide dog. "Who's your friend, Tex?"

"This is Bobby. Bobby is Tye's oldest son," Tex introduced. Ghost held out his fist and Bobby bumped it with his own.

I nodded at the kid. "Nice to meet you, Bobby. Want to sign my cast?"

The kid's eyes lit up like I'd offered him a hundred bucks. "Mom has a silver sharpie in her purse. I'll be right back." He raced off almost vampire-fast and was rummaging around in his mother's purse as she tried to fend off his hands. She plopped the huge bag on the ground, and Bobby was basically buried to his waist as he searched around in the bottom looking for the elusive sharpie. His mom, Willow, waved at me, shaking her head in bemusement.

Finally, Bobby emerged from the bag, triumphantly holding the silver sharpie in his hand. He raced back over, uncapping the pen before he'd even come to a complete stop. I held my arm down, and he gently held it in his tiny hands. "Does it hurt?" he asked solemnly.

I smiled and shook my head. "Not too much."

He nodded, slowly writing his name in silver. He even gave it a swirling underline. He looked up at me, grinning. This kid. His destiny felt too big for such a tiny body. I felt it in my bones. "Can the other kids sign it too, if I promise to make them be gentle?"

I sat down on the grass. "Sure they can."

Bobby ran off, and Tex settled down beside me. "He feels like an Alpha, you know. I have my money on that one to take Brody's place when he's ready to retire."

Ghost nodded in agreement, but he didn't sit. He seemed poised and ready to attack at any moment. I appreciated it. For the second time in as many months, I found myself surrounded by a town of potential suspects. Though I was going to wipe little Bobby from that list.

The first kid he brought over was a little girl, probably about ten or so, the same age as Bobby. "This is Suze," he introduced, handing her the marker and pushing her in my direction.

I smiled softly, making sure to hide my fangs completely. "Hi, Suze. Do you want to sign my cast too?"

She nodded hesitantly, stepping closer. She knelt beside me and wrote her name in a shaky scrawl. Then she put a little smiley face next to it. I grinned, forgetting to hide my fangs. Her eyes went wide, and she scrambled back on her butt. Bobby was right there though. "It's okay, Suze. She's not gonna hurt you, Dad said. She can't help the fangs anymore than Mr. Tex can help that he can't see or that Tommy can't help he's a jerk."

I almost choked out a laugh. Suze seemed to weigh his words, then nodded. She smiled, patted my shoulder, and said, "Seeya." Then she was gone. Not one for conversation apparently. She was the first in a series of kids who came over, each writing their name on my cast. Brody came over and gave me a beer, kissing my head but wandering away to talk to the rest of the members of his Pack.

On my third beer and twentieth kid, I began to run out of space on my cast. A little girl called Lulu was currently writing her name on my cast, the letters too big and not well-formed, but boy she could talk. "And I said to Tommy that he was being mean and that I didn't like it when he threw sand at me but he just laughed so when he wasn't looking I put sand on his sandwich because it's called a sandwich, you know?" She giggled at her own joke, and I'm not going to lie, I thought it was hilarious. "And he said I was dumb because I couldn't read or write properly and I said it was 'cause I had dels-dyse, ugh. The words are around wrong?"

"Dyslexia," I corrected softly.

"Yeah, 'cause I had 'slexia, but he was a jerk 'cause he was just bad, you know? And he thinks he's king of the playground because he has a bunch of people who follow him around and tell him how good he is, but not Bobby. Bobby always sticks up for me," she said dreamily, and I guessed Lulu might have a crush on Bobby, Hero of the Playground. She looked up, and her eyes went wide. "Uh oh." She was on her feet fast, fear marring her adorable face. I looked at what her so scared and saw a man storming towards us. He had the same yellow hair and blue eyes as Lulu. Definitely her father.

"Louise, get the hell over here now," the man barked. I stood, not liking his tone, but I didn't stop the girl going to her father. "Stay away from my kid, Death Dealer."

I put my hands up placatingly, even though I wanted to punch him in his sneering face. Look, you could learn diplomacy in a day. "She was just signing my cast, sir. I promise I am no threat to your daughter."

He raised his lip in disgust. "Your very presence is a threat, Bloodsucker," he growled, and Ghost was suddenly there, looming ominously between us. He didn't say anything —well, couldn't say anything—but his presence was enough. The man threw him a disgusted look and then dragged a scared Lulu off, roughly pulling on her arm.

"One day I am going to kill that man," someone said beside me, and I looked down at Bobby in shock. He'd appeared from nowhere, but he was standing at my side. He was staring pure death at the retreating back of Lulu's dad. "He's bad. I can feel it in my bones. The Alpha says we can't do anything because there's no proof that he's bad. He's just a bully. But Brody doesn't see how Lulu flinches whenever someone jumps out at her. I know he's bad. I know it here." He thumped his tiny chest. Tears of frustration shone in his eyes, and I put my hand on his shoulder. I looked over at Ghost, and I saw a similar frustration there.

I squeezed Bobby's shoulder. "Leave it with me," is all I said, but Bobby looked up at me, his eyes looking too old to be in such a young face, and nodded solemnly. He trusted me to take care of it.

Brody appeared behind me too, I could sense it when his presence enveloped me. He put a hand on Bobby's other shoulder.

"Bobby, your Mama is looking for you."

The boy nodded and walked toward the mess of children that indicated his family. His shoulders were slumped and I hated it. Brody hissed out a breath between his teeth. "I hate that fucker," he growled, wrapping his arm around my waist and pulling me close. "If his wife would even attempt to make some kind of complaint, I would have him flogged and cast out. But she doesn't say a thing. His son is so beaten down he won't even look at me, let alone approach one of the Protectors. One day soon, Lulu will have to make a move and save them all. That's a lot of pressure for a little kid to shoulder, but she has the heart of a lion, that one."

I nodded, some of Bobby's frustration bleeding into me. I wanted to go, break both that man's arms for holding Lulu so roughly, then blow out of this place before the inevitable fall-out. But that wasn't what responsible adults did. I looked at Ghost and he quirked a brow. But maybe we'd pay him a visit anyway.

When Lulu's dad stormed off, I watched the rest of the crowd. The easiness had gone, and I was back to being the town's number one monster. I resisted the urge to sigh. People had started to drift away just after Lulu and her family left, and I noted their faces. Sure, they hadn't stormed off with him, but they were close enough that it was probably more than a mere coincidence. Coincidence or not, it didn't count as proof. Still, I made sure to commit their faces to memory.

I felt eyes on me and looked over my shoulder to Brody's mother staring daggers at me. She didn't leave, but the pure distaste on her face was enough to make my gut churn. I just quirked an eyebrow at her. These people were my Pack now too, and I refused to be chased away. Not by a bully and not by the death stare of a bigot.

I strode over to the grills beside Brody, the smell of red meat making my mouth water. I stood in front of a small red-headed man with an apron on that said 'BBQ Beast.'

"Alpha Mate," he said as he handed me a plate, bowing

his head in supplication, much the way that everyone did with Brody. It shocked me a little, and I wanted to tell him it was unnecessary, but a tiny shake of Brody's head stilled my tongue.

"Hi." I looked on in awe at the giant steak he placed on my plate. It must have come from a buffalo or something because it was huge. It was also barely seared and it made my mouth water. I looked over at the little red-haired man. "Do you know, I used to be a vegetarian? Didn't work out so well for me, right?"

The man looked at me with huge eyes, then he snorted. Then he was full on laughing and Brody was chuckling along beside me. He hip-checked me down the line to where all the sides were set out on a trestle table.

I heaped my plate with every carb-laden food on that table, which believe me was a lot. With my plate filled high, I stood and waited for Brody and Tex to be finished. Ghost stood beside me, his hands empty.

"You sure you don't want anything?" I asked, frowning when he shook his head again. The guy was a huge wall of solid muscle. I figured he must always be hungry. I spotted Annie in line behind Tex. Ghost saw the direction of my gaze and began shaking his head, but it was too late.

I gave him a fangy grin. "Annie! Come and sit with us?" I yelled to the other woman, and she waved and smiled back. Ghost just gave me an unamused frown, which honestly just made me laugh harder.

Brody came over, kissing my cheek. "Are you tormenting my best friend, Red?" I just wiggled my eyebrows and shrugged. "Nah, it's okay. He needs a good shakeup. He's too set in his ways."

Ghost's scowl switched to Brody, and he huffed out a sigh and gave him the finger.

"First lesson in ASL. That one means fu—"

Annie arrived, bounding over all smiles. She handed her plate absently to Ghost and hugged me. "God, I'm so glad you are okay. I've seen what happens when one mate dies, and the other one just pines away, and it's fucking awful. Not that I wouldn't have been sad that you were dead, because I would have been. You're pretty cool. But you know, Brody is my cousin and my Alpha."

I wasn't sure if I needed to respond to that tirade of words, and when I looked over at Ghost, he had a snarky expression on his face.

One point to Mr. Silent but Deadly.

Annie took her plate back off Ghost, giving him a bright, beautiful smile that left him looking a little stunned. "Thanks, Casper," she teased, and Ghost gave her a mock snarl.

I grinned again, and Ghost gave me another wary look. Yeah, buddy, that look was totally warranted. Call me the Love Doctor, because I was going to matchmake the shit out of these two.

22

I went three whole days without getting shot at, blown up or otherwise murdered in my sleep. Instead of feeling relieved, I felt more on edge. I was riding Brody the Horse—I mean, he was shifted into a horse, not hung like a horse. Though actually... Anyway, I was riding him up to the top of the rise, the only place in town where you got proper reception. I needed to talk to Walker. I missed his voice. I missed his face. I hadn't realized how much I now just wanted him around. I even missed X and the dirty innuendos. I missed Nico and our bonding sessions. I missed Dark River and my life there, even though I was learning to love Brody's town. It just wasn't home.

I slid from Brody's back and grinned as he shifted back to a man. "You know, when I said I wanted to ride bareback, I didn't mean you should turn into a horse," I teased, giving him a saucy wink. He laughed, kissing me so hard that my back bowed and my chuckles turned to moans. I pushed against his chest, determined not to be distracted by my sexy Alpha. I tucked a hat on my head and pulled up my hoodie. Today was overcast, and I felt like I could get away with the look. I didn't want to scare the guys that I'd had a mental breakdown and shaved my head.

I pulled out my phone and hesitated. I FaceTimed Walker, because I missed his face, and held my breath as it rang. I hadn't gotten any messages from Judge saying they'd been executed for their impudence or anything like that. Still, I wouldn't breathe until someone answered on the other line. It rang, and rang, and rang before the call finally dropped.

Brody turned back and frowned. "Try X," he said, and I flicked through my phone for his number. Finding it under Fucking Hot Asshole in my phone, I rang it, my heart in my throat. When he answered, I almost whimpered with relief.

"Love, is that you?" he said, staring at his phone intently.

I gave him a self-conscious wave. "Hey X."

He let out a huge shuddering sigh. "Woman, you are a sight for sore eyes. I've seen more wang bunking with these two than I have in ten years, and I gotta say, I miss your sweet face." Someone grumbled something from the other side of the room, then Walker was there, pushing his face into the camera view.

"Raine?" he said like he just couldn't quite believe it was me. X rolled his eyes and held the phone out further until I could see all three of them. Both Nico and Walker had huge dark circles under their eyes. Had they been feeding? Sleeping?

Instead of asking these questions, I just smiled at him. "Hi, Sheriff. You look like shit, but fuck I miss you."

He grinned at me sadly, his face lighting up like I'd given him the best present ever. "I miss you too."

X made a gagging noise in the background. "Fuck me, you guys are so sweet I am going to get the diabeetus. Though, I miss you too, Love. I'm ready to be done with this place and back in your little utopia. Has the shifter been good to you? They pull out the whole welcome wagon for you up there?"

I looked at Brody, who was frowning. I silently told him to keep the last few days on the down-low from the guys. They had enough on their plates. "It's been great. I miss you guys though."

Nico cleared his throat, his brows drawn together. "Raine, what happened?"

I gave him my best innocent look, moving my hand to my chest. My cast-covered hand. Whoops. Brody just shook his head.

"Raine..." Walker was using his no-nonsense Sheriff's voice. Uh oh.

"Do not make me compel you," Nico said, his voice as exhausted as his face.

That's what convinced me. Whatever they imagined

would probably be worse than the truth. Though I did almost die, so maybe not.

"Raine," Nico prompted again.

I pinched the bridge of my nose. "I'm pretty sure you can't compel me over FaceTime, Nico." I wasn't actually sure at all. "Look, it's no big deal, okay? I just accidentally broke my arm."

They all spoke at once, except X who was looking past me to Brody, whose arm was still in a sling. I'd have to ask him why the injury didn't affect his horse form. The answer would probably be 'magic' but one day I was going to find someone who could tell me the science behind all this shit.

"If it was an accident, why is your Alpha all bandaged up too?" X said, and I poked my tongue out at him.

I shouldn't have called them. This was selfish. But now I had to tell them. "Someone is kinda trying to kill me and they accidentally on purpose exploded Brody's house with us inside. But I'm okay. So are Brody and Tex."

There was silence on the other end of the line, and the beauty of FaceTime meant I could see them all gaping at me like codfish. I pressed the button that would take a picture of the screen. I was keeping that one and doodling dicks beside each of their mouths.

"What makes Brody think it wasn't just an accident?" Walker asked, his voice cool and professional, but his eyes burning embers of rage.

"Probably the fact someone tried to shoot me with an ash arrow the previous day."

Well, the stunned mullet soon gave way to anger, outrage and everyone talking at once. I thrust the phone at Brody, so he could field the questions. He pressed his lips together in a thin line, his eyes promising retribution of the sexiest kind.

"Enough!" he shouted, and it echoed down the mountain. "She's fine. I have people looking into these attempts on my mate's life. She didn't want to burden you lot with this extra worry and she is too kind-hearted to drag away Angeline's last hope for survival because someone was trying to kill her. Again."

X just began to laugh. "You know, when I left the Enforcers, I was worried I'd be bored. But I gotta give it to you, Love. You are never, ever boring."

Well, I was glad that my ability to inspire murderous urges was keeping one of us entertained.

I wrapped up the conversation quickly after that. Not because I didn't want to speak to them anymore, but the more they asked questions, the more dire the whole thing seemed. Plus, I didn't want to look like a complete sissy and cry about how much I missed them.

I got an update on Angeline's case, and when their faces all went completely blank, I knew it wasn't going as well as they'd all hoped. Titus had taken some persuasion to help their cause, which meant Angeline had been trapped in the Vampire Nation dungeons for nearly a week. I shuddered to think what they did to prisoners, given what they did to Dark River when they were just 'investigating.'

My heart ached for my old friend. I had been the herald of nothing but pain for her. I just had to hope she was strong enough to hold out until they were persuaded to release her. I had no doubt in my mind the guys would get her out one way or another.

After they'd extracted several promises to stay out of trouble—they said it like I chose to get blown up—I hung up. I looked up at Brody, and his face softened. He wrapped me in his arms and held me close to his chest.

"Don't give me those big sad eyes, Rainey. They'll be back before you know it." He kissed me softly, and a wave of contentment washed over my body. I could get used to this mate thing. It was a dose of Valium when my emotions ran riot. "Let's go. Ghost will be starting to fret like a mother hen if we don't get back soon."

Ghost had indeed lived up to his title of Protector. I don't know when he slept, but he only left me when I was with Brody. We walked back down the hill hand in hand, Brody not shifting forms. I could have picked him up and ran home in half the time, but I was discovering that in Nîso, all I had was time, so why not walk home average Joe-slow?

I had to admit, before being turned into the undead, I wasn't much of a nature girl. The idea of camping gave me hives. Once, when I was seven, I ran away from home because I was a brat and my parents wouldn't buy me a Ken

Doll—those monsters! I packed a backpack of Barbies and underpants, and ran away to the back yard. I'd slept in my play teepee for thirty-five of the longest minutes of my life before I packed up my Barbies and my underpants, decided Ken just wasn't worth it and went back to my room. The whole thing had scarred me against the outdoors forevermore.

But walking through the mountains around Nîso was beginning to change my mind. The whole place was beautiful —rugged and wild, just like Brody. I could appreciate the thought of sleeping under the stars, surrounded by my shifters, and making love under the moon. Maybe one day soon, when I wasn't being targeted by a psychotic murderer. It was a situation that was turning out to be more common than I'd like.

When we reached the back porch of the temporary house we were staying in, Brody stilled when he heard the low hum of voices inside. He sniffed the air, then relaxed. Whoever it was, it was a friend, not foe. We strolled into the living room, and I grinned when I saw Annie was sitting on the couch beside Ghost, talking animatedly to the huge Protector without drawing breath. Tex was sitting on the other side of the room, looking like he was trying to hold in a laugh.

"And I said to him that just because he weighed as much as a Mack truck didn't make him a better Protector than me, and that everyone knew you were the best one we have which was why you were guarding the Alpha Mate, and that he was like our twenty-fifth best Protector so he needed to shut his mouth. Then he took a swing at me!" She clutched a hand to her chest like she was still outraged, but she seemed to miss the murderous look on Ghost's face. Whoever they were talking about was going to get his ass kicked before he knew it. "So I kicked him in the balls so hard he's still talking in falsetto! Talk about delusions of grandeur, amiright?"

Ghost nodded, and then he seemed to realize we'd returned. Tex had known all along, and now he wasn't even trying to hide his grin. He bounded over, knocking his leg into the couch and hip-checking the kitchen table. He was still learning the layout of this house, which meant a few bruises for a while. I'd already promised to kiss every single one better.

"How was everyone?" he whispered as he came over and kissed me. I wrapped my arms around his chest and heaved out a sigh. I missed them so badly it hurt, but with Tex's arms around me and Brody's hand still in mine, the burn in my gut wasn't quite as intense.

"They're fine. They look exhausted but they're working hard to free Angeline. Brody totally let it slip about our troubles," I pouted. Tex kissed me tenderly.

There was a distinctly feminine sigh in the room, and I looked around Tex's shoulder to where Annie was watching us from the couch. "God, you guys are so sweet. Don't you wish you had a mate, Ghost? This lucky bitch gets two. I'm so jealous," she said with a laugh. Ghost's face was so full of painful longing as he stared at her, but she didn't notice, she was too busy looking at us. Before she could see, Ghost had his face schooled back into that nonchalant mask.

I smiled at her. "Trust me when I say that sometimes it's right there, under your nose the whole time." At Ghost's furious look, I grinned. "That's what happened with me and Tex, anyway. We'd been friends since we were children. Then one day, boom. It was like every feeling I'd ever had about him suddenly made sense."

Ghost was still giving me a stern, slightly panicked look, so I let it go. I'd planted a seed. It was up to him to make it grow.

Brody just shook his head and walked into the living room. "What have you got for me, Annie?"

All the jovialness left her face, and in her place was someone else. It was like someone else had possessed her body. She was cold, unemotional, all business, no hint of the teasing woman that had been sitting in her place a moment ago.

"We have dissidents."

Brody waved a hand at the window toward the rubble that was his house. "Duh."

Annie rolled her eyes, a little bit of her normal personality leaking into her professional demeanor. "I mean more than one, jackass."

"Alpha Jackass to you," Brody growled, but there was no heat in it.

"There is a whole subgroup of dissidents who want you

out. They were trying to arrange a coup and set your mother up in your place until one of the younger Alpha contenders could step up. Someone they could shape to their... ideology."

Tex was sitting cross-legged on the armchair, his long legs creating the perfect armrests. I wanted to crawl between them and curl my body into his. "How do you know this?"

Brody looked between Tex and me. "Annie is my best spy. It is stupid to think that everyone is in love with the status quo. Annie is my ears on the ground. She blends into the background almost as well as Ghost."

Annie winced. "I hate it when you call me a spy. Sounds so sleazy. Like I should be wearing a trench coat and a bad fedora while I rat out my fellow Pack members. I prefer Pack Satisfaction Representative." Now it was Brody's turn to roll his eyes, but Annie continued. "I went along to one of their meetings, though I kept my head down. I didn't see your mom there, so I can't be sure she's involved. I want to say no," she said softly.

The more Annie spoke, the closer I stood to Brody. In the way of hate groups, they wanted Brody dead and wanted to do it in the most brutal, public way possible. They wanted to execute him on the steps of the Meeting House. As more and more of the details were revealed, I stepped closer and closer to Brody until I was basically on top of him. He wrapped me in his arms without hesitation.

"Ringleaders?"

Annie's mouth twisted. "I couldn't pin just one. But they

all seemed vaguely surprised by someone trying to blow up your house. I got the impression that they'd mostly been getting together to whine, bitch and daydream about your head on a platter up until that point. I don't think it had been preplanned by the collective. Just one person going a bit rogue. They are ready to double down on the effort though. They have been inspired to act." She looked at me and smiled. "If it makes you feel better, they seemed to be developed enough that they must have begun long before you were on the scene. You just added fuel to the fire; they are definitely anti-everything that isn't shapeshifter and 'normal.'" She spat the word like it was poison on her tongue.

Brody only seemed vaguely perturbed about the idea that there was a hate group that wanted him dead.

But I was furious. "When do they meet next? I could go in and wipe them all out like that." I snapped my fingers. We all knew it was true, and my normally pacifist heart was burning right now with the thought of someone wanting to kill Brody. To kill my mate. The predator in me wanted to shred some things, which simultaneously revved me up and terrified me.

A small huff of laughter passed Brody's lips. "Aw, Red. You are a lot of things, but you are not a killer. It would haunt you for eternity. What if you got a person who was only coming for the first time and doesn't necessarily agree with whatever they were saying? An innocent? The teens that are caught up in the fervor of older generations, who haven't had time to understand just how wrong it all is?" He hugged me tightly. "You aren't a remorseless killer, and that is one of the things I love about you." He leaned close, trailing his lips until they were just beside my ear. "But I appreciate that you want to protect me, mate. I love you." A wave of happiness passed through my chest, and I realized it was the bond. It felt like he was thrumming it with his fingers, pushing emotions around in there. My eyes snapped open to stare up into his beautiful dark eyes.

"That's weird. Did you just poke around my insides?"

He laughed. "Well, a few times now. Remember last night when I put my—"

"LAAAA! Too much information," Annie yelled, and Ghost let out a hissing laugh.

My eyes felt like they were open too wide and all the blood in my body was in my cheeks. I tried to do the same thing, but with love and a good chunk of lust. I concentrated on the feeling in my chest that I considered the bond. It was pure and good. The bond had no negative emotions attached. It was just a connection, wrapped in the pureness of love. Then I thought about how much I loved him, how hot I was when his body was pressed to mine. Then I took a deep breath out and pushed all those feelings toward that spot.

I legitimately felt Brody's skin ripple, and Tex basically jumped from the couch with a yelp.

"Out. Everyone out. Ghost, gather the Protectors and

bring them over in two"—Brody looked down at me consideringly—"three hours. Pup, you can stay."

"Thank fuck," Tex grumbled, but there was heat in his voice.

Brody was using his Alpha voice, so everyone was moving before he'd even finished. Annie and Ghost were both giving us knowing smirks.

The door hadn't even shut behind them when Brody spun me in his arms and kissed me like his life depended on it. His mouth devoured mine, and then I felt Tex behind me.

"Bed," Tex muttered, and Brody grunted, lifting me effortlessly into his arms and striding down the hall toward the bedroom. Tex was out of his clothes and on the bed before we'd even reached the room, and Brody passed me down into his waiting arms. My feet didn't even touch the floor. Tex wrapped his arms around me, and I straddled his hips, kissing him with hard, frantic movements. He peeled my shirt off with deft hands, barely breaking the contact with my lips. His tongue thrust in and out of my mouth like a foreshadowing of what was about to come. His fingers found the waistband of my cutoff shorts and he unbuttoned them, slipping his fingers inside. He'd memorized my body like his own, and found my clit with unerring accuracy. He flicked it and I bucked like I was electrified. He rubbed slowly, building his pace until I was panting. I could feel Brody's eyes running over my face, watching my pleasure as it built to almost painful heights. I wanted someone inside me now.

I let out a panting, pathetic mewling noise, but that was enough. Brody was behind me, dragging off my shorts. He pulled me to my hands and knees, and I felt his rock hard cock at my entrance. He slammed into me, his length stretching me until it burned so damn good. He let out a sigh of relief, just sitting in me, buried to his balls. My eyes were rolling around in my head, and he wasn't even moving. Instead of pulling back out, he wrapped his arms under my torso and dragged me down Tex's body a little more until I was face to cock with Tex's body. I looked up at the wild grin on his face. Brody didn't tell me to suck his dick—Brody wasn't that kind of lover—but he slid all the way out, slamming back in one last time before he set a slow, deep rhythm that had me panting. Tex held his dick as I slid him into my mouth, drawing him out in time with Brody's thrusts and my own panting moans.

I took Tex deeper and deeper into my throat with every slide, until he had his beautiful inked hands wrapped in the blankets as his body bowed off the bed. "Fuck!" he grunted, and I hummed my agreement while he was deep in my throat, making him make an animalistic noise.

Brody picked up speed until I was being slammed forward onto Tex's cock, and my orgasm was threatening to shatter me in two.

"I'm going to come," Tex groaned, and I pulled him out of my mouth, wrapping my hand around his dick and striking at his femoral artery with my fangs. The thrill of my bite had him coming all over my hand and his abs, and the magic in his blood had me coming on Brody's dick, gripping down hard as he still pounded into me. He let out a guttural groan, his thrusts losing their finesse until it was just wild, disjointed fucking. He came on a roar so primal, I was pretty sure they would have heard it in the center of town.

I collapsed onto Tex's abs, uncaring that I was lying in a pool of bodily fluids. "Note to self. Do not send lust down the bond in mixed company again. Holy hell," I panted. Brody pulled out, wrapping his body around mine, uncaring how close his face was to Tex's still semi-hard dick.

"Not recommended."

Tex grunted. "You may as well have grabbed my dick and pulled it. It was..." He shuddered with pleasure again, just at the memory.

"It's like an invisible finger stroking your G-spot out of the blue," Brody clarified. Well, yeah, that would definitely do it.

Tex's cock was now hard again near my lips. I leaned forward and licked it from base to tip, just because I could. "How can you possibly be hard again?" I muttered.

Tex laughed. "I am always hard for you, Raine. Let's go shower. I'll clean off this mess with my tongue." His fingers brushed over the stickiness on my chest. "I still need to be inside you," he purred, and it made goosebumps run over my skin. Tex's voice when he whispered dirty fucking things was a wet dream come to life.

Brody rolled to the side, letting me and Tex up. He slapped Tex on the ass, then me. "Take care of our mate," he mumbled, then he was snoring softly.

Let's just say I felt clean and so, so very dirty by the time I fell back into bed, Brody on one side and Tex on the other. Surrounded by my mates, I couldn't imagine life being better in that moment.

I was learning the alphabet in sign language, watching Jeopardy and eating Cheetos in a tank top and a pair of Tex's boxer briefs like the multitasking goddess I was, when there was a knock at the door. Ghost frowned as he stood from where he sat across from me, walking warily toward the door. His body was tense, but whoever it was couldn't be too bad, because he still opened it.

His big body blocked entry to whoever was standing on the other side. "Aren't you going to let me in, Pierre?" a smooth, cool voice asked—a voice I didn't recognize but should have. "Move," she said, and Ghost frowned, but moved to the side. Brody's mom strolled into the house like she owned it, her regal posture making it easy to see she was the daughter of an Alpha and the mother of another. She oozed power, but not to the same degree as Nell, and definitely not the same amount as Brody.

I looked down at my outfit and scowled at Ghost. I was pretty sure this was payback for all the Annie matchmaking I was doing. Kelly walked stiffly in behind her mother, her eyes screaming apologies and her body tense. She mouthed, "I'm sorry," behind her mother's back, and I gave what I hoped was a forgiving look back.

"Death Dealer. I thought it was time we spoke without my mother or son around to interfere."

I held my head high, although my tighty-whities were covered in orange Cheeto dust prints.

"My name is Raine. Maybe we should start there." I tried to channel my own take-no-shit mother at that moment. If I expected an 'only if you call me Antoinette' moment, I was going to be very disappointed. She merely sniffed and sat down in Brody's chair. Damn, this political posturing thing was about as subtle as a brick to the face.

"Fine. I wanted to come and say personally that I had nothing to do with the destruction of my son's house. I would never endanger him like that." She smartly omitted the fact that she didn't give a fuck if I lived or died, but the subcontext was there. We all got it.

"And the ash arrow?"

She looked at me, her eyes glinting. "What of it?"

I gritted my teeth. "Did you have something to do with the ash arrow that was aimed at my head?"

She scoffed. "If it had been me shooting arrows, I would not have missed."

It was official. I wanted to punch her in the head in a very violent manner. I gave her a very cold smirk, doing my best to channel the cold menace of X. "Well, congratulations. If that's all, I have some very pressing engagements that I have to attend."

"Final round of Jeopardy?" she sneered.

Kelly made a strangled noise in the back of her throat, like she was wondering if she yelled for help whether anyone would save her mother before I ripped out her throat. I looked at Ghost, whose face was completely blank. A canvas that said the woman in front of him wasn't worth his emotions. Hell, I might have been reading a little much into that, but I liked to think he was on my side.

I shook my head. "No. All the shit you are talking is making me gag. I need to go and vomit."

Kelly sucked in something that may have been a gasp and a burst of laughter, or may have been her choking on her own tongue.

Antoinette got to her feet, her cold face suddenly heating with rage. "Listen to me, you parasite. If you opened your eyes, you would see that my son almost died because of you. If he spent more time here being an Alpha to his people, rather than fucking some cheap cunt in a town filled with Death Dealers, he would have known that there was a coup being incepted. If he hadn't been indulging in necrophilia, he would have been able to crush these malcontents with the force they deserved before it had even reached this point. You are a drain on his very life force, and you will never be anything but a drain. You will never give him an heir, you will never properly lead this Pack as an Alpha Mate. You will never be anything more than an irritating threat to everything we've achieved here. Do us all a favor and crawl back into the coffin you came from, corpse."

With that, she whirled and left, and I stood there dumbfounded.

I finally summoned up the right words. "Well, even as a bloodsucking corpse, I will still be more important than you, you pompous old hag!" I screeched after her, even though the door had slammed shut at the beginning of my epic comeback.

Kelly shook her head, never taking her eyes off me. "I'm sorry, Raine. She's wrong. About everything. Just don't let her get inside your head." With that, she chased after her mother. How that creature had spawned the good-natured Brody and Kelly was beyond me. She was a freaking piranha.

I looked at Ghost, whose face was stormy. "Hey Ghost, what's ASL for 'Fuck you and the horse you rode in on, bitch' in sign language?" I asked, and he just nodded his head with a gesture in her direction that needed no interpretation.

Fuck it. I was going back to bed. Bullshit took it out of me and now I needed a nap.

23

I woke up in the middle of the day, which was odd. Normally, I slept like the dead. Har har. I rolled over and pouted when Brody's side of the bed was cold. I rolled out of the blankets and went to check if he was still around. I didn't know how long his meeting with the Protectors would go for, but I put pants on just in case they'd reconvened to the living room. Ghost would have a fit, and Brody would get all growly, which I found stupidly attractive. On second thoughts, maybe I should've left the pants off.

Grinning to myself, I walked toward the kitchen, but I couldn't hear any other heartbeats. Boo. When I reached the living room, I could hear Brody's voice as he strolled up the driveway from the street. I grinned wider. If his business was over, I might convince him to have round three—or was it four?—for the rest of the afternoon.

I opened the fridge and pulled out a can of whipped cream. Yeah, this would definitely help with the convincing. I turned, smiling, as I heard heartbeats reach the room.

"Hurry the fuck up, they're almost here," an unfamiliar voice whispered, then I was being electrocuted from the inside out.

It all went black. Again.

I snapped back to consciousness screaming. Unlike the last time I woke up from being unconscious, which was only a freaking week ago, when I had drifted gently from the blackness with a peaceful feeling of being surrounded by my mates and lovers. This time, I woke to what felt like my flesh being melted from my bones with a blow torch.

I screamed, but it was muffled by cloth stuffed halfway down my throat. Luckily I didn't need to breathe, or I would have been dead. Still, I tried to scream for help around the rag.

"You can quit the screaming, bitch. You aren't even on Pack lands anymore. No one can hear you scream. Hell, even if someone could, they wouldn't give a shit."

I screamed that he could go to hell, but it was muffled. So I told him that he was worse than a maggot and that his face looked like the herpes virus infected an intestinal worm and his face was the spitting image of what that worm shat out. It didn't make sense, but cussing him out kept the panic at bay.

The sun was burning me; that was what it had to be. Or maybe they had legitimately set me on fire, but I couldn't smell smoke or any kind of accelerant. So I had to assume it was the sun. And given the amount of my skin that felt like it was being flayed, I'd probably been stripped down to my underwear. Now I was doubly glad I wore underwear.

My eyes were scrunched closed, which was a blessing. But it meant I couldn't see my attackers, or how many there were, or where I was. I couldn't process anything but the searing of my flesh.

Someone stood over me, blocking the sun from touching my skin momentarily. It gave me a brief reprieve so I could just breathe. Well, theoretically breathe because I was still gagging on the rag in my mouth. Whoever was blocking the sun leaned down and plucked the rag from my mouth.

Someone further away let out a frustrated grunt. "For fuck's sake, I'm sick of listening to her screaming. Just go put her under the tree already," the voice, a man's voice, grumbled.

Whoever was blocking the sun grunted his assent, then he dragged me over rocks and sticks, which scraped against my already burned skin. I whimpered as the pain made me gag.

Noticing, the person dragging me stopped, and hefted me into his arms. "Don't bite me," the person—a guy, but young if his voice was anything to go by—said softly in my ear. "I'm so sorry. I didn't know this is what they wanted. You gotta tell the Alpha I didn't know they'd do this. I've gotten a message out to Annie—I know he'll come, but if you rat me out now, they'll kill us both. Well, re-kill you." The words were hushed, a barely audible whisper. "I didn't know. I just thought we'd all just sit around forever and bitch about how bad the Alpha was while drinking beer. I didn't know they'd do this." He repeated himself, but I'd tuned him out as we'd reached the shade. I let out a relieved sigh as the burning stopped, giving my body time to heal itself.

I didn't give the kid the words of reassurance he seemed to desperately be seeking, because fuck him. But if I could, I would try and get Brody to spare him. Maybe.

"Come away, kid, before she eats you," someone chuckled. That was the third voice. "She's trapped there until sundown, and then they'll be here for her. You never know how you'll catch vampirism from nasty fucking Death Dealers."

Someone laughed. "Can't send you home to your mama with the worst STD on the planet."

Rage bubbled in my chest. Rage and fear and frustration at the unfairness of it all. I gritted my teeth. "You know what, you bigoted pieces of shit, you are all nothing but sheep, following each other off a cliff because you are too stupid to turn away before you plummet to your deaths," I spewed back at them, my nerve endings buzzing with trapped power. I wanted to tear off their heads. I wanted to fucking bathe in their blood. I was sick of this shit. Sick of being tormented, tortured, attacked. All I wanted was a life where I could love and be loved. Was that too damn much to ask of the universe right now?

Tears of anger pricked my eyes and I blinked them away. I wouldn't seem weak in front of these assholes. I'd let my body heal, then I would kill every last one of them myself, even if my skin melted off in the sun in the meantime.

After a moment, there was silence in the camp. I could still hear the heartbeat of the kid near me, obviously not taking the advice of the rest of the douchebags here to run away while he could. But I didn't eat kids. He didn't know that, but he knew that when the cavalry arrived, it was probably better to be near me and not them. Because Brody would tear them to pieces, and all that would be left was their entrails littering this forest. I smiled a little at the thought.

"What the fuck?" the kid whispered.

I huffed out a frustrated noise. I couldn't see, and I needed to see. I was a fucking easy target sitting here with my thumb up my ass. "What?" I growled to the kid.

"They're... I mean, I think they're trying to..." He trailed off again. "They're pretending to be sheep."

Someone bleated, and I blinked. "What?"

I could almost taste the kid's confusion on the air. Magic swirled through the clearing. "Shit, now they're shifting to sheep. Clint is fighting it, but he can't stop the change." Another magical pop, and another bleating baa.

Um. The kid was right. What the fuck?

"Did I do that?" I asked, but how the kid would know was beyond me. Couldn't be a coincidence though, right? "What about you? Are you feeling sheepish?" I snorted, the hysteria finally beginning to kick my ass.

Even the kid let out a honk of laughter. "No? I mean, I don't think so?"

"How do you feel about lettuce?"

"Uh, not as good as steak?"

I nodded. Whatever was happening, it wasn't affecting him.

He tugged at my arm. "Whether they are sheep or not, we need to go before sunset. I don't want to be slaughtered, and no offense, but I don't think you can take on a whole squad of Enforcers."

I spun on him. "What?"

His heartbeat became fainter as he took a big step away. "That's what Clint and the others were doing. A call went out to all the shifter mercs that they wanted you. Clint heard about it from one of his old biker buddies. He said we were going to be rich, and we'd be rid of the Alpha and the Death Dealer as a bonus. I mean, it's not like I don't like the Alpha, but Dad said you were evil and you'd infected his mind with your undead pus—" He snapped his mouth closed, and I had to laugh.

Seriously? This was the propaganda they were spreading? If they hadn't almost melted my flesh from my bones, and you know, tried to sell me to a psycho, I'd be in hysterics. But right now, no matter how misguided he'd been, the kid was right. It was time to go. I did not want to see Lucius again any time soon.

However, that meant I had to rely on one of the people who had kidnapped me in the first place to get me home. I was fucking doomed, but I figured that between the kid and Lucius, I'd take my chances with the kid and hoped the fact I could tear him to pieces and Brody would eat him alive would deter him from making any more bad choices.

Ugh. I hated this. "Okay, look. I'm going to level with you. I don't trust you even a little bit, but I'm between a rock and a psychotic ancient vamp, so you're the best I've got. I need you to play guide dog for a bit, but I swear, if you push me over a cliff, I'm coming back to haunt your ass until you beg for death, got it... What's your damn name?" I prompted.

"Colton."

"Got it, Colton?"

I could hear him shifting from foot to foot. "Yes, ma'am."

"Raine. It's just Raine. Let's go."

I stepped out of the shade of the treeline and sucked back a scream as my body sizzled with third-degree burns. The sun was still up, cooking my already tender flesh like bacon. Dammit.

Clint snapped his fingers. "Wait, I've got an idea." He raced away, and I had a moment of panic that he was just going to run off and leave me out here alone. That was what I'd do in his position. I'd run and hope the Enforcers slaughtered me before Brody got here and found out how I was involved. But Colton, bless his misguided little heart, returned to me almost instantly. I heard the slide of metal on metal, then he was thrusting something into my hand. "Umbrella!"

He sounded so proud of himself, I couldn't help but smile back. "Good idea." He led me towards a car, and then he hesitated. I could hear him shaking his head. "I don't know what to do. If we drive, we could run across the Enforcers coming up the mountain and we'd both be dead. If we go down the mountain on foot, we'll be slow and you'll be exposed to the sun too much."

He sounded so uncertain, so scared, I reached out and patted his back. "It'll be all good, Colton. I haven't survived this long to go down so easily. How well do you know the mountain?"

He hesitated. "I know it okay. We are about seven hours on foot from the Pack lands. About a two-hour drive, but most of that is down the mountain and there's only one road in and out, and it heads in the opposite direction to Pack lands. I know I could eventually get us home on foot," he said firmly, convincing himself more than me.

He sounded so young in that moment that I revised his age downward. "Colton. How old are you?"

"Fifteen." He hesitated. "And a half. I'm big for my age," he defended.

Shit. He was a baby. Now I was doubly glad I didn't eat

him. I wanted to go and kick all his co-conspirators sheepy asses for bringing a baby into their stupid plot. As if sensing the direction of my thoughts, Colton said quietly, "What about them?"

I scoffed. I hoped the Enforcers felt a little like lamb for dinner, but I didn't say that. "We'll get back to Pack lands, and Brody will send some Protectors to pick them up to face whatever the Pack considers justice. Unless you turn into a sheepdog?" Still, Colton hesitated. I remembered what he said about his dad saying I was evil. "Is your dad one of the sheep?" I asked softly.

"Yes," he whispered.

"Go and get him. We can take him with us."

Colton reached down and grabbed my hand as if to stop himself from doing just that. "No," he said softly. "I hate him. I hope the Enforcers eat him. It would be better for Mama, and Lulu." He didn't say it would be better for him too, but I knew it would be. I heard the pain in his voice.

"You're Lulu's brother?" I remembered what Brody said about Colton's dad beating down his son until he never thought about going to the Protectors. I could scent the shame that wafted off him.

"Yes." The sadness in that word spoke volumes.

I didn't know what to say. I was barely a responsible adult. I didn't know how to deal with someone else's trauma. So, I took a leaf out of X's book of social etiquette. "Want me to kill him for you? No one would ever know. We'll just say I did it in self-defense?"

Colton let out a manic little laugh but he didn't immediately say no. Eventually, he heaved a sigh that was so full of torment I wanted to hug him. "No. The Alpha will take care of it. They'll have a trial and everyone will know what a sociopathic piece of shit he really is and Lulu can grow up happy."

I grabbed his hand and squeezed. "Okay. Now lead on, Lassie. I wanna get home as soon as possible because it feels like these mountains have eyes."

I clutched the umbrella to my body, angling it so only my feet were getting burned. It wasn't quite big enough, but luckily the woods were quite dense so only small patches of sun poked through.

We walked for hours in silence, worried that the Enforcers would be early, or my kidnappers would turn back to human and track me back down. Colton moved with purpose, and I found that oddly reassuring. He lifted me down over ravines, whispering directions to make up for my lack of vision, and I'd only fallen on my ass six times. I'd take that as a win.

We'd been walking for about four hours, and I was tired and hungry. Tired I'd deal with, but the hunger was going to be a problem for both me and Colton soon. I reached down into my chest and tugged at the mate bond. I'd done it periodically every so often, just so they knew I was alive, even if they couldn't find me yet. The rush of love I always got back made me want to cry. My eyes welled up. Dammit. Enough. Hunger was making me emotional.

Colton tugged my hand. "Are you okay?"

My fangs punched out as I heard the whoosh of his blood now we'd stopped walking. Ugh. Not good. "I'm fine. Hungry. We should keep going; I can hold out."

Colton hesitated. "You can, you know, bite me if you need to?"

I laughed, and it was a sharp, wild peal as the predator reared her head. No. We did not eat kids. "Thanks, Colton. But no. I have rules, and one of them is not to eat anyone who can't legally drink. Thank you though. I know it had to be scary to offer."

I kept walking before the blood-fuelled predator in me took the choice out of both our hands. Colton wanted to argue, I could sense it in the wild rush of his blood, but eventually, he followed along beside me. Then he stopped again. "What the... Oh shit."

I crouched down, listening for predators, and instead the pressure in my chest built and built. My mate bond. My cavalry was here. Oh shit indeed. I ripped up my blindfold in time to see a giant snake launch itself off the back of a tiger and wrap around Colton. Shit, the kid wasn't joking—he was big for his age, but he didn't stand a chance against a pissed off mega-python.

Tears flowed down my cheeks as the dull light burned my

eyes, but I made a grab for the snake that was my mate. My Tex.

"Tex, stop! He helped me, it's okay." But Tex was in a frenzy, no longer listening to me as he constricted Colton so tightly his eyes were starting to bulge. I looked at Brody. "Stop him?"

But Brody just roared back at me, herding me away. They'd obviously gone completely feral. Fine. I tried to replicate the feeling I'd had before I turned everyone into sheep. I let the power fill my chest before I spoke. "Tex. Stop!"

Tex stilled, relaxing his coils. Colton sucked in a deep gasping breath, his face going from puce back to a regular color. I stared at my unexpected savior and noticed he looked a lot like his little sister. I slapped his back. "Big breaths, Colton." I turned to Tex, who was shifting from snake to man, and as soon as the transformation was complete, I threw myself into his arms. He grabbed me and held me tight, his face buried in my neck as his body shuddered with adrenaline.

"God. I thought you were dead. I thought you were dead again and I couldn't handle it."

I kissed his chest and then arms were wrapped around me from the back as Brody pulled us both into his arms. "Jesus, woman. No more. I can't take it anymore," he whispered against the back of my head as he held me, and by extension Tex, close. He sucked in a deep breath of my scent, and then straightened his spine. He whirled on Colton, who shrank back, falling to his knees and tilting his head to the side. "My mate said you helped her. Explain."

As Colton explained the whole sordid thing, from the formulation of the plan to steal me from the kitchen with a UV pulse to the back of my head, which apparently rendered vampires unconscious, to Clint arriving with me in the back of his pickup, burned and red, and staking me in the sun. Brody had growled so ominously at that, goosebumps flared across my skin as the primordial part of my brain screamed 'DANGER!'

Poor old Colton looked like he was going to piss himself, but he held it together. Colton told them about secretly texting Annie when they staked me in the sun, then the fact he moved me to the shade and stayed with me.

When he got to the part about everyone turning into sheep, Brody looked over at me, his eyebrows raised. "Well, that's an interesting development, one which we'll talk about later. Continue, Colton," he said, the power in his voice not giving Colton any choice. He got to the part where he offered to feed me, and Tex tensed beneath me. I rolled my eyes even as Colton explained I wouldn't.

Tex wrapped his hand in my hair, pulling me closer. "Feed, baby," he whispered soothingly, and he didn't have to ask me twice. Healing my burns had made me starved; I felt like I was running on nothing. To the point I moaned and came when the first hint of his blood hit my tongue. It was like nirvana. Like the best thing that had ever touched my tongue. Tex's arms banded tighter around my waist as his blood whispered through my veins, giving us both pleasure. I had to stop, or this was about to get seriously un-PG rated. I pulled back and licked the wound. I hadn't been gentle, and I felt a little guilty. Though, judging by how hard he was underneath me, Tex probably didn't mind.

Brody cleared his throat, and I shifted off Tex's lap. Colton was looking at me wide-eyed, and I looked everywhere but at him. I chastised myself that there was nothing wrong with what I'd just done. It was natural, but still.

Brody just grinned at me. "We should move. I can't sense anyone else close by, but I'll be happier when we are back on Pack lands anyway." He looked at Colton. "We will talk about your involvement when we get back to the Meeting House. While I'm thankful that you helped my mate, you were involved in a treasonous plot." Colton winced and my heart kind of went out to the kid. "I understand your circumstances, and I will talk to the Elders on your behalf."

Colton nodded, his face a mask of hopelessness. I went over and put my hand on his arm. "I got your back. Don't worry."

He gave me a wan smile. "You have pretty eyes, without your blindfold," he said softly, looking at me a little awed.

Brody growled low. "Watch it, kid or I will kick your ass for making goo-goo eyes at my mate. Tex still wants to constrict you and eat you alive, so I'd keep those thoughts to yourself," he threatened, but there was laughter in his voice. I winked at Colton and wrapped my arm around Brody's waist. He leaned down and kissed me. "I love you, Red. Let's not do that again, okay?"

Tex made an annoyed noise. "She's a magnet for trouble. Thank god we've got backup. She's enough to give one man a heart attack."

I blushed and gave him an annoyed look, but he was grinning back at me with so much love, I couldn't help but reciprocate.

Brody kissed my head. "Everyone shift. We'll run home. I want to be as far away from here as possible before dusk." He looked at the sky. It wasn't far enough away from nightfall for my liking. Tex turned into his ginormous snake and Colton into a giant hare. I raised my eyebrows. Well, okay then.

Brody shifted into his tiger, and Tex slithered over, wrapping his huge bulk around the giant tiger. It was the strangest thing I'd ever seen, the three of them before me. I picked up Colton's discarded clothes, slipping them on over my own. The kid was huge, but his clothes would provide some kind of protection from the late afternoon sun, even if I did have to run holding my pants up with one hand. I put on his sunglasses and the polarization helped, but the light still burned my eyes. I squinted, letting in as little light as possible while still being able to follow the shape of Brody's tiger. Brody fell into step in front of me, keeping an eye on both me and Colton. Tex lifted his head from the striped back of Brody, looking at me with his snake eyes, his forked tongue flickering out to taste the air. I blew the snake a kiss and ran on, a heavy cloak of fear starting to coat my body. Although I wasn't safe in Nîso either, at least there was only one threat. Out here, I had my back exposed to an enemy far more dangerous than some malcontents.

We ran impossibly fast for an hour, and when I felt the magic of the Pack lands border, I could have cried with joy, if I wasn't already crying from the injuries to my eyes. But because this was my life, that happiness was destined to be short-lived.

24

Sometimes, I wondered if I'd pissed off some kind of deity by not dying when I was supposed to. By waking up in a ditch after I was murdered, did I screw with the circle of life so bad it was set to punish me until I was definitely dead for good?

I struggled to stop as five Enforcers stepped from the shadows, blocking our path to the border. My heart sank even further when I realized one was Raul, Lucius's second-in-command and the dick from my house.

I wanted to cry. I was so, so close. "Colton, stay behind me," I whispered, and he hopped back to me. We slowed, and Tex slid from Brody's back.

"Ah, I would like to say it is nice to see you, but that's a lie. You are never where you are supposed to be, are you fledgling? If you come now, I will leave your animals alone,"

Raul sneered, and Brody roared. One of the Enforcers laughed.

I bared my fangs at the smarmy asshole. "Listen, Douche Canoe, I'm not going anywhere with you. You have no rights over me—I've done nothing wrong."

Raul laughed like I said the funniest thing ever. I'm glad he appreciated the moniker because I was never going to call him anything else. "Stupid bitch. We aren't here in an official capacity. Lucius wants you, and he always gets what he wants. He is going to break you slowly, and if I am lucky, he will let me watch."

I screwed my nose up at him and hoped he couldn't hear the roaring of my heart or see the shaking of my knees from back here.

I spoke as softly as I could, without moving my lips. "Colton, you need to get across the boundary and then run as fast as you can to the Protectors. Get Nell to call Judge, then Nico and Walker." I sucked in a deep breath through my nose. "I'm relying on you, kid. I hope for everyone's sake that you really don't want me and your Alpha dead."

The hare stared up at me with big, brown, unblinking eyes. Jesus, I hope he could understand me in this form like the guys, and it wasn't something you grew into. Finally, his long bunny ears twitched, and he shot off like a blur toward the barrier. It drew everyone's eyes and one of the vampires gave chase.

Colton zigzagged, throwing the vampire off his pace a

little. It gave me time to get there, and I crash tackled the chasing vamp. I took him to the ground, more from surprise than finesse, and I rolled with him until I connected my knee to his balls. But he was a professional, and it would take more than a little kick to the nuts to keep him down. Tex was suddenly there, constricting around the vampire's head. The Enforcer just pulled him off and tossed him across the field where he landed with a heavy thud.

"Tex!" I shouted, and the snake lifted its head. I let out a sigh of relief. Thank god. My distraction was enough that the vampire had me in his arms, my body locked tightly in his hands. Raul just looked bored.

"He can run as fast as his little rabbit feet can go, but it still won't be fast enough," Raul sneered, moving slowly to keep my Alpha in his sights. "Easy there Alpha, or I'll rip her head from her shoulders. End your abominable little love affair."

I scoffed. "He's full of shit. If he killed me, Lucius would rip him apart like a bug."

The guard behind me huffed a laugh, but it wasn't a pleasant sound.

I stared hatred at Raul. "Let them both back across the border and I'll come with you willingly. Everyone already know it's you, Colton will tell them that. You have nothing to gain from killing them other than bringing the wrath of the Convocation and Titus down on your head."

Invoking the name of a man I'd never met was probably a ballsy move, but I had to try.

Raul just looked bored. "I'm pretty sure that Titus wouldn't care if I killed some half-breed shifter."

Brody shifted back to a man. "No, but Alexander would care if you killed his only offspring."

Raul reared back at the mention of this Alexander. Who the fuck was Alexander? "You lie."

Brody grinned a feral smile. "Maybe. But are you willing to gamble with the chance? He hates your kind. You know what he did with the last vampire who crossed him? Kept him for a thousand years, tied in his cave, burning the flesh from his bones. When the vampire healed enough, his flesh pale and golden again, the pain finally gone? He'd sear it off all over again. For one thousand years. Just think about that as you consider your next move."

Ugh, as someone who'd just felt like they were melting in the sun, the thought made me want to vomit. I must have made a heaving noise because the Enforcer pushed me away from him a little but not enough for me to wiggle out of his grasp.

Raul frowned at Brody. "You can go. Take the snake with you."

Brody laughed in his face. "I'm not going anywhere, fuck-face. Not until I've torn you all apart and feasted on your hearts."

I wanted to kick his ass. He needed to run, to go behind

the border that would protect them. They were outnumbered. Outskilled.

We were so fucked.

That was until hot blood sprayed all over my arms, the Enforcer holding me dropping his arms and flopping to my feet. Shit, had I done that? I looked over my shoulder to the feral grin of Judge. Nope. That was all my Killer. I couldn't hold back the smile that lit my face, and Brody took advantage of everyone's distraction and launched at the vampire closest to him, shifting in midair. His scimitar-sized claws pierced the Enforcer's chest and he crushed his skull in his huge jaws, big fangs popping through the guy's head. While I understood that vampires were immortal, I wasn't sure how anyone could survive that. Brody didn't waste time playing with his food, as he leaped from the body of the shredded vampire to lope over to me, looking as graceful as he was deadly, blood all around his maw.

Judge made his way back to me and Tex was reared up in front of my feet.

Fuck, I loved these men. We were now even, and I let myself breathe a little easier. Raul looked like he personally wanted to turn us all into confetti, but he hesitated. A good tactician would run right about now, but Raul looked like a dumbass. He stepped toward us, pulling his dagger from his hip. His eyes were completely on Judge, the cruel twist of his lips screaming hatred. "I've wanted to cut out your heart for a long time, Judge," he sneered, but Judge looked completely unperturbed. He looked like this was just another day in Deadsville for him. He circled Raul, dodging the swift slashes the Enforcer leveled at his gut. The remaining uninjured Enforcer stood behind him, not interfering. Raul, despite being a dickhead, was an accomplished fighter, and Judge was out of practice. When he didn't dodge a slash to his arm quick enough, blood quickly soaking his shirt and dripping down his arm, I stepped forward. Only Tex tangling his huge snake body around my legs stopped me from diving into the fray.

"Let go Tex, I have to help him!" I hissed, and he shook his snake head.

A noise from the edge of the clearing drew my eyes and the eyes of the other Enforcer. Even Raul was momentarily distracted, allowing Judge to slice quickly across his face before he could pull away.

Walker and Nico stepped from the treeline, and I almost sagged with relief. Nico was at my side in an instant. "Leave, Raul, before I have you on trial before the Vampire Nation," he growled, sending shivers down my spine. My ancient vampire was pissed. He was savage when he got in this mood, and I'd only ever seen flashes of it around his normal affable nature. But it never paid to doubt that it was there.

Finally outnumbered, Raul sneered at me, his grin disconcerting. "I will see you again, fledgling." The other vampire bent down and picked up his fallen comrades, nodding almost respectfully to Judge and Nico, then following quickly behind his psychotic leader.

Walker had me in his arms the moment the Enforcers left. He held me so tightly, it was like he was trying to consume me. "Raine," he said, a whispered plea, though I didn't know what he was pleading for. Instead, I kissed him deeply, tasting the fear and desperation on his tongue.

Nico pulled me from Walker's arms and kissed me with a desperation that bordered on manic. His tongue tasted every inch of my mouth, devouring me with a passion that he must have kept locked way, way down inside. I kissed him back just as furiously. Life was too short, especially mine, to not take advantage of every ounce of love and passion that was given freely. I moaned as he pressed me closer, his hard body compact against mine.

He groaned, pulling away to rest his forehead against mine. "I haven't been able to get you out of my head. You've haunted all my dreams and my nightmares, Raine Baxter." He hugged me tight, the hard ridges of his body almost perfect under my hands. I pulled away, and he let me go with a touch of reluctance. Something niggled at the back of my brain, and I searched for threats in the trees.

"It's okay. You guys got here just in time. We can all go home." I hesitated. "But first we should go into Nîso and make sure everyone knows that there are traitors in their midst."

Nico grinned. "Wolves among the sheep?"

My shoulders tensed but I grinned over my shoulder. I

pushed Tex toward the border, and Brody went before us. As I stepped over the magical ward, Niso embraced me.

Nico stayed on the other side. He grinned at me. "Clever and beautiful. I should have known." His feral grin was not the sweet expression I was used to seeing on Nico's face.

But I'd definitely seen it before, on the face of his twin. "Lucius," I breathed. Judge and Walker leaped toward him, but he was ancient and powerful. He moved out of their grasp as easily as if they were fumbling toddlers. "Beautiful and clever. I now see what tempted my brother to break his self-imposed monkhood."

"Where's Nico?" I growled, and he laughed, quirking an eyebrow. I frowned, going to step back across the ward so I could shake the answer from him, but Brody's hand around my arm stopped me.

I glared at Lucius, but he just grinned back. "Oh, don't make that face, Beauty. Nico is fine. Probably angrier than a cut snake though." He pointed at Tex and laughed at his own joke. "He's making his way here now, your precious Angeline with him. Though, I might just kill her anyway for the way she treated you."

I shrunk away from the fervent look in his eyes. "Please don't."

"I will be seeing you soon, Beauty."

Then he was gone.

I stood around in shock, my eyes bouncing from Walker to Judge. Walker looked shaken. "We traveled all the way here together. I never once suspected he wasn't Nico." He was shaking his head over and over again.

Judge growled as he stepped across the ward. "They've been impersonating each other for millennia, don't take it to heart. They are very good at it. Lucius can only play at being good, though. He always slips eventually." Judge walked over to me, picking me up so I could wrap my arms and legs around his body, and kissed me deeply, despite the fact our enemy had just had his tongue in there. If anything, it made him kiss me deeper, as if he was trying to chase any trace of Lucius away.

Finally, he let me slide down his body, and turned to Tex. He kissed him just as deeply, sighing when we were both in arm's reach. "Let's get this shit over and done with, Brody. I want Raine back in Dark River where I can watch over her."

Brody nodded, and we moved back through the Pack lands to Niso. Brody lifted a cellphone to his ear and began talking in hushed tones to whoever was on the other end. The guys spread out around me and I sighed at the rightness. Except...

"Where's X?"

Walker sighed. "Are you sure about him? I mean, the guy has the mouth of a sailor and the personality of a shark."

I just smiled. Yeah, I remembered his mouth pretty fondly.

"He's in the cells beneath the Vampire Nation headquarters. He got a little, uh, verbose about the length of time it was taking them to find an innocent woman innocent. There was a bit of a tirade about how he'd rather be home with his head between your thighs," Walker grumbled, "and not 'jerking off a bunch of dusty old pricks.' Direct quote. They wanted to chop off his head, but Nico and Titus managed to talk them into a few days to cool off in the cells instead."

I couldn't help the grin that spread across my face, and Judge laughed. I briefly worried about Nico, enough that I nudged Walker to call him. He dialed the number and handed me the phone.

"Walker! Lucius is impersonating—"

"Hi, Nico. We know," I interrupted softly. "I was worried about you, though. I thought he might have hurt you or something."

There was silence on the other end of the phone.

"Lucius is many things, but in his own twisted way, he loves me. He is my twin. But he likes to torture me in other, more inventive ways," Nico said from behind me, echoing his words down the phone.

I spun on my heel and there was a disheveled looking Nico, easily stepping across the ward into Pack lands. I hung up and handed the phone back to Walker as I ran toward Nico. When I reached him, I hesitated. Lucius had kissed me while pretending to be Nico, but I had never reached that point with the man himself. Nico reached out and ran his fingertips down my cheek. I leaned forward and kissed his lips softly. He let me, his breath escaping on a soft sigh. "You are okay. I can't tell you how happy I am to see you."

Fuck it. I launched myself at him, and kissed him. I traced the seam of his lips, begging for entrance and he happily complied. Our tongues battled as we kissed, and it was raw and primal and absolutely perfect. He groaned as his hands sank to my lower back and pulled me closer.

And as much as my mind rebelled at the thought, I couldn't help but compare his kiss to that of Lucius. I broke off the kiss and stepped away, breathing heavily. Nico's eyes searched mine, looking for something, but I couldn't figure out what. I hoped he couldn't read my thoughts. I hoped none of them could.

I hated Lucius, but he'd set my body on fire, just as much as his twin did.

25

When I walked into the middle of Nîso flanked by three other vampires and preceded by two shifters, every eye snapped to us. Given that the Alpha was in his tiger form, everyone knew shit was going down. Or maybe it was the fact that Tex was completely naked, which was causing a stir because some of the women on the street were openly ogling him. I bared my teeth at them, and zipped to Brody's house and back with two pairs of pants from the dresser. One for Tex, and one for Brody when he shifted back from the tiger.

Tex laughed as he stepped into the tight jeans that still sat tantalizingly low on his hips. I swear, he didn't look any less drool-worthy now that he wasn't naked. I frowned, but I couldn't help but follow his ink down to where he was zipping up his pants.

"Why are you so damn sexy?" I grumbled, and he just grinned. I looked over my shoulder at Judge who was watching Tex just as hungrily.

"Damn, I have missed you two," he mumbled. I leaned back and kissed him quickly. I'd missed him too.

I spun back around and caught up to Brody. One step behind, that was where I was meant to be as his mate.

I spied Ghost striding towards us, his face a thunder-cloud. He signed angrily at Brody, and then he looked at me and signed even more angrily. "Uh oh."

Brody just pulled the huge angry pale man in for a hug. Ghost still frowned as he stood stiffly in his arms. "Don't be angry, brother." Brody looked over at me. "I might have just skipped out of here without telling anyone but Tex you were missing. He is chastising me like a nagging old housewife. Also, he said you better stop getting your ass injured on his watch otherwise he's going to give up his life as a Protector because he sucks at it so bad."

I couldn't help smiling at Ghost. "Don't sweat it, big guy. Not your fault. I attract trouble like bees to honey."

Someone muttered, "Amen" behind me, but I ignored them. I did give Brody the stink eye though. "You shouldn't have run off like that though. Ghost is right. You have a responsibility to your Pack." I talked a good talk, but there was no way I wouldn't have done the exact same thing in his position. Which was why I wasn't Alpha of Anything.

Annie appeared, with Colton on her heels. She barrelled

up to me and wrapped me in a hug. I hadn't realized we were at the hugging stage, but I went with it. "Thank god you're okay, again! I swear, if you were my mate, I'd lock you in my room and never let you out. You've given me gray hair and I only just met you!" she accused angrily.

I laughed, but when I looked up at the Elders lining the steps in front of the Meeting House, all the mirth left me. Nell looked pissed, but it seemed to be for the people next to her, and a little bit for her grandson. Thank god. If looks could kill, Nell's wrath would flay me alive.

Her eyes landed on me and she gave me a small smile. Then they landed on Nico and she full on grinned.

"Nico, you honor us with your presence," she purred, and I didn't know whether I should chuckle at the saucy gumption of her, or be a little jealous at the way he was smiling back. I took the higher ground. He was old and he was bound to have a history with the fiery Matriarch of Brody's Pack.

"The honor is mine, Matriarch."

"Nell, please."

Nico nodded his head in assent and stepped closer to me, resting his hand on my spine. "You too? My my, child. You have quite the collection," she cackled. "To be young and horny again. I think I might be a tad envious of you."

Brody shuddered. "Matriarch, please. We should get down to business," he said sternly, but Nell just winked at me before all mirth left her face.

She nodded, and let out a sigh. "We have spoken to the

boy." She indicated Colton, who was hiding behind Ghost and Annie. Someone herded a small flock of sheep into the town square. "They are unable to shift back."

She looked at me, and I shrugged. I wasn't overly perturbed about the people who were going to sell me to my enemies permanently being sheep. Karma was a bitch. I didn't know how I'd done it, so I didn't know if I could undo it. It felt a little like Brody's Alpha power, and I said as much. Brody went over to study his former Pack members, speaking to them quietly. Finally, he just shook his head softly.

"I can make them submit, but I can't keep them trapped in any form for a long period of time. It's... unnatural."

I really had nothing to add to that. "I can try and make them change back if you want me to? It didn't do anything to Colton and he was standing right beside me."

Brody looked between me and them. "The issue is that they show no signs of being in there. It is like they are really sheep, not a shapeshifter in the form of a sheep. There's no higher intelligence in their little sheep brains."

I wanted to snort, but I didn't. I had to remember that these bigoted, torturing assholes were probably people's sons, husbands, fathers. I held out my hand, not sure why except that it would look more impressive. "Return to your asshole human forms."

Nothing happened. I tried again, trying to push that power from my chest. "Shift!" I boomed. Seriously. It was impressive. So impressive, that everyone but Brody shifted. Even Nell and the Elders.

Oops.

Brody stared at me. "Well, this is interesting, isn't it?" Then he looked at the men who'd changed back from sheep. They looked fine, except maybe a little shaky. Walker helped secure them all in handcuffs until they were kneeling on the grass at Brody's feet. An assortment of animals stared at me, and I felt awkward as fuck. "Can you make them shift back, please? I'm starting to freak out," I whispered to Brody.

He looked at his Pack, and a flash of worry passed through his eyes. He was worried he wouldn't be able to make them shift back. To be honest, I was a little worried too.

"Shift!" he projected, and my skin rippled. So much power. One by one they shifted back, and I heaved a sigh of relief. Thank fuck. I didn't know how I would've been able to explain to the Canadian authorities that an entire town of people had disappeared, but we had a really awesome zoo here now, complete with lions, tigers and bears, oh my.

I watched Ghost transform from his snow leopard back to a man, and he gave me a pouty look. I lifted my hands, hoping my expression said, 'hey, I was only doing what I was asked.'

The problem with a mass shifting? Everyone lost their clothes. I was basically standing in the middle of a nudist colony. Luckily, the people who'd shifted into smaller animals just picked up their discarded pants and put them back on. But those who shifted into bigger animals had shredded their clothes. That was a lot of wang flapping in the breeze, and no one seemed to care. I looked over at Tex, who just grinned at me. He had grown up human, so he understood that a hundred people didn't just stand around naked, but fortunately for him, he couldn't see all the pasty skin. I looked at my feet and tried not to look guilty.

Nell was staring at me like I was the Antichrist or Cthulhu or something equally as horrifying. She slid her dress back over her arms like she hadn't just been naked before the world. Probably wasn't even the first time this week. I really needed to lose these human sensibilities. "Are these the men who attacked you, Alpha Mate?"

I looked at the kneeling men, all shooting venom in my direction. "I don't know. I was blindfolded. Is one of them named Clint?"

Brody pointed to an older man, his beard streaked with gray. "Speak," I said, using my new found Wizard of Oz voice.

"Fuck you, bitch," he growled, and I grinned.

"Yeah, he was definitely one. Now make that one say I have STDs and that I like to bite kids," I sneered as I pointed to the guy next to him. Under the intense gaze of his Alpha, the guy repeated my words. I flipped him the finger, probably not very regal but immensely satisfying. "Guess Colton still gets to go home to his mama, unlike you pricks." I pointed at Lulu and Colton's dad. "Him too. Not going to lie, I think I'd get some satisfaction in tearing out his throat."

Judge let out a hum behind me. "I second that."

Both Nico and Walker gave him a quelling look. They had no standing here. This was the Pack's system of justice, not ours. Well, maybe it was a little bit mine now, as Alpha Mate and everything.

"That is not our way. Well, not just yet," Brody said softly. He looked down at the men with sad eyes. "Do any of you want to speak in your own defense?"

Clint spat in the direction of Brody's bare feet. My sad Alpha curled his shoulders infinitesimally, and it was only because I was beside him that I even noticed.

"Will anyone speak for them?" His eyes found a woman in the crowd, one clutching tightly to Lulu's hand, fear and hope warring in her eyes. But she didn't speak. Brody nodded. "So be it. You are all sentenced to banishment. You will be warded from the Pack lands of your ancestors, and gelded so that you may never breed your own Pack."

Tex audibly swallowed behind me. "Did he just say gelded? As in neutered?" he whispered to Judge, and even I felt pale. That seemed like an intimate kind of punishment.

Nell nodded. "It will be done, Alpha." Ghost stepped forward, along with a couple of other huge guys who I assumed must be Protectors too, and they roughly pulled the traitors to their feet.

Brody turned and grabbed my waist, walking me away a little bit. "Go home, Red. Sleep. Catch up with your other men. I'll be here for a while, and you still need to feed and rest." He kissed my temple and I let my head lean into him. I wanted to support him, but I felt tired to my very bones. Every part of me ached from the sun, my eyes felt like they'd been flash-fried and then stuck back in my skull, and I just wanted to curl up in someone's arms and let them take care of me.

Nico touched the tips of his fingers to where my hair was missing. Oh shit. I'd forgotten about my hair. It was a testament to my life that no one had mentioned the fact that I was channeling Sinead O'Connor 'til now.

"It'll grow back. I think."

He nodded, seemingly unperturbed that I was rocking basically a five o'clock shadow on my head. It made me love him a little more. It made me love them all a little bit more.

"I have to stay and try to smooth over this fiasco from the vampires' point of view. It helps that their Alpha loves you, but the Elders hold a lot of sway and are far more traditional than your lover," Nico said softly, and I nodded. I grabbed his fingers and gave them a light squeeze. I bowed respectfully to the Elders and walked out of the crowd with my head held high, each and every single person in town watching me as I left.

When I was finally out of the eyesight of the crowd, I let the tension ease from my body. I shuffled slowly back up the slight incline back toward Brody's temporary house. Walker wrapped his fingers in mine, and Judge had his arm around Tex's shoulders. He leaned over and kissed Tex's temple tenderly, then turned to me. He leaned in, brushing his lips against mine, before biting the swell of my bottom lip hard.

"Enough already, Rainy Day. No more of this dying thing. I can't stand it anymore." He looked past me to Walker. "I have to go and play Deputy Doofus for one more day, but then I'm handing this fucking badge back and spending a week between our girl's thighs. No arguments."

I laughed even as heat rushed to the apex of my aforementioned thighs. He was so damn handsome, I kind of wanted to strip off his clothes and take him on the footpath. Gravel rash and all.

Walker nodded, giving Judge a crooked smile. Who knew that he would take his deputation so seriously? God knows, he hated commitment, but he seemed to be changing his ways. "Thanks, Judge," Walker said quietly, and I could tell that he really meant it. Judge had stepped up, and I couldn't love him more than I did at that moment.

Judge's face lifted into that crooked grin that made my heart flutter. "You owe me one, and I intend to collect."

He turned to leave, and I stilled him with my hand on his arm. "How did you get through the wards anyway?"

Judge's face shut down. "Miranda."

I knew it had to have been the Witch Miranda. Gah, she was like the ghost of Christmas past that kept coming back over and over again. "What did she want in return?"

He shook his head. "She cursed me to love someone more

than I love myself. I told her it was too late. I already did." Then he winked and he was gone.

Tex let out a soft sigh. I echoed it. Walker just shook his head. "Smooth bastard. Let's go, Raine. I need to have my arms around you as soon as possible."

As we got closer to Brody's house, Tex lifted his arm to look at an invisible watch that he wouldn't be able to see anyway because he was freaking blind. "Oh, would you look at the time? I forgot I have to, uh go to my, uh shifter training class."

I raised an eyebrow at him. "Shifter training class? Seriously?"

Tex just grinned, flashing me shiny white teeth. "Uh-huh. Have fun, you two."

With that, he walked away back down the hill, whistling happily like we hadn't just all almost died. I shook my head at his retreating back, before looking up at Walker and grinning. "And then there were two?"

He smoldered down at me, then I was scooped up into his arms and he was running at the speed of light towards the spare room in Brody's temporary house. I didn't know if it was luck or his vampire senses that led him to a room that was currently unoccupied, but he'd known. He kicked the door to the bedroom shut behind us, spinning me and slammed me into the wall beside it. His mouth was everywhere suddenly, sucking, teasing, devouring me. I sucked in a panting breath as I tried to sort through the sensations. His eyes glowed that luminescent green as he tore off Colton's shirt. Whoops. I'd get him a new one.

He took my nipple into his mouth, sucking hard, nipping at it like he was a starving man before moving onto the next one. My fingers pressed into his shoulders as I held on for the ride, my legs holding him tightly to me.

"I don't want to wait for the perfect time. You are perfect, Raine. Perfect for me. Anything we do will always be perfect, even when we aren't. I love you, Raine Baxter. I loved you the moment you stumbled into that diner looking like a hot mess."

His hands found their way into my panties, finding my clit and brushing his thumb against it. "Yes," I breathed as my body jolted against his palm. "I love you too. Please," I whimpered as he slid a finger inside me, stroking my core. He pushed another finger inside me and I moved against his hand, matching his thrusting rhythm as his mouth found mine again and his lips punished mine with a brutal, desperate kiss.

He spun me around, falling onto the bed behind us, his body caging me in. He tore off my underwear, tossing them over his shoulder as he traced all the curves of my body like a blind man. His tongue followed the path of his fingers. He tasted every square inch of me with a manic intensity.

"I need you, Walker," I panted as his mouth found my clit and nipped it gently. I bucked off the bed toward his face, then he grabbed me beneath my hips and devoured my core. He alternated between sliding his tongue in and out of me and swirling it around my clit until I was whimpering.

"I wanted to take this slow and easy. I wanted to worship you as you deserve, but I can't, Raine. I just can't. I need you too much," he said, his voice pained as he thrust his hips against my leg and I felt the very hard results of that need.

I was panting. "We've waited long enough. Hurry up and make love to me already." I sounded grumpy and needy, and it made the bastard grin. He stripped off his clothes, throwing them in the direction of mine until he was naked and glorious in front of me. Jesus. He was so damn radiantly hot. Broad shoulders, a wide, muscular chest, that tapered down into washboard abs and a narrow waist. He was like every teenage dirty dream I'd ever had. He slid his body up mine until he could taste my lips again.

"Walker," I whispered pleadingly between the teasing kisses he was bestowing on my face. Fortunately, it was only his kisses that were teasing as the crown of his cock found my core and he slid home in one, long, hard thrust. I keened a noise that probably wasn't overly human as he slid back out and slammed himself home again.

"Fuck, Raine," he gritted out. "You feel like heaven."

I grinned as he swore, and I dragged his head down so I could take his full lower lip into my mouth. I scraped my fangs, cutting it up and we both moaned as I pulled the abused flesh into my mouth, sucking hard. We moved together in a rhythm so perfect, a rhythm that could only be created by the two of us, together in this moment, and honestly, I wanted to cry. Instead, I screamed as he shifted one of my legs to his shoulder, folding me in half like a fucking sweater and reaching places that made my eyes roll back in my head, all without breaking our kiss. My body cradled his like we were made to fit together, and I scraped my nails down his back until it broke the skin, making him grunt louder and pound harder. Oh, my sexy, sexy Sheriff liked it a little bit rough? I filed that away for a time when he wasn't hitting just the perfect spot that made me scream as I came all over his cock.

But Walker wasn't done, and I should have known he had the self-control of a monk. He pulled out briefly, flipping me onto my stomach and slipping a hand under my hips to pull me higher, then he slid back into me, barely losing his rhythm. I whimpered as he hit all new places, his fingers moving from my hip to my clit as he drove me into the ball of his hand with hard thrusts. Like he had played with my body a million times before, he worked the orgasm out of me. Then finally, he thrust in harder and harder, until he was roaring his own release, biting down on my neck as he came. The feel of his fangs sliding into my flesh had me coming again.

We both collapsed forward, and he held himself up on his elbows even as he heaved in breaths, then he rolled off me, pulling me into his body as he did.

"That was better than I could have ever imagined."

All I could do was nod. He was like the pied piper of

orgasms. He crooked his finger and they just poured from me. I laughed silently at the image of him blowing a whistle, calling forth my orgasms.

"Worth the wait," I said softly, snuggling into his chest.

He kissed the top of my head. "Uh-huh. But I would have waited forever for you if I had to."

As I laid in his arms, his body spooned around mine, I thought that perhaps I had been waiting forever for him too.

26

When I drove away from Nîso, its town lights flashing in the rearview mirror, I was conflicted. On one hand, so far Nîso had only brought me fear and pain. I missed Dark River and my home. On the other hand, I was leaving a big chunk of my heart there too, although he promised he would come back to visit as soon as he'd wrapped up everything after the trials and banishment, as well as sniffing out any more conspirators. Still, after spending so many days together, it felt wrong to leave him.

It was a feeling I'd have to get used to because Brody might love me, might be my mate, but he loved his Pack too, and I would never make him choose. On the plus side, he let me borrow his car and actually drive it. I couldn't keep the huge grin off my face as I pressed the gas and the car rumbled to life under me like a monster.

"I can hear you grinning from here," Tex laughed, though he was holding onto the sissy-handle on the door awfully tightly.

The car hugged the curves of the winding road like it was built for it, and with my now inhuman reflexes, driving was almost as good as sex. I drove too fast, but it wasn't fast enough. I swerved around a deer with ease, the roads empty except for wildlife, and I just enjoyed a quiet moment that reaffirmed I was alive. This, and being loved by my guys, were the simple things that chased away the pain of my death. I hadn't even thought about my old life lately, probably because my new life had been a little stabby itself, but when I did think about my human life, it was never with longing or regret anymore. I missed my family. Nothing would change that. But did I ever want to go back to being Mika McKellen again? Never.

When I pulled up in front of my house, Tex scrambled out of the car so quickly he was basically a flash of slightly green skin. "You drive like a lunatic, woman!" he growled, and I just grinned. He stomped towards the house, and I followed him laughing. I hadn't driven that fast.

Judge was standing on our stoop, waiting for us, something that looked a lot like love shining in his eyes. Not that he would ever say the words, but he didn't have to. I didn't need the validation of the three words when his actions told me a million times over every day.

Tex reached him first, and Judge gave him a punishing kiss, filled with yearning and need. Then he pulled away and looked at me, reaching out and tugging me into his arms so quickly my head spun. He kissed me with all those four-letter words no one wanted to say out loud. I grinned against his lips as I felt Tex stand behind me, his body pressed right along my back as he buried his face in my neck.

"Seriously. This is a respectable neighborhood. If you are going to do perverted things on the doorstep, we may as well make it an orgy on the lawn," a familiar voice said from behind us, and a grin spread across my face even as Judge was kissing me.

Judge gave me a crooked smile. "I'm beginning to see why Walker hates him so much. That really is annoying." He reached down and adjusted his hard cock in his pants. He looked over my shoulder. "You offering, asshole?"

I looked over my shoulder, past the hot look in Tex's eyes that said he wasn't opposed to an orgy in the front yard at all, to the grinning face of X. Fuck, he looked like sin on a stick. He raised his eyebrows and his fingers flew to his zip. Before I could stop him, he was standing there with his pants around his ankles. "I never say no to an orgy."

I rushed over to him. "Jesus. Put your pants on before Walker comes around and arrests us all for public indecency."

X had no shame, just waggled his eyebrows. "Is he bringing handcuffs?"

I laughed because let's face it, I had the exact same thought every time I saw him in his uniform. "Will you put your pants on so I can hug you already?" I mock growled.

He grinned, showing way too much fang. "Why don't you take your pants off and I can give you a hug that will blow your mind?"

My arousal perfumed the air at his words, but I glared until he sighed, pulling up his tactical pants and buttoning them safely. Well, at least with the illusion of safety. He opened his arms wide and I stepped inside them, appreciating the huge width of his chest because that was as high as my head sat without heels or a step ladder. When he leaned down and put his cheek on top of my head, I melted a little. "It's good to see you, Love."

I stepped out of his arms reluctantly. "Let's go inside. I'm looking forward to sleeping in my own bed."

X nodded solemnly. "I'm looking forward to sleeping in your bed too."

I whacked him with the back of my hand but grinned at him over my shoulder as we went inside. Judge grabbed my bags, punching X in the shoulder in some manly display of affection on the way past. I briefly wondered what it would be like if those two ever had sex. Who would top? My vagina did a little Mariachi dance at the thought and I shut it down before anyone got the slightest hint of the direction of my thoughts.

I stepped into my little cottage and sighed happily. It felt like home. Tex bustled in behind me, and my ears picked up the sound of X whispering, "It's good to see you, Snakelet." As I looked over my shoulder, the big former Enforcer leaned down and nipped Tex's earlobe, making him shudder.

Damn. There went any chance of keeping my arousal under wraps. I hustled to my fridge and pulled out four beers. "Where's Walker?" I asked Judge, hoping everyone could be diverted from my errant pheromones. Judging from Tex's hooded gaze, I wasn't doing a good job.

Judge smiled at me crookedly, coming to take a beer from my hand, leaning down to kiss me softly. "He's at the station, making sure I didn't fuck anything up too badly in his absence. He said to tell you he'd be over later to make sure you were okay."

"And Nico?"

X answered this one, though how he knew was beyond me. "He's making sure Angeline gets resettled, and is updating the Town Council." He sauntered closer. "So, it's just the four of us. Whatever could we do?"

He reached into the pocket of his tactical pants and pulled out a long length of silken rope. Judge gave him a warning look. "X..."

X just grinned and pulled out another length from the pocket. I looked down at his pants. "Are they like Mary

Poppins' bag or something?" I looked between the two of them. "Why is Judge glaring at you like that?"

He leaned forward, taking my hands in his. "Have you ever heard of Shibari, Love?"

I screwed up my nose. "Like the sushi?"

X threw back his head and laughed. He laughed so hard that I thought he might have passed out if he'd actually had to breathe. I tried to pull my hands away, but he held them firmly, but gently. "No, Love. Not like sushi. It's an art form really. I find it quite relaxing." As he spoke, he wrapped the ropes twice around my wrists, pushing it through and tying a knot. It happened so quickly, I wondered if I'd imagined it. They weren't tight like you'd imagine. "It was originally a way to tie up criminals in Japan, but I think it serves a far better purpose right now, don't you think?"

Judge was shifting from foot to foot, but I could feel the desire in his stare as X lifted my hands over my head and ran the length of rope down my back. Judge lifted a hand to stop him. "You have to ask first, X. This isn't the nineteen hundreds anymore. Do you want X to tie you up, Rainy Day? He won't do anything you don't want or I'll feed him his own balls. I'm right here." I looked at Judge, then back at X. His eyes were clear and earnest, but with a heavy dose of lust that made my skin prickle.

X stepped closer until his body was pressed against my front. He passed the rope around my waist, his hands working behind my back to create complex knots that passed under my breasts and over my shoulders. "What do you say, Love? Want to play? I promise you'll like it, and all you have to do is say stop and we'll go and drink tea and watch Monty Python. Scout's Honor."

"You were never a Boy Scout," I breathed.

His smile was wicked. "You're right. But I'm pretty sure you are still going to enjoy my version of the three-finger salute," he whispered against my lips, then shifted down to kiss the curve of my shoulder, his hands moving quickly and with an assurance that seemed to chase away my nerves. Tex had stepped closer to Judge, and Judge was quietly describing what was happening.

The rope moved down to my waist, and X breathed in my scent.

He looked over his shoulder at Tex. "Come here, Snakelet. Keep our girl entertained while I finish these knots."

Tex was beside me in a moment. His lips were barely an inch away. "Okay?" he whispered, the heat of his breath cooling on my lips. I nodded, and I felt X's fingers trace up the inside of my thigh.

"Say the words, Love. Snakelet needs to hear you."

"Yes," I breathed on a sigh as he kissed the back of my knee. He undid my jean shorts and slid them and my panties down my legs. He let out a small groan at the sight of my dripping pussy but went back to the task at hand. He laddered the knots down my leg in a complex pattern. Even I could appreciate the art the silken rope created next to my skin.

"I've wanted to do this since I stepped foot in your house. It was like you bought it with me in mind," X said, looking over at Judge with a raised brow. Judge's face was completely impassive, but his eyes were blazing with heat. "While you were away, I made a couple of minor modifications, Love. You'll never even notice unless we are doing what we are doing right now." I had no idea what he meant until he jumped and clung on the exposed cross beam of my cathedral ceiling. Oh. He'd installed shiny gold rings to the cross beam.

He was sexy as hell as he hung there by one arm and threaded the ends of two ropes through the rings suspended from the beam. Tex knelt in front of me and took my silk-covered nipple into his mouth, my camisole strapped tight to my body. I moaned, the sensitivity of my nipples increasing tenfold. X jumped down, his body pressed against my back as Tex lapped at my breasts. He'd dampened the silk, and when he blew cool air over the area, I moaned loud, my nipples pebbling painfully.

"Ready, Raine?" X murmured in my ear. He never called me by my name, and I nodded in my shock. He reached down, ran a hand over the globe of my ass, then smacked it hard. "Come on, Love. Remember, you need to use your words."

I moaned as he ran his hand over the area he'd just slapped. "Yes," I hissed.

He smiled at me and kissed me tenderly. "Good girl. The safeword is Baton, in honor of the one up your Sheriff's arse," he chuckled as I frowned. "Just say the word, beautiful, and it all stops." Then he pulled the ropes and I was pulled off my feet. My body twisted to the side and X hummed in satisfaction, like an artist seeing his hard work come together for the first time. Judge walked over, holding my body to his chest, making sure the ropes didn't pull against my skin too hard. X stopped raising me when I got to about three feet off the floor.

Cock height.

There was a delicious dance between pleasure and pain that had me panting as the silk rope tugged against my flesh. X pulled one final piece of red ribbon out of his pocket, binding my foot on the leg that was already crisscrossed with ropes, and using the ribbon to attach it to my hands behind my shoulders.

He stepped away, sucking in a breath between his teeth. "Fuck, you are the most beautiful being I've ever seen, Raine Baxter."

With my left leg pulled tight behind me, my toes almost touching my fingers, and my right leg hanging loose to the floor, I was bared to them all. I'd never felt sexier than in that moment, displayed like a butterfly on a board, every single one of them looking at me hungrily.

"Snakelet, on your knees. You look hungry," X commanded, and Tex dropped to his knees beside me eagerly.

I don't know how he did it, but X had made me exactly face height for Tex.

Tex licked up my thigh, his tongue running over the tender flesh exposed between the ropes. When he reached my upper thigh, he nipped the bulging skin. This felt so good, I wasn't even worried that my thigh looked like a trussed ham. When he buried his face in the exposed core, I bucked, but I was suspended in place. I tried to pull him tighter with my other leg, but X made a disapproving noise that had me stopping instantly. "Uh uh, Love. Don't make me tie your other leg. I'm taking it easy on you right now, given this is your first experience as a rope bunny." He knelt beside my head, bending down so we were eye level with each other. "Are you enjoying this?"

"Yes," I groaned as Tex's tongue ran over my clit. Shit. X leaned forward and kissed me like it was the first time and the last time. There was a desperation in his kiss that made my chest hurt. Then he stood up and moved away. He looked hotly over at Judge, and there was a fire in his eyes when he looked at his friend that I hadn't noticed before. "She's all yours."

Judge looked between X and me, then took X's spot by my head. He leaned forward, his hands running over my restrained body in awe.

"He always was a fucking artist," he murmured. "But you were already the perfect canvas." My skin prickled where he touched, every stroke heightened by the burn of the ropes. He leaned forward and kissed me, pushing me back into Tex's plundering mouth. He kissed me deeply, somehow in sync with Tex. My climax came out of nowhere, thundering over me in a scream. Judge looked down at Tex, his face glistening with my release, and his eyes got even hotter. He shed his pants in an instant, and Tex followed suit. Judge looked down at Tex, his eyes appraising the other man in all his naked glory. And fuck he was glorious.

"Take your mate, Lover Boy," he commanded, and Tex lined his body up with my exposed core.

"I love you," Tex moaned as he pushed inside me, and I whimpered with pleasure. I wanted to scream and cry and make freaking animal noises with how good it felt. I closed my eyes and let my head hang forward as the sensations washed over me like nothing I'd ever felt before. I felt confined and free.

Judge's cock tapped against my cheek, and I opened my eyes. "Open for me, Rainy Day. I can't wait to fuck that beautiful mouth."

I parted my lips as he slid the solid length of him into my mouth slowly. He looked over his shoulder at X. "Are you not joining in?"

X had his cock in his hand, stroking it slowly but with a tight fist. "No. When I have Raine, it will be just me and her, and I will make her scream my name so you'll even hear it from the diner. We'll have plenty of time to all play together."

Well, if that didn't sound like commitment, nothing did. I

swirled my tongue as Judge slid out of my mouth, making him groan and push in further. I swung gently between them, the silk ropes biting my skin and my eyes on X where he was stroking his dick. It was the hottest experience of my life.

Tex must have been getting close, because his pounding thrusts were getting wild, slamming me into Judge's cock in time with his movements. Tex's hand slid around and flicked my sensitive clit, and I came again, moaning around Judge's cock, making the man in question groan, moving in shallow rapid thrusts until he was coming too, shooting hot spurts into my mouth. Finally, Tex gripped my hips, burying himself deep inside me as he came on a roar.

I hung there panting as I tried to get my brain back online. Holy fucking shit. Tex crawled forward to kiss me, his tongue swirling around my mouth to taste Judge's cum. Then he flopped onto his back.

"Fuck."

I had to agree. X strolled over, his shirt gone and his own release still glistening on his chest. He undid the ropes until I was lowered back to the ground, and then he gently undid the knots with deft fingers. When I was completely free, blood rushing back to areas where it had been restricted, he scooped me into his arms and walked me to my bedroom.

"You did so good, Love. You were perfect," he murmured, his hands running over the indents in my skin from the ropes reverently. We'd just reached the door of my bedroom when there was a knock at the front door. I wiggled out of X's arms, though he tsked disapprovingly, pulling my gown from the back of my bedroom door and wrapping it around myself. I was glad to see that Judge had cleaned up all the ropes because I didn't know how I'd explain that to Walker or Nico. Given the time, it could only be one of those two.

If I'd been thinking clearly, if my brain hadn't been addled by hot sex, I'd have wondered why either of those two would knock. Instead, I answered the door like an idiot.

Then I screamed.

27

There was a severed head on my doorstep. I slammed the door and bolted for the kitchen. Judge grabbed me in his arms, bundling me behind his back as X opened the door again, his knives out.

When he looked down, he saw it too. Instead of freaking out like a damn sissy like me, he cocked his head to the side.

"Well, that's certainly interesting."

"Interesting?" I screeched, making Judge wince. He stepped forward, assured there wasn't any threat, and then he stared down at the head on my stoop too.

"Is that...?" he asked X.

"Yep," X agreed.

I hadn't taken the time to examine the face, and now I needed to know. "Who the hell is it?" I yelled from my spot behind the island bench in the kitchen.

"It's Raul," Judge yelled over his shoulder.

Shock made me take a step back. Raul? As in, Lucius's second-in-command? "Asshole Raul?" I double-checked, not that we knew any other Rauls.

X nodded. "You better call your Sheriff and the Old Man. They are going to want to see this."

I grabbed my phone and scrambled for my bedroom. My kitchen was still way too close to the thing bleeding on my front step.

Walker answered on the second ring. "Sorry, Raine. I'm coming now, just got caught up on everything that happened and doing the paperwork. Judge kept the peace, but he isn't big on filling out the appropriate forms," he said, his exasperation evident.

I swallowed hard. "You better hurry, Walker. There's a head at my front door."

"Pardon?"

"There's a severed head on my welcome mat," I repeated. Silence sounded through the phone. Then there was a whoosh of air, probably because he was super-speeding to my house. My suspicions were confirmed when I heard him talking to X and Judge moments later. I didn't want to leave my room, didn't want to be anywhere near anyone's severed head. I was really strange about dead things. I always had been, even growing up. The irony that I was now a dead thing wasn't lost on me. But as Raul showed, there was undead, and then there was dead-dead.

I hadn't smelled the blood, hadn't sensed an intruder leaving a pretty little present while X had me hogtied to the ceiling. That freaked me out almost as much as the head. "Can you guys just move it?" I yelled out to them. I'd be happier if it was gone, and I could burn my doormat and hose down my front step and forget the whole thing ever happened.

Walker must have leaped over the head like a gazelle because he was suddenly in the room with me. "I'm sorry, I can't do that, Raine. It's a crime scene now. I have to ask, is there anyone who would leave severed body parts at your front door?"

I huffed out a strangled sigh. "Only X, and he was with me the whole time." I hoped that Walker didn't notice the slight blush that spread across my cheeks. Couldn't a girl just have five minutes of breathing room? Lie down and sleep in her own bed? It was always death or debauchery these days; I just needed a few hours of downtime.

Walker leaned forward, kissing my forehead as he wrapped his arms around my waist and pulled me tight. "How about you take Tex and head over to the diner? I know Bert and Beatrice are waiting to see you. I think you've stolen their golden child position. Used to be me, you know," he growled completely non-threateningly.

I nodded and walked out to the living room to find my purse. I tried to resist the urge to look upwards at the rings hanging from the ceiling. I didn't want Walker to know I'd been up to all sorts of BDSM shenanigans quite yet.

As I grabbed my purse, Nico arrived, along with Catherine and Grim from the Town Council. Nico stared down at the head of the former Enforcer, his face so grim it was almost desolate. "Open the mouth," he said softly, and X leaned forward to follow his command. X raised his eyebrows when he pulled out a perfectly folded piece of paper, but Nico just looked forlorn.

"How did you know?" Catherine asked softly, her eyes studying the head and its placement critically.

Nico shook his head. "It's not my first severed head. He likes to leave a note, like a message in a bottle thrown out to sea."

Catherine's eyes narrowed. "He?" she asked, but I could tell by the look in her eye that she already knew who he was talking about.

"Lucius."

X opened the note, reading silently as his eyebrows rose further and further toward his hairline. "Well, who needs messages in a bottle when you can send love notes in the skulls of your enemies?" He looked at me, a wild, vicious smirk on his face. "Have to say though, Love, I feel like there's only room for one psychopath in your group of admirers and I was here first."

My feet froze to the floor, and I turned rigid. My brain refused to comprehend what he was telling me. Walker grabbed the note, his brows doing the opposite of X's and dipping low over his eyes in a frown as he read.

"What's it say?" I whispered.

Walker shook his head, but X had no such qualms. "It says, 'I can't get you out of my head, Raine Baxter. Speaking of heads, here is what will happen if anyone lays a finger on you again. I will lay them at your feet for judgment. Lucius.'" X screwed up his nose. "Beautiful, right? But I think he might like to work on his courting game. Severed heads are so faux pas. Doesn't he know it's dick pics and Netflix and chill now?"

Every person in the vicinity stared down at X in something that looked a lot like bewildered horror. He seemed completely oblivious. I shook myself from my frozen state, picked up my purse and got out of my house as fast as possible. I'd had enough. I could take no more without suffering from a complete meltdown.

When I made it to the diner, it felt like I hadn't been there in a month rather than a week. Beatrice's face lit up with happiness as I walked in the door, the bell tinkling above my head. Then she noted my pasty—well, pastier—complexion and ordered my usual from the kitchen, quickly making me a Type-O float.

"Lass, you are a sight for sore eyes. It is good to see you back here, safe inside your town once again now all those Enforcers are gone, may they all get dickrot and die." If we weren't in a restaurant, I was pretty sure she would have spat on the ground. I didn't have the heart to tell her that they weren't really gone, just on a temporary sabbatical. I'd basically adopted two former Enforcers, and the most dangerous, most psychotic one of them all was now sending me severed heads and beautiful love notes.

I fell onto my Type-O float like a starving woman, and Beatrice gave me and my sudden paleness a hard look, like maybe Brody had been neglecting me.

"It's been a rough year, Beatrice. Next year has to be better, right? It's all going to be puppies and rainbows and unicorns and mind-blowing orgasms, right?"

Beatrice gave me a wan smile. "It's all you can hope for, Lass. Now, will any of your beaus be joining you for dinner tonight?"

I shrugged, and I looked over my shoulder as Tex strolled through the door. "Better make it a plus one."

Beatrice gave me a motherly look that she somehow laced with pure sass, and pointed to a booth. "Take your usual booth. Unless the apocalypse has arrived, they will all find their way to you eventually. Even the shite-talking Brit." She gave a fond grin as she spoke about X. I really had to ask how he'd wooed her over like that.

Tex grinned in her general direction, and she smiled back at him, though a little frown appeared on her face when she realized he couldn't see her. It was easy to forget with my self-assured shifter. He leaned forward and kissed me, finding my lips with such ease that I understood why people forgot. "You okay?"

I sighed and nodded, sucking down a fortifying slurp of my milkshake. Damn, I'd missed these. "I'm okay. What's one more psycho trying to take my head?"

Tex frowned. "I don't think he wants your head, babe. I think there are other parts lower that he has his heart set on." He looked like he wanted to vomit at the thought. I couldn't blame him really. I wanted to vomit as well.

Cheese fries and ice cream appeared in front of me, and a burger appeared in front of Tex. "Bert made them extra cheesy. I think he missed you too, Lass."

I grinned at her because I couldn't help it. Even in the face of the shitshow that was apparently my life, I found that I was happy here.

The door opened, and the look on Beatrice's face at whoever entered the diner had my heart pounding. I looked over my shoulder, and my heart flip-flopped sadly at the sight of Angeline. She looked a little worse for wear, her eyes flat in a way they never were before, but I guess a week in Lucius's tender care would do that to the most hardened of people. Her hair was a mess, and Cresta would have been horrified, if she wasn't so relieved that Angeline hadn't been executed on the spot. I'm pretty sure she would be ecstatic even if Angeline had been shaved bald. I ran a hand over my head. Oh yeah.

I made a note to hit up Cresta for wigs or something. It

was going to be a long century of looking like a neo-nazi otherwise. Beatrice was in front of Angeline, hugging her to her ample bosom like she was sure she was really a ghost and not our Angeline.

Her Angeline, I should say. I turned back around and tried my best to keep my promise to her. I was going to do my best to be invisible so I didn't make her more miserable than she already was. Tex reached out, wrapping his hand in mine, our bond pulsing with love and just a touch of anger at the way Angeline had treated me. That made my lips curl in a shadow of a smile. I loved him so damn much.

When Angeline stopped in front of our table, my heart was thundering in my ears. I didn't know if I had it in me to take another emotional hit today. Squaring my shoulders and taking a deep breath to fortify my feelings, I looked up at Angeline.

Her eyes were flat, but I could see the pain in them, or maybe that was just a reflection of my own. She seemed a little more gaunt, a little paler, and when I looked at her hands, they trembled softly.

She seemed to be waiting for me to speak, but I didn't know what to say. So, instead of letting the uncomfortable silence drag, I swallowed hard and whispered, "I'm glad you are okay." She'd survived, and that was all anyone could ask for.

She nodded, her face still that weird, blank mask. "I am. Walker told me you insisted that they come and campaign for my freedom, that your Executioner was the one that managed to sway Titus, so I thank you." Her words were robotic, but the world of pain that coated her words like oil still hurt my heart.

I just nodded once. I didn't want her thanks or her gratitude. "You were my friend."

She flinched like I'd struck her, and I guess even being my former friend must have been abhorrent to her now. She reached into her pocket and I tensed. Call it my life right now, but I suddenly had flashes of her pulling out a stake and driving it through my heart.

Instead, she dropped a bunch of keys on the table. I knew the keys, of course. They were the keys to The Immortal Cupcake. I looked from her to the keys, and back again. She put her fingers on them almost reverently, then pushed them my way.

I just stared at them until she spoke. "I'm leaving. I'm giving you the store."

My eyes flew back up to hers, and I shook my head subconsciously. "No."

She raised an eyebrow, just a hint of the old Angeline in her expression, and my heart cracked. "No?"

I hissed out a breath. "You can't leave. I feel... You can't... Ugh!" I tripped over my words, unable to get any coherent reason why she shouldn't leave to pass my lips.

She smiled down at me sadly, but it didn't reach her eyes. "Dark River is no longer my home. It is a place filled with bad memories and constant reminders. I need to leave. Whether you take the cafe doesn't change anything except..." She took a deep breath. "Except as some kind of restitution for what Alice did, for how I treated you afterward. If being taken by the Enforcers taught me anything, it was what it was like to truly fear. To stand there and be judged for someone else's actions. I did that to you, even if I didn't mean to, even if I was mourning, and it wasn't fair. So take the keys. Even if you never use them and the store stays locked up forever. Take them so I can selfishly appease my own guilt."

I swallowed hard and my eyes welled with tears. I didn't know what to say to her, so I just reached out and pulled the keys closer to me, removing my hand so quickly that they may as well have been silver dipped in garlic. She closed her eyes in relief.

It all felt so wrong. "I'll watch the store until you get back," I said quietly, but she just shook her head.

"I'm never coming back, Raine. There's no going back, only moving forward." Then she was gone. She didn't say goodbye, and I didn't get to say anything else. Like the fact that I forgave her. She was just gone. I turned to Tex, and he pulled me to his chest so I could cry in peace.

28

It shouldn't have surprised me that Beatrice had been right. If I sat in the booth at the diner for long enough, my guys would come and find me. It may have been Brody's fault though, rather than the pull of my magical lady charms. Brody had sensed my distress and called Tex, who had filled him in on what had happened that morning. I was in rare form to get a head and a cafe in one day. Lucky me.

I could hear Brody cussing over the phone, and then he hung up, and I had no doubt he was calling Walker. Like my knight in shining armor, he'd appeared at the table with a gust of displaced air. He looked between Tex and me, then down at the keys on the table that I was avoiding like a tarantula, and pulled me out of the booth and into his arms. He kissed the hell out of me, then slid me back down, hopping into the booth after me until I was jammed between him and Tex. I was about to ask why we were all on one side of the table when the door opened, and Judge and X swaggered in like they were made of sin and violence. Who needed sugar and spice?

They slid in opposite me, Judge leaning over to kiss me softly on the lips, and X doing the same. In public. In front of Beatrice. I flushed, my cheeks turning pink when I noticed her giving me a knowing look. Gah. Do not think about the ropes. Do not think about the ropes.

I looked up at X's face, and the shit-eating grin he gave me told me he knew exactly what I was thinking about. Dick.

I cleared my throat and willed my blood to cool. "Where's Nico?"

X grinned. "Like that already, is it? Well, I guess I can deal with one more banger in your little mash."

I blinked at him. Was I supposed to know what the fuck he was talking about? Judge just rolled his eyes—he seemed to do that a lot around X—and elbowed him in the ribs. "Like you have a choice, asshole. You're smitten."

X looked completely offended at the term smitten, but when he looked at me, he did look less like a sociopath. He looked softer. Beatrice bustled over and placed steaks in front of Judge and Walker. Apparently, no one even needed to order anymore. She placed this weird, puffy monstrosity in front of X, and he looked up at her like she'd just hung him the moon and the stars. I might have been a little jealous.

"Tsch. Don't give me that look, Redcoat. Bert was just

experimenting and we didn't want to poison the good customers."

X was still staring at her adoringly. "You made me Toad In The Hole? Beatrice, Love. Would you marry me?" Yep, I was definitely jealous.

She rolled her eyes at him. "T'was Bert who made it."

He looked over her shoulder. "Bert! Marry me, you talented bugger," he yelled, and every person who wasn't already staring at our table turned to look. Beatrice tapped his cheek in a motherly fashion and walked away muttering to herself in Scots.

X dug into his food with abandon and we couldn't help but stare.

"I have to ask, what the hell is a Toad In The Hole?" Tex mumbled around a mouthful of food. Gross. "It sounds like a sex position."

The huge scarred Enforcer gave Tex a lascivious look. "I can show you exactly where to put your toad later, Snakelet."

Walker choked on his steak and looked between us all again. "Did I miss something?"

I shook my head. "I'll tell you later. What are we going to do about You-Know-Who and the head?" Walker looked resigned, and cast a look between Judge and X. "We are going to have to call in Miranda."

Both guys looked like they were going to choke.

Fuck. Me.

. . .

I was beginning to think that Miranda waited outside Dark River for us to call. Just loitering there in the background, hoping that we would be stupid enough to invite the fox into the henhouse. Which we did because she had a skill set that apparently rivaled no one else. When she saw my lack of hair, she winced.

"Fashion statement?"

"Brain surgery," I said flatly. We'd parted on reasonably good terms last time, but Brody had been there to keep her happy and I wasn't flanked by her two former partners/lovers/whatever the fuck they were.

She shrugged and turned her attention to Nico, but I saw the way her eyes swept over X and Judge. I looked at X, trying to gauge his expression like it would give me the secrets to how he was feeling. I should have known better. His face was all business—well, if 'paid killer' could be considered an expression.

Miranda did her best professional face too as she faced Nico. "What can I do for the Town Council of Dark River?"

"I need two houses and The Immortal Cupcake warded against Lucius." His eyes quickly darted to me. Miranda placed a hand on his arm, before Nico could move away. Her eyebrows arched prettily, and she looked between Nico and me. "You too?"

She appraised me and seemed to find me wanting, yet again.

Nico kept his expression cool. There was no love lost

between vampires and witches, apparently. "What is the cost?"

She looked at him appraisingly. "You know the answer. A vial of your—" She stopped herself. "No. A vial of her blood."

Nico was shaking his head. "No."

I didn't see what the big deal was. I'd had barely a taste of Nico's blood, and it was like drinking tequila in a hot tub after not eating for a week. It blew your socks clean off and then flung them into the next state. Honestly, if she wanted my weak fledgling blood, then I was all for it. Was I a little worried she might do voodoo on it and make my tits fall off? Maybe a touch.

"Sure. I don't see why not."

I'm not sure if it was the calculating look in Miranda's eye as she grabbed my hand and palmed her ceremonial dagger, or the sight of my blood itself that made me feel a little clammy, but suddenly a cold sweat ran down my spine. The ceremonial knife slid right through my flesh like it was butter, and I didn't feel a thing until I watched it bleed. And then that bitch hurt. She must have clipped a tendon. To distract myself, I looked at the swirls of the knife, the blackened indentations that were probably dried blood and I was suddenly really glad that I couldn't get hepatitis anymore.

When she'd filled a tiny little glass bottle of my blood, she released my wrist. She gave Judge a cool look. Guess they still weren't BFF's. "Are you going to lick it clean like last time?" she said haughtily.

X laughed, a cold humorless sound, and grabbed my hand. "Waste not, want not, right Love?" And then his tongue lapped over the cut in a way that was completely pornographic and went straight to my lady bits. He lapped at it like it was an ice cream coated nipple, and I suddenly forgot what we were doing and who I was.

Judge was still having a stare-off with his former lover, Nico was looking at us like we'd all gone mad, and Walker was pinching the bridge of his nose like he was wondering if he could retire to the mountains somewhere and become a hermit. Only Tex was focused solely on me, and that was probably because I was so wound up by X's tongue bath I smelled like McDonald's after a hunger strike.

Finally, the silent stare-off between Miranda and Judge must have reached its climax, because the witch shrugged and got to work, warding everything.

We did the whole knife door ritual again because it was hard to ward a place to keep one vampire out. It was easier to ward all vampires out and then make exceptions. "Unless you have some of Lucius's blood just lying around?"

I looked hopefully at Nico, because how could I do this ritual at The Immortal Cupcake and keep it open? Then I mentally slapped myself. I wasn't reopening The Immortal Cupcake. I wasn't going to step into my friend's life like I had the right, after it was my fault her world turned to shit.

When I said to skip The Immortal Cupcake until we got some of Lucius's blood, Miranda had grinned. "You say that like he'd just hand it over. Good luck, fledgling. Witches have been trying to take Lucius down since he subjugated his very first one over a millennia ago. The beast is meticulous about not leaving behind any part of his DNA for our uses. But if you do manage to get some? My coven will pay you whatever you desire to have it."

Duly noted. It would be nice to have some bargaining power over the witches, though I wanted nothing to do with supernatural politics. I just wanted to stay in my small town, have copious amounts of sex with way too many hot guys and live a reasonably happy eternity. Was that too much to ask?

She held up my vial of blood to the moonlight, twisting and turning it as if she could divine all my secrets just from looking at it. Hell, maybe she could. It just looked like blood to me, leeched of its ruby color by the starless night. She opened up her interdimensional vagina portal and smiled at me. "I will see you soon, Raine Baxter. But damn, you have an ugly shaped head. For the sake of us all..." She paused, and my scalp began to itch. When I put my hands up to scratch it, I felt handfuls of my hair. I looked at the locks, the same ruby color they'd been before. She looked between X and Judge. "Take care of them."

Judge stepped forward and halted her with a hand on her wrist, and she looked down at the appendage with such sad, resigned longing. Hell, maybe she had loved Judge once, rather than just wanting the thrill of the chase like Judge had suggested. I bared my fangs. I didn't care if she'd just restored my hair, Judge was mine.

I must have let out a tiny growl, because both Miranda and Judge looked over at me, and X laughed hysterically.

Judge reached out and handed Miranda a second vial. "Payment. We are square."

Miranda nodded, tucking it into the pouch that hung on her waist. Then the slit collapsed in on itself and she was gone. I looked at Judge, who would be a mean poker player because his face gave nothing away.

"Payment?"

He nodded, coming over to wrap an arm around me. He didn't look nervous or guilty or anything like that this time. "To secure my way through the ward at Nîso the first time. Brody was there, it was all above board, but I would have gutted her and used her blood to cross the ward if she'd disagreed. You were dying. I needed to get to you."

Fuck me. Be still my beating heart, because that was the most romantic thing I'd ever heard that contained the words gutted and dying. I kissed him gently. "Let's go to bed," I said softly, walking with him across the threshold of the house. He held his breath, waiting for the zap to his nuts that always happened after the last time Miranda had done a ward for me. But nothing happened. I let out a relieved sigh, but I remained cautious. I wasn't stupid enough to think that Miranda was suddenly over her love/hate relationship with my sexy as sin drifter. When everyone was through the door,

I let out a relieved sigh. I struggled to keep my eyes open as I walked to my bedroom. I could hear the guys chatting in the kitchen, but none of them tried to follow me. Somehow they must have known I wanted space. Or maybe they just preferred each other's company to the sound of my snores. Either way, I was beyond caring. I wanted a nap and several days of uninterrupted sleep.

When my head hit the pillow, I was out like the dead. Literally.

Tex making coffee woke me, and I slipped out from under Judge and Walker's assorted body parts to shuffle to the kitchen. My body had decided it had slept enough, and now it was screaming for caffeine.

As I shuffled through my living room, someone knocked lightly on my door. I was going to blame the lack of caffeine and my confidence in Miranda's wards for opening it like a dumbass.

Standing at my door was a youngish guy, with pale skin and big black eyes. He was looking at the ground, perplexed, and I looked down too.

Fuck.

"Did you realize there was a severed head on your doorstep?" the man asked, and I sighed.

"No. But I can't say I'm surprised." I didn't recognize the

face, which was both a relief and a cause for concern. "Can I help you with something?"

The dude might have had a young face, but he had a real big energy. He also had a rapid heartbeat that marked him as alive, and some serious heat blowing off him that he could almost be a furnace.

The man grinned, and I felt Tex come up behind me, his body vibrating with... something? Fear? Terror? Excitement?

I didn't want to take my eyes off the stranger to judge what it was.

"Forgive my rudeness. I am Alexander. I believe you have found my progeny?"

Alexander. Alexander? Why did that name sound familiar?

When the shoe dropped, all the blood left in my body dropped away from my face and fell to the floor.

Holy Mother of Fucking Dragons.

About the Author

Grace McGinty is eclectic. She has worked as a chocolatier, a librarian, a forensic accountant and finally a writer. Like her professional career, the genres she writes are also eclectic. She writes romance, reverse harem romance, fantasy, contemporary young adult and new adult books.

She lives in rural Australia with her crazy family, an entire menagerie of pets, and will one day be crushed by the giant piles of books that litter every room.

Head over to www.gracemcginty.com and join my mailing list for sneak previews into what I am working on and to stay up-to-date with new releases and giveaways!

Not ready for this to end?

Check out Pleasantly Undead in Dark River, available in ebook, paperback and hardcover now!

Made in the USA
Columbia, SC
22 August 2023

ef7d5006-381d-4f76-99c6-ebc4905116c7R01